THE CUTTING TIDE

ROBERTA L. GREENWALD

The Cutting Tide

CUTTING LESSONS – THE EMOTIONS OF LOVE

I'm a rookie at this game of love – existing before in complacency with the same ole song and dance. Never reaching or wanting or exploring for myself. Never thinking it was there for me. But with the changes of the tide, so too, have I changed. Maybe for better, maybe for worse – the jury is still out.

Testing the waters to see how deep, cold and rocky my footing feels beneath me. Why does the seabed always appear safe, with only soft sand meeting the soles of my feet? Why can't sharpness cut at my flesh immediately, screaming out its warning, allowing me to retreat from a more heart-wrenching blow?

But instead, it masquerades cleverly – sensuously – giving no warning to the danger that lies ahead. Allowing no simple fix – but only a cutting of the extremities. A shark-like incision, ripping to the marrow of the soul, taking one too many bites from my already shattered existence.

And we vow to ourselves, that it will never happen again! We shroud ourselves in a thicker wetsuit – this time with a layer of metal reinforcement – smugly believing that we *finally* have learned all the lessons that life has thrown our way **– but the riptide pulls us out again.** *Remember*…. the subconscious challenges…. *remember*. Swim across the current, not with it!

The lesson is that you will survive if you remember what to do in the face of confusion, not wanting to be dragged down this time – not wanting to be swallowed up in shame. In the deep recesses of your being, you find a mustard seed of fight left in you, finding the will to survive, breaking free of the restraints that try to imprison you.

And this time the victory is yours – maybe not always, but this time…. breaking free of the force that you think will surely be your demise. You pause and breathe deeply in relief.

The relaxing swim back to the shore is triumphant, as you regain your composure, sitting on the beach that has left your thighs brush-burned from the sand. You are a peace again. All is right with you and the universe, as you gaze out over the diamond-glistening sea.

But the playful waves beckon and wink at you, desiring that you would never leave…. inviting you to dance upon each crest…. and you ever-so-carefully submerse your feet in the water again.

TO MY FATHER, ROBERT - WHO WAS MY HERO AND MY FIRST LIFEGUARD. I LOVE AND MISS YOU DADDY!

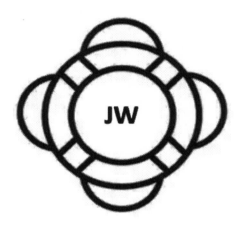

Lifeguard

GREATER LOVE HAS NO ONE THAN THIS - THAT SOMEONE LAY DOWN HIS LIFE FOR HIS FRIENDS. JOHN 15:13

I DEDICATE THIS BOOK TO:

FAMILY AND FRIENDS WHO HAVE GONE ON TO ANOTHER CRYSTAL SEA.

THE CUTTING TIDE

CHAPTER 1

"Wait a minute. I'm getting in the car now!" Dex yelled, hopping in the front passenger's seat by his sister Sarah, as he threw his backpack to the seat behind.

"What took you so long? It's always this way when I want to leave," she complained in frustration, knowing her brother was never punctual.

"Oh come on… Sarah, admit it, you are not always on time either, and you know it," Dex grinned.

Sarah looked at her brother and just shook her head, realizing it was worthless to pursue the subject with him. They were going to the beach for several days before they said goodbye to summer, and hello to a life at college.

Sarah and Dex were fraternal twins, and they typically got along as equally well as they fought with each other. They had never been apart, other than a few nights here and there to be with a friend or to attend a sports camp. But now things were changing. Different colleges and interests were pulling them apart – at least, until they would see each other again over holiday breaks.

"Why don't you pull in up there?" Dex pointed. "Gotta use the bathroom."

Sarah just sighed and looked at her brother. "Seriously? It's only been 45 minutes."

"Yeah, I know. Too much to drink before I left," he grinned sheepishly, slipping from the car in a hurry.

"Ok, but after this stop, you're driving," she yelled.

"No prob, sis. Got it covered!" Dex answered over his shoulder, as he ran to the convenience store door, yanking it open as he darted in.

Two hours later, Dex nudged Sarah on the arm, waking her from her slumber. "We're here sleepy head. Let's get our stuff unloaded."

Dex had already grabbed his bag and was making his way up the front steps of his parent's beach house. Unlocking the door, he walked to the closed vertical blinds and pulled them back, taking in the glistening ocean in front of him.

"Beautiful…" he simply breathed.

"I agree…" Sarah replied as she stood beside of him out on the deck, knowing that they not only shared a fondness for the beach house, but also the ocean that was their constant summer companion since youth.

"Why don't we get ready and go out to dinner? I don't know about you, but I'm starving," Sarah moaned, feeling her stomach suddenly growling.

"What did you have in mind?" Dex asked, looking at his sister for the answer.

"What else? Crabs!"

"Sounds like a plan."

"I'll be ready in 30 minutes," Sarah announced, already making her way to the bathroom.

"That would be a first," Dex teased back with a laugh, escaping to his parent's bathroom with his duffle bag in tow.

CHAPTER 2

Michael and Nancy Miller had owned the beach house, that they affectionately named - The Dancing Seahorse - for over 20 years. Three generations – all loving and going to the Eastern Shore of Maryland - their parents, them, and now their children. Just as their parents took them to Marlin beach, so did they take Dex and Sarah, instilling in them a love for Blue Crabs with Old Bay Seasoning, fries with Malt vinegar, and all the other specialties and treats of the wooden boardwalk that the town was famous for.

The Miller's built The Dancing Seahorse on the inheritance money that Nancy had received after her grandmother's passing. It had always been their dream to build a beach house and the generous gift from her Nana had just speeded up the process.

Michael was an architect by trade, so he insisted on building the beach house stronger than what was required by the city's code. Even though several other dwellings that had been built close by hugged the sand, he insisted that their house be built on stilts along with hurricane force windows and doors. The roof was steel reinforced, and the house was outfitted with hurricane shutters on the outside that could be closed with manual crank handles or electrical switches if the power was still on.

4

The inside of the beach house was laid out in a way that was timeless, not showing 20 years of age. The kitchen and living room areas flowed as one with no walls or obstacles disrupting the view of the ocean in front of them. Three bedrooms and two bathrooms completed the inside of the house. Balconies on the outside, wrapped three quarters of the structure, with weighted patio furniture strategically placed in groupings for sitting and dining.

Nancy was a third grade elementary school teacher. Her lengthy and successful career was not only rewarding, but allotted her the luxury of having time off in the summer with her children. Many weeks were spent at the beach house with Dex and Sarah, and her husband Michael would show up for long weekends after he was done working in Baltimore – Monday through Thursday.

The days were filled with the children on boogie boards in the ocean or building sandcastles, while the adults sat on low-slung beach chairs under their umbrella, each reading a great novel or magazine as they watched over Dex and Sarah at play.

A nap - for the adults - usually concluded the day at the beach, as the sun drifted lower on the horizon. Typically, Dex and Sarah would start whining about being hungry; so the towels, chairs, umbrella and beach toys would be packed up for another day, as the caravan made their way back up to the beach house.

An outside shower and hose would wash the sand from all the carried items along with their feet and legs, and then the assortment of necessary beach things would be replaced in a free standing shed situated near the lower part of the house.

Nancy would scrutinize her husband and children after their rinse-off, making sure no sand would be clinging and dragged into her clean home. It was a ritual that a shower was in order right away once they entered the beach house - with wet bathing suits being hung in the bathtub after the scrubbing was completed.

The children would resist, acting as if they did not want to comply with her strict wishes, but they grew to love the routine and reward afterwards of a good meal and maybe a board game or movie before bed. Sometimes, they would go to the boardwalk with their parents or even go out to dinner, but not often. Family time was to be spent at home, and it seemed to be enough for all concerned.

Michael always resisted leaving his family at the end of his routine visit. He would wait until late on a Sunday evening after the sun had set, before packing and making his way back to Baltimore for another week of work.

The deck by far was a calming force for him. The smell of sea air and citronella candles filled his senses as he sipped on his Tanqueray, tonic and lime. A kite could be seen floating aimlessly through the drifting breeze. Seagulls would squeal out and match the rhythm of the kites, dancing and swaying amongst their tails. Children would play on the darkened beach, running with sparklers, causing an array of light that would glow quickly before going out.

He never wanted to say goodbye after a memorable weekend with his family. But work beckoned early on a Monday morning, and it was rare that he would take off more time - other than the extended weekends he would allot himself.

CHAPTER 3

"I told you I would only be 30 minutes," Sarah said matter-of-factly as she grabbed her keys and headed towards her Mazda.

"Yes you did. I guess there is a first for everything," Dex smiled jumping in the front passenger's seat, placing his flip-flopped feet on the dash.

Sarah gave him her warning glare, playful but firm. " I say we just go to the Crab Shack and get the *all you can eat* special with the corn, fries and hush puppies."

"Sounds good to me. I know mom and dad won't be taking us there in a few days, so why not?"

The wait was close to an hour as the many patrons stood in line or mingled outside with a drink in hand until their table was called. Sarah and Dex were only 18 and drinking alcohol was not allowed; that was, unless secretly gotten by someone older while they were at a party without their parent's knowledge. They had been the lucky ones, heeding their parent's warning about drugs and staying active in sports and academics instead. With an occasional beer here and there, but for the most part, they walked the straight and narrow.

Both had dated, and Dex had a steady girlfriend, up until two weeks prior. The typical speech came up about college and not being tied down to his girlfriend, or she to him. Neither seemed to bulk too much, and both were ready for the break up. There had been sex for Dex and his girlfriend, but they both agreed it was time to discover college and new relationships. Sarah, on the other hand, only had a few dates here and there, but no exclusive boyfriend. She figured that college would be a whole new chapter, and the time to meet someone new, even though her mother had constantly impressed upon her that her studies came first if she wanted to be an architect like her father.

Dex was average in height with brown wavy hair and blue eyes. He was athletic in build and fairly tan from all the days spent outdoors at the beach, with a light sprinkling of freckles running over the bridge of his nose. Only for several months in the winter did he fade out in color.

Sarah was shorter than her brother, but equally as athletic in build. Even though they were twins, their looks were different. Her hair was sandy blonde and took on even lighter hues during the summer with sun-kissed highlights, from spending the majority of her time outdoors also. She too had blue eyes, but hers were lighter in color than her brother's who's were steel blue. Both were attractive with friendly depositions, and each one had beautiful straight teeth that displayed sunny smiles. They were liked, and fairly popular in their individual and mutual social circles, being very active in high school.

"Right this way. I can seat you inside or out. What do you prefer?" A young pretty waitress asked of the pair, who was only a year or two older than Dex and Sarah.

"Let's sit outside," Sarah suggested as she already moved in that direction.

"I agree. I can hear good music playing on the back deck," Dex mentioned with curiosity, as the waitress escorted them to their table.

After being seated, they ate their fill of over a dozen crabs each, with all the sides and several refills of sweet tea. Neither was shy eating as much as they liked, because they were young and weight never seemed to be a problem. The music played and they talked of college and the past few months, and what they anticipated happening once they were in college and apart.

Sarah watched several couples dancing close, wondering if she would ever meet someone to dance with in much the same way. Dex looked around tapping his fingers restlessly on the table, totally bored with the whole thing and just waiting for his sister to give the word that she was ready to leave.

"What do you say we get outta here?" Dex asked, looking at his sister who appeared to be in trance as she stared at the dancers.

"Huh? Oh, sure," Sarah smiled. "I'm just enjoying the evening."

"I can see that," he winked. "But I'm ready for something else besides this *boring* dancing. So let's get going," Dex insisted, as he got up from the table ready for the next activity.

"Sure, Dex. Whatever you say," she answered, rolling her eyes at her brother. Sarah reached for the cash that was stuffed in her jean's pocket, laying it on the table for their dinner, hurrying to catch up as the two walked away.

CHAPTER 4

"Now that was some meal. Boy am I full," Dex grimaced, as they walked back to the car grabbing his stomach with both hands.

"Me too," Sarah agreed. "How about a walk on the boardwalk? I think I can beat you in a few games of Skee-Ball."

"You do now, do you?" Dex laughed with a raised eyebrow, being up for the challenge. "Why don't you park the car back at the beach house first and we will walk to the boards. It is such a pretty night. What do you think?"

"Sure, but I will need to use the bathroom first after all that iced tea!"

Dex laughed, grinning at his sister warmly. "You are such a girl. You know that? I saw the way you were looking at those dancers at dinner. You wished you were up there too. Didn't you?"

Sarah looked at Dex with a knowing smile as she drove back to The Dancing Seahorse. "Maybe I did, and maybe I didn't. None of your business!" She yelled as she ran from her car, taking the steps by twos into the house.

The boardwalk was alive with noise and activity. Many vacationers were squeezed together - shoulder-to-shoulder - on the overcrowded, wooden sandy deck that smelled of tar and salty sea air.

Maryland is known for their world-famous boardwalk that is a mixture of small hotels, condominiums, beach shops and local popular food eateries that hug into small spaces - one by one - on the wooden strip. The outside wall is built with a cement barrier, hoping to control the tempestuous sea from strong storms when it overtakes the beach and meets the boardwalk, wanting to run over its barrier. A train and bicycles compete in the morning, but the train wins out in the evening when the bicycles are not allowed.

All who walk on the boardwalk make a mental checklist as to what foods one has to consume as they pass from one eatery to the next. The tasty fries, crab cakes, pizza and homemade ice cream – just to name a few - were the top contenders year after year for Dex and Sarah as they would return to the beach with their family.

Both had decided on ice cream – Sarah picking a swirl of chocolate and peanut butter in a sugar cone, while Dex picked mint chocolate in a regular cone with sprinkles. Not that they were hungry after eating so many crabs, but it was tradition – and a tradition that they shared and loved. They laughed as they licked their cones quickly, not wanting the sweet concoction to run down their chins.

"Well you were right, Sarah. You are still the Skee-Ball champion," Dex announced, giving her the honor that she so much enjoyed hearing about.

"Ha, what are you up too?"

"Can I convince you to ride on the tilt-a-whirl with me?" Dex begged, knowing Sarah hated the fast moving rides.

"Are you freakin serious? I will probably throw up after eating all of that ice cream, if I get on that ride!" she laughed, remembering it had happened many times before.

"You'll be fine," he reasoned, patting her on the back as they made their way to the ticket both.

The tilt-a-whirl kept making quick jerking circles as the base lifted and lowered on an angle, one too many times for Sarah's liking.

"I really need off of here, Dex!" Sarah yelled over the blare of the loud dance music playing, as the ride continued to bump and tilt, throwing her sideways towards her brother in the fast-moving seat.

Dex laughed loudly, watching his sister being pissed off, but loving her reaction. "It's almost over. Look – it's coming to an end now," he reassured, as it made one last jerky lap.

Dex helped Sarah from the ride. She walked slowly holding her side, moaning the whole way off the platform before jumping to the ground.

"I will *never* do that again! I don't know why I *always* give into you!" she said with a sideways irritated grin, feeling as if she was going to throw up.

"Cuz we're twins, and you can't say no to me."

"Oh yes I can!" Sarah insisted, knowing that for the most part what he was saying was true. Dex was her best friend. From the time they were born, she had his back and he had hers. She was only 5 minutes older than he was, but for her - that was enough to feel like his older sister that needed to always watch over him.

"Why don't we go back to the beach house? I think Scrabble is in order."

"Dex, seriously? You know it is hard to beat me in Scrabble," Sarah announced. "You want to lose now in that too?"

"We will see... I have been practicing," he answered giving her a playful grin.

"You can't practice Scrabble!"

"Well, sister, you obviously don't know everything," he quipped as they made their way back to The Dancing Seahorse.

They had left a couple of the lights on inside, but not the deck ones. Sometimes the mosquitoes were drawn to the outside lights, and their parents had taught them that keeping them off would resolve this problem until the citronella candles could be lit.

Dex pulled back the heavy set of patio doors, leaning over the metal railing and looking towards a few children who were still at play on the sand near the shoreline.

"Quite a breeze out there tonight. We may not want to light the candles, after all. I doubt they would stay lit anyway."

"No worries, we are still playing Scrabble though, right?"

"Of course," Dex confirmed with a smile, turning his attention back to the dining room table and the already set up game. "You didn't waste any time, I see."

Sarah smiled ready for the challenge of beating her brother. "Can I get you a coke?" she offered, grabbing one too.

"Sure. And that bag of pretzels that you brought from home?"

"Seriously? I just don't know where you put it all!"

Three rounds later and the conclusion was in – Dex won two games and Sarah beat him at only one.

"Want to go for round four?" Dex asked as he gathered up the Scrabble tiles placing them back in the cloth pouch.

"I'm exhausted," Sarah admitted. "It's 2:15 a.m. and I want to go to the beach in the morning. You are the winner, Dex. I guess you have been practicing," she conceded as she rolled her eyes, yawning loudly.

Dex grinned. "You believed that? Seriously? You can't practice Scrabble!"

Both of the siblings laughed until their sides ached. It was good to be together for a few days before their parents showed up for the weekend.

College would separate them, but their hearts would always be bound together – just like the tiles on the Scrabble board.

CHAPTER 5

Sarah could hear the many noises of the beach as she stretched and woke up. She had opened her window during the night wanting to hear the waves crashing on the shoreline; but now she was still tired and didn't want to be awakened by 10 a.m. by the sounds of the shore, seagulls, and kids yelling in the distance.

"Oh my... I guess I am up now, whether I like it or not," she resigned, sitting on the edge of the bed and slipping into her flip-flops.

She made her way to the kitchen, rummaging through the cabinets and refrigerator for something to eat. She decided on granola cereal that her mother kept at the beach house, and one of several bananas that she had brought from home. Coffee was never to her liking, although Dex was already a fan. He enjoyed the flavored, cold brews that were way too expensive in her opinion. If he wanted one, she would walk with him later to the coffee shop a few blocks down from the beach house.

"You up already?" Dex yawned, scratching his butt cheek through his athletic shorts as he made his way to the table. "I thought I would hit the beach this afternoon, but since you are up already, I guess I will go with you now."

"Do whatever you want," Sarah replied absent-mindedly, looking up from her cellphone that she was always busy with. "Did you know my new college roommate is from England?"

"Hmmm, that's cool. Hope you can speak her language," Dex teased.

"*She speaks English like we do, silly*," Sarah replied, looking at her brother to see if he was being serious, since he always said stupid things to make her laugh.

"Well, I'm sure she would argue that since Americans butcher the language," he added, while pouring himself some of the cereal, throwing a whole banana on top without cutting it up first.

Sarah looked up at Dex, lost in her thoughts about college. "I hope she won't be a pain-in-the-butt. I didn't think about that."

"It will be fine. You will see," Dex added, looking at his sister in a somewhat sympathetic way.

"Everything ok?"

"Yeah, everything is fine. Something just feels sorta weird - that's all. Maybe I ate too much last night."

Sarah began to laugh. "*Really? You know you did!*"

With breakfast completed, Dex and Sarah donned their bathing suits and made their way to the outside shed for the beach chairs and the umbrella. She had packed a cooler of ice, water, cheese and grapes, along with a beach bag of suntan lotion, beach towels and crackers. Dex's contribution was his towel slung over his shoulder and his flip flops that were his constant companion. Even when it was cold outside, he would wear them – at least inside.

As they turned to walk away from the shed, Dex remembered what they forgot. "Hey, we forgot the boogie boards!"

"You want them?" Sarah asked in surprise.

"Sure, why not?"

"Ok, I just wasn't sure if you wanted to go out today. It seems a little rough when I was looking out from the deck."

"You worry too much, you know that?" Dex added, looking at his sister in a half-hearted way.

"Whatever. Go get them," Sarah instructed, as she waited for Dex to grab the boards and return.

He hurried back, half out of breath. "Gotta start jogging again. The ladies won't want me once I'm at Towson, if I don't do something soon to stay in shape. Been lazing around too much this summer."

Sarah looked at her brother realizing he was kidding. "You know that is *not* the case. Too many will want you, and I *know* you will be blowing up my phone with the details."

Dex laughed. "You too, Sarah. I know you will make lots of friends at Maryland."

They trudged their way through the sand and sat up their beach camp near the shoreline.

"Maybe we are a little close," Sarah assessed, looking at where the other beachgoers were located with their things. "I don't want the water rushing in and getting everything wet once the tide comes in."

"Sarah, its all good," Dex reassured. "We are just fine."

CHAPTER 6

Dex and Sarah sat under the umbrella that was blowing a little too much in the morning breeze. The flaps were snapping loudly from the wind pushing against them.

"I think I better do something about this umbrella," Sarah said in frustration, as she got up off her low-slung seat and packed more sand around the base of the umbrella, hoping it would not blow away.

"Just look at the water. A little rough, but great for riding the waves, don't you think?" Dex asked, as Sarah was brushing the sand off of her hands.

"I could take or leave it. I'm just enjoying sitting here, chilling and watching people."

Just at that moment there was a simultaneous whistle from all the lifeguards, high above their lifeguard stands. They were motioning for the beachgoers, that were situated close by their stands, to report to them for some important information and updates.

"We better go see what that guy wants," Dex said, as he rose from his chair.

"Sure..." Sarah replied drowsily, half asleep and relaxed as her twin pulled her to her feet, groaning and walking by his side.

They moved with the others and crowed around the lifeguard who had since jumped down from his stand, talking with his hands on his hips with authority.

Sarah took notice to his muscular tan chest and well-fitting royal blue shorts with Marlin Beach printed on the backside. He wore sunglasses, had a brimmed ball cap on that revealed a few brown curly locks, and a whistle dangled from his neck. He was quite handsome. She noticed a tattoo above the inside of his right wrist that looked like a life preserver with initials inside of the circle. Her parents would have never allowed Dex or her to get a tattoo, but she felt somewhat intrigued by it. She wasn't sure how she felt about the tattoo, or even if she found it attractive, but one thing she knew for sure - the lifeguard made her heart flutter - with or without it. Sara assumed he was a few years older than she was and totally out of her reach, but for some reason he unnerved her.

"Ok, my name is Lance and I called you guys here for a reason. You see - there are riptides out in the ocean today. For anyone not knowing what that is," he pointed outward towards the waves, "it's like a river running vertically through the ocean - out from the shoreline. If a riptide grabs hold of you, you got to remember to swim sideways from the pull of it. Never allow it to pull you out further. Bad things could happen. That's all I am saying…" he said distantly, to the group standing around him.

Lance motioned to the sign attached to the lifeguard stand, which showed more information about riptides. A young child interrupted him as he spoke.

"Can we still swim? Can I ride the waves with my boogie board?"

"Ah, sure. But you gotta be careful, little guy," Lance said with a smile, bending down and bracing on his knees, as he made eye contact with the young boy. "Ok, folks, enjoy the beach, and be on guard for those riptides!" he warned once more as the group departed, making their way back to where they were all camped out.

Sarah looked back, giving Lance a lingering parting glance that rested way too long on his bathing suit, and then proceeded upward to lock with his dancing brown eyes that were now minus sunglasses. He smiled at her and she felt embarrassed that he knew she was looking him over from head to toe. *How silly*, she thought in embarrassment. *He probably has a different girl everyday. No one would want skinny me with barely any boobs*!

Dex had already made his way back to their umbrella and chairs. "What took you so long? Let's get in the water. I am really hot and sweaty."

Sarah grabbed her board, following Dex into the foamy swell. "Are you sure? It is so cooold!" she yelled, as she followed her brother beyond the initial break of the waves, jumping up and down and trying to avoid the water's blasting spray as it washed over her body.

"Don't be a sissy. We have done this many times before, Sarah. You will get used to it. Come on," Dex yelled, diving under the snap of the waves with his boogie board in hand.

They swam and played in the ocean, enjoying the exhilaration of the water temperature that was no longer cold to their skin. Several people were pulled from the surf by the lifeguards, as Sarah and Dex happily rode the waves and were oblivious to any potential danger around them.

"I don't know about you, but I am getting hungry," Dex mentioned with his hair full of sand, trying to pump the water from each ear, as he walked from the ocean pulling his boogie board behind him. "How about we break for some lunch? And maybe later we can walk to the coffee shop for my iced coffee?"

"Definitely," Sarah answered, feeling rather hungry herself.

She opened the cooler and her beach bag, extracting the things she had packed for each one of them to eat, handing Dex a paper towel along with his share of the food. They dined on the crackers, cheese and fruit; and washed it all down with a couple swigs of water from the ice-cold water bottles she had packed.

"Sarah, I'm just gonna rest a little bit and then we will get the coffee," Dex explained sleepily, as he laid face down on his beach towel ready for a nap.

"Sure, Dex, whatever you say," Sarah answered in a daze, feeling a snooze was in order for her too, as she glanced over at the lifeguard stand once more, realizing Lance was gone on his apparent lunch break.

Some time later, Dex poked Sarah in her side with his foot, waking her from a deep sleep. "Man, were you snoring," he teased with a toothy smile and his arms crossed, taking his seat back beside of her in the sand again. I went up to the beach house to use the bathroom and now I am wide awake."

She smiled at her brother, still trying to wake up. "Dex, you are so full of energy. Much more than I have at the moment. You know that?"

"Yeah, I guess I do," he answered without much regard, wiping the salt spray from his sunglasses. "That lifeguard is back over there," he gestured with a tip of his chin. "He's been busy dragging out all the little kiddies today."

"Unlike us who can handle are own?" she grinned.

"Something like that."

"Are you ready for that coffee now?"

"In awhile. Just enjoying the time sitting here," Dex replied, closing his eyes and breathing in deeply of the sea air.

"So, I'm not that bad of company?" Sarah asked, staring at her brother who seemed deep in thought.

"You know I pick on you, sis, but it is all in good fun. I will miss you when we leave for college in a few weeks," he answered tenderly, turning towards her again.

"Really, Dex? I never thought I would hear you say that, but you know the feeling is mutual. It is going to be strange being apart, right?" Sarah questioned, locking her sky blue eyes with his steel blue ones.

"Yeah, it will feel strange. But it will be a good thing for both of us, if I can concentrate on my studies," he laughed, trying to lighten the serious mood.

"If you ever need to talk or come visit, Dex - just let me know."

"Yeah, you too. I will always be here for you – you know that, right? That is, if you ever need me."

"Thanks, Dex. That means a lot," Sarah said, as she reached for her cellphone that was buried deeply in her beach bag. "Hey lean in. I want to take a selfie of us."

"Sure," Dex answered with a smile, leaning in towards his sister with heads pressed together, for a memory-making picture of their last summer spent together at Marlin Beach before college.

CHAPTER 7

The sun was shining brightly with barely a cloud passing in the sky. The wind continued to slap the umbrella around, making it almost impossible to keep it open any longer. Sarah got up from her chair and straightened the umbrella, kicking and packing additional sand around it, hoping to steady it for the final time of the day.

"How about one more time on the boogie boards?"

"Are you kidding?" Sarah remarked. "I thought once was enough with the size of those waves."

"Oh come on, we used to play in the surf all day long just a few years ago," Dex added with a playful sideways grin.

"You're right, but there is always tomorrow, and maybe it will be less windy. I just noticed a few kids getting dragged out of the water again," Sarah said with her hands on her hips, surveying the scene in front of her.

"That's what happens at the beach, sis, everyday. You know that."

Sarah grabbed her board already running for the shoreline, turning to look at her brother. "Ok, Dex, let's go for it!" she yelled excitedly, running full steam ahead, and diving in before the cold ocean water would impact her senses.

Dex was right behind, laughing all the way, trying to run and dive out further than Sarah was with her board.

The paddled out, riding one wave after the other, immensely enjoying the time they shared together. They were both athletic and well versed in the water. It had been a part of their lives since they were born, and their father had taught them well how to swim and be careful in the ocean.

And then the tide changed...

"Dex, I am getting sucked out in a riptide!" Sarah yelled in a terrified panic.

"Stay calm. Paddle sideways like the lifeguard said!" Dex yelled in her direction, as he still held on to his board.

"I can't Dex. I can't!" she yelled back, feeling the pull of the riptide taking her out at a swifter speed - faster and faster - deeper and deeper.

Dex let go of his board and began to swim at a break-neck pace, trying to reach his sister. He was sucked into the current and it was strongly tossing and dragging him out even further, as his arms wildly thrashed above his head, out of control. He began to cough as water rushed over him, as he still attempted to bob up and down above the waves.

"Help someone! Help!" Sarah screamed to shore, knowing that they were both in serious trouble.

Lance could hear Sarah, and jumped down from the top of his

lifeguard stand, running and shouting for additional help from his fellow lifeguard in the adjacent stand. They immediately jumped in the ocean, leaping over the surf with their rescue buoys in hand.

"You go after the girl," Lance yelled and instructed, as he pointed towards Sarah, before he swam swiftly in the direction of Dex.

Lance swam swiftly through the turbulent surge, pushing ahead as fast as he could in Dex's direction, keeping his eyes focused only on him. A huge monstrous wave erupted and crashed violently over Dex, making him scream out in a shrilling, piercing cry of pain. He was flung to and fro through the break of the wave – and then tossed in the air like a rag doll. Lance watched in disbelief at what he didn't anticipate happening. Dex lay motionless, face down in the water, sinking below its depths.

Lance tried to remember the exact place that Dex went under, as he continued swimming towards him and the riptide loosened its power. His lifeguard training taught him the necessity of never losing site of a person in trouble in the ocean. He kept plunging and diving with his arms outstretched under the water, trying to find him through the darkness of the sea. And then the riptide began again with its fast outward flow, revealing Dex once more - with another flipping and crashing of his lifeless body.

Lance threw himself in his direction with one last desperate attempt, risking the safety of his own life as the buoy flung from his body. He reached Dex and the buoy again, turning him over, trying to give him mouth-to-mouth recitation as he paddled sideways against the riptide, finally breaking the hold the strong current had over him and Dex.

Sarah had already been taken to shore and was placed on the edge of the beach in the wet sand. She propped herself up on her elbows, crying out in disbelief, as she looked out at the scene unraveling in front of her. "Where is my brother?" she asked with an anguished cry, not even realizing she had several cuts on her forehead and legs from the lashing of the current that had flung her to the seabed floor.

"He is coming out now," the lifeguard with her answered, as Lance continued to drag Dex's lifeless body to shore, trying to give him mouth-to-mouth recitation all at the same time.

A crowd gathered by the water's edge, watching the whole spectacle unfolding. "Call 911 stat!" Lance yelled loudly. "Unconscious male," he announced in the direction of the guard making the call.

Sarah gasped in disbelief. "What is going on? What is wrong with my brother?"

 She began to get up from the sand; not caring about her own condition, as the other lifeguard gently pushed her back down. "Miss, please sit down and stay here. You have some lacerations. We are attending to your brother."

Dex was a distance away and Sarah could not see the extent of the injuries that her brother had sustained. He was unconscious and cut badly on his temple and the side of his chest. Blood was flowing freely from those areas as well as his mouth, nose and one ear. Lance covered him with a nearby beach blanket that someone had thrown in his direction, and continued to give him CPR as he waited on the ambulance. "Please get back!" he yelled to the nosey onlookers who had no business being there.

Soon, the roar of an ambulance was a short distance away. Parking quickly with the squeal of tires, a team of several paramedics ran to the scene with a gurney in hand. "You need to all get away!" one shouted to the crowd, as he bent down to assess Dex.

"What happened?" he asked Lance who was still doing heart compressions on Dex's chest.

"He got caught up in a riptide. The waves thrashed him about pretty badly, before landing him on a large jagged rock formation. He won't come to. I have been giving him mouth to mouth and CPR since I got to him."

"Thanks, we will take over from here," the paramedic directed, as he placed oxygen on Dex's face and quickly rolled him onto the gurney that was laying in the sand. The other strapped him down in place, and then the two mutually lifted the stretcher, transporting him to the ambulance that was ready to depart.

Sarah hid her face with her hands, tightly shutting her eyes in fright, wanting to block out what was happening. "My God, where are they taking my brother Dex? Please tell me what is wrong?" she cried out in a total state of shock, realizing something was terribly wrong.

Another ambulance arrived with two paramedics, rushing to Sarah's side – ready to attend to her cuts. "Miss, please hold still," they instructed, as they washed the sand from her wounds with a bottle of sterile water. "We are going to take you to the hospital now. Someone is taking care of your brother, but we need to see that you are alright also."

"I don't care about me. I am fine! It is Dex that I am concerned about," she cried, trying to get up again.

Lance walked over to the where Sarah was sitting in the sand. She looked up at him, squinting with her hand shielding her eyes from the lack of wearing her sunglasses. *It was the lifeguard,* she realized, *who had called the beachgoers to his stand, to talk about the riptides that day.*

He bent down, propped up on his knees that were brushed burned from rescuing Dex. "I am so sorry about your brother."

Sarah stared back at him in confusion. "Is he going to be ok?"

Lance's glance went from Sarah and then to the paramedic in charge of her, not sure what to say. "He is in good hands now. Please try not to worry," Lance added with a weary smile, touching Sarah's arm in a comforting and yet reassuring way.

She glanced down to where he had touched her, surprised by the gesture. She noticed his forearm with the unique tattoo that resembled a life preserver with the initials "JW" inside of it. She had never seen anything like it before today, and wondered what the significance of the initials were all about.

She looked back up at him into his sincere, brown eyes that seemed to hold genuine concern. "I need to be with my brother," she pleaded, with tears streaming down her swollen, brush-burned face.

"I know you do, and you will soon," Lance promised sadly, as they hoisted her onto the gurney, whisking her away to the awaiting ambulance.

CHAPTER 8

The loud blaring, endless squeal of the ambulance, sounded its warning as it pulled into Channel Ridge Regional Medical Center. Quickly, the gurney was unloaded and taken through the back entrance of the hospital into an awaiting operating suite, where a surgical team was prepped and ready - to do emergency surgery on Dex.

It was determined from his assessment on the way to the hospital that Dex could not breathe on his own and was barely holding on to life. An emergency intubate procedure was necessary, which the paramedics performed while he was still onboard the ambulance. They placed a tube down Dex's throat, and then he was hooked up to a portable ventilator. There was no other choice, and it had to be done just to keep him alive. X-rays and a CAT scan later, verified that he had internal bleeding caused by the deep cuts and lacerations he withstood in the ocean from the sharp jagged rocks, along with a severed spinal cord. Sadly, he had very little brain activity remaining.

The surgeons that were waiting on Dex's arrival at the hospital felt it was imminent to perform surgery immediately. The main purpose of the surgery was to control the bleeding in his brain as well as his abdomen, but to also determine the extent of his other injuries. They knew the percentage of survival was very slim, but decided the risk was worth taking to try to save the life of the young man.

Mike and Nancy were called and informed about the horrific accident that had occurred for both of their children - not only Dex, but with Sarah also. They were spared the full set of details; only knowing they both had been hurt. A private helicopter service was contacted, and airlifted them to the hospital, not even certain - God forbid - if they would make it in time.

Nancy was given a sedative before getting on the helicopter, by their family doctor who met them at the airport. She was in a state of shock, not dealing well with the uncertainty of what was happening with her children.

Mike had to be a strong stable force for her, as much as he wanted to break down himself from the reality of what was happening. He kept a strong arm wrapped securely around Nancy's shoulder as they boarded the chopper.

"This can't be happening, Mike. They are my babies," she sobbed, looking at him with pain-filled, frightened eyes.

"It will be ok," he comforted, patting Nancy's hand for support. "I am here with you. We will get through this together."

Nancy fell asleep as the blades of the chopper beat out a steady rhythm and rose high in the air, making a direct path straight towards the hospital. Mike looked out of the window and felt tears streaming down his face.

"God, please save my children," he breathed, hoping for a miracle.

The second ambulance raced into the back parking lot of the hospital. Sarah was not to be contained even though she had been given a sedative as well. "I need to get out of here!" she yelled. "I need to find my brother!" she screamed, unable to be comforted.

Sarah endlessly repeated that she wanted to see and be with Dex from the time she had been placed in the ambulance. "You need to calm down, miss. Being this upset is not going to help anything or anyone," the ambulance driver insisted, knowing his request was in vain. Her gurney was removed from the vehicle and taken through the same doors that her unconscious twin brother had been moved through. Sarah immediately sensed him and his pain, as they rushed her through the busy hallway, causing her to cry again. She was whisked away to her appointed examining room, purposely being kept away from where Dex was having surgery. A nurse covered her quickly with several warm heated blankets, trying to deal with the shivering that was now occurring.

"Please tell me that Dex is ok, God...." she pleaded to the heavens above, as she waited alone, crying in the semi-darkened room. Nothing, or no one, could console her from the empty, gut-wrenching, broken-hearted agony she was feeling.

As the lights were raised fully by Doctor Reynolds, he entered the room with his nurse right behind, causing Sarah to awake with a start as she tried to sit up. "Sarah, I am Dr. Reynolds. I am here to look at your lacerations from you accident."

"I do not need any help," she gritted out angrily. "Please just tell me where my brother is," she begged helplessly, as the nurse gently pushed her back down on the table for the doctor's evaluation.

The nurse glanced quickly at the doctor in silent anticipation, knowing the situation was complicated in the least. "Your brother is being attended to. For now, we need to focus on you and determine if you need some stitches," he answered with a kind smile.

Sarah moaned, as the nurse lowered the blankets, giving Dr. Reynolds full view of the cuts covering Sarah's arms and legs. He also examined her forehead with its superficial scrapes that appeared to be not too serious.

"I feel that everything is going to be ok, except for this one area on your leg. I do feel we need to sew this up," he pointed out, as he and the nurse washed and sterilized Sarah's leg and prepared it for the stitches. A simple numbing with several prinks of a needle, and five stitches later with a bandage in place, and they were finished with the procedure.

"I am going to give you a tetanus shot since you haven't had one in awhile - along with an antibiotic. All should be fine in a week, when you will need to come back to the hospital and have your stitches removed."

Sarah was very groggy from the whole event. "I am very tired, doctor."

"That is quite normal under the circumstances," Dr. Reynolds answered, as he encouraged her to rest. The lights were lowered again as the medical team left the room. Sarah drifted off into restless sleep that still had her fighting for her life in the ocean - and Dex was nowhere to be found.

The helicopter landed on the roof of the hospital, as a team of crisis intervention personnel was there to meet and escort Mike and Nancy to an awaiting office. Mike knew that this was not a good sign and he needed to be strong for Nancy.

"Have a seat, Mr. and Mrs. Miller," Dr. Peterson greeted, as he stood up from his desk and reached out to shake Mike and Nancy's hand. "My name is Dr. Peterson, and I am a neurologist here at Channel Ridge."

"What is this about?" Mike asked in concern.

"Mr. Miller, I have some good and bad news."

Mike lowered his head, sighing and breathing deeply, bracing for the worst. Nancy's mouth opened wide in anticipation, as she placed her free hand over it, waiting for the blow that she knew was coming.

"Your daughter is fine. A few bumps and bruises, and some minor lacerations that required several stitches, but other than that - Sarah will be ok."

"Well, thank God," Mike expressed in relief.

"But Dex, is not so fortunate."

"Oh nooo," Nancy cried out in fright. "What is wrong with my Dex?"

Dr. Peterson paused. This conversation was never pleasant with a family - no matter who the patient was, or the events surrounding the tragedy.

"Your son was in a horrible accident while he was in the ocean. He was caught up in a riptide. A series of waves overcame him, and flung him repeatedly into a very large jagged rock formation under the ocean. It badly punctured and cut into his side and forehead. The force of what happened severed his spinal cord," he informed sadly, knowing he had a son of his own. "He took in a lot water into his lungs and lost a lot of blood in the process."

Nancy quietly cried, just shaking her head in disbelief.

"I am sorry to inform you of this, but your son is in a coma and he barely has any bodily functions remaining. We have determined that he is brain dead. We did emergency surgery on him as soon as he arrived at the hospital, so that we could stop the internal bleeding that existed. We were able to get the bleeding under control in his cranium as well as in his abdomen, but unfortunately the blood loss has been too great. Unfortunately, that is why his brain function has stopped and his organs are beginning to fail."

"Do something, Mike," Nancy pleaded, grabbing her husband's hand, a little too firmly in earnest fear and desperation.

"Can he survive like this?" Mike asked, looking intensely at Dr.

Peterson for the answer he sought.

"If your son survives, we feel he will be in a vegetative state and never regain conscious. He will never walk or talk again. I must be realistic with you - chances are very slim that Dex is going to make it. He is on life support."

"Oh my God, oh my God, nooo!!!" Nancy screamed at the top of her lungs. "My wonderful son. You cannot let this happen to him, doctor!" Nancy exclaimed loudly rising to her feet. No amount of sedation would contain her raw emotions and the impact of the news.

"I am so sorry, Mr. and Mrs. Miller. Would you like me to page the Chaplin for you? Maybe he could provide some comforting words during a difficult time like this," Dr. Peterson offered, as he rose from his desk chair.

"That will not be necessary," Mike answered solemnly, as Dr. Reynolds approached the door ready to leave.

Dr. Peterson turned back to face the Miller's one last time before leaving the room, remembering what he reluctantly needed to add. "We did notice on your son's records that he had signed up to be a organ donor. Are you aware of that?"

Nancy began to cry again. "Please don't talk about this, like it is over. Please, please, don't make us have to say goodbye to our son."

Mike nodded at Dr. Reynolds, giving him permission to leave. He turned to hug Nancy once the room was empty and the door was shut, leaving them alone with their grief as his wife cried without end.

"Nancy, I have nothing to say right now. I have no words as to what we should do..." he said quietly in anguish, knowing he felt weak and unable to cope himself.

Her eyes were deep pools of despair, and she was emotionally drained to the point of not being able to respond to her husband either.

They sat together for some time, just holding the other and crying softly. Words were not spoken as they prayed silently, pleading for God to undo the past 24 hours and make it all go away.

CHAPTER 9

It was some time until Mike and Nancy could regain their composure. A kind Chaplin by the name of Rev. Roberts knocked on the door and asked to come in and speak with them for a few minutes. Nancy resisted, but Mike felt it was best to allow him to give them counsel, even if they felt they didn't need it.

"Mr. and Mrs. Miller, I am not a doctor, and I cannot give you medical advice. But I feel this is a time where we must turn to God and his wisdom - in circumstances such as this."

"Rev. Roberts, why would God allow this to happen to our son?" Nancy asked in desperation.

"I do not have the answer, Mrs. Miller. I wish I did - but only God knows," he said with a sad shake of his head. "Why don't we pray and ask God to grant you both strength and wisdom with what you need to do," he encouraged.

The three stood in a circle holding hands. Rev. Roberts led the pray. "Dear Heavenly Father. Grant the Miller's the wisdom to know what to do in this difficult situation. May your peace be over them and their family. In your precious name we pray this. Amen."

Rev. Roberts gave them both a hug, along with his business card that had his name and phone number imprinted on it. "Call me anytime, day or night. I am always available if you need me."

"Thank you," Mike replied solemnly. "That is very kind of you to offer."

"That is the least I can do," Rev. Roberts answered sincerely, as he left the Miller's alone again in the room.

It was some time until Mike and Nancy felt strong enough to leave Dr. Peterson's office, as they headed down the hall to the nurses' station to find their daughter.

Several of the staff were busy helping other people inquiring about their loved ones, as Mike and Nancy approached the large circular desk area. "May I help you?" the over-worked, middle-aged nurse asked, as the Miller's stood next in line.

"Yes, I hope so. We are trying to find our daughter, Sarah Miller. She was brought here by ambulance."

The nurse looked on the computer for the information they sought. "Sarah is in room 319 – right down the hall on the left," she pointed in the general direction.

"Thank you," Mike answered, as he wrapped his arm securely around Nancy's waist, leading her to their daughter's room

The lights were dim, but still slightly on in the room, giving Sarah a quiet environment to rest and regain her strength in. Nancy immediately ran to her side, unable to keep from touching and holding her.

"Sarah, it is mom. I am here and so is dad," she whispered, waking her daughter from sleep.

"Mom?" Sarah answered groggily, trying to sit up again.

Mike gently pushed her back down on the bed. "Sarah, you must rest. We just wanted you to know we are here now."

"How did you get here so quickly?" Sarah asked in dazed confusion.

Mike looked at Nancy, trying to find just the right words to say. "We received word of the accident, and we flew here by helicopter to the hospital."

"You did? *I am not in that bad of shape*," Sarah answered in surprise, trying to focus in on all that was happening. Sarah looked at her parents with concern, sensing something was terribly wrong. "What is it? Is it Dex? Is that why you came here by helicopter instead of driving?" she asked in alarm, this time insisting that she would sit up in the bed.

Mike and Nancy sat in the two chairs adjacent to the bed "Sarah, we really do not know how to tell you this."

"Oh my God, then don't!" Sarah screamed, knowing that what she was sensing was turning into a harsh reality.

"Please Sarah, calm down. This has been very hard on all of us," her father continued with a pat to her arm to steady her, trying to be the rational force where chaos now existed for mother and daughter both.

Sarah began to sob; not wanting to hear what she knew was coming. "Daddy, I can *feel* Dex is in trouble. Remember we are twins. I have always had that connection with him, as he has with me."

"I know, sweetie. I know," he replied sadly, while continuing to have his hand on her arm. "But we have some decisions to make and you are a part of this family. You do need to know what is happening."

The tears began spilling from Sarah's eyes again. "This should have never happened. I was the one pushing to go to the beach one last time with Dex for a few days before you guys showed up," she said with downcast eyes filled with regret. Her gaze returned to look sadly at her parents. "Just tell me. What is it?"

Mike braced himself for the blow that he knew was coming. "Sarah, your brother is in very bad shape. He was severely injured from the riptide that flung him against rocks in the ocean. The jagged rocks tore into his head and side. He is in a coma."

"No, no!" she gasped in disbelief, not able to grasp the reality of what her father was saying. "This can't be. It just can't be that bad!"

"Yes, Sarah, it is. Dex is dying. His spinal cord was severed, and he is brain dead and on life support."

"I will not accept this! You need to get him surgery to fix this! My God, we can't just let him die!" she sobbed.

"It isn't that simple. We just had a meeting with his doctor who explained everything to us. Dex did have emergency surgery to stop the bleeding as soon as he arrived here at the hospital, but he has already lost too much blood. The doctor explained to your mother and I that he will never come out of the coma or be able to walk or talk again. He will be in a permanent vegetative state if he survives. Do you want that for Dex?"

"Daddy, that is very unfair of you to ask me that question. I love Dex very much and I cannot make a decision about his life. Maybe a miracle will happen and he will recover. Doctors have been wrong about things like this in the past," she rationalized, not wanting to accept the truth.

It was some time until Sarah was calm again and resting peacefully. The nurse, who came in and took her blood pressure, felt it was in her best interest to have an anti-anxiety drug administered under the circumstances, after discussing all that had happened with the attending physician.

As Sarah slept, Mike and Nancy left the room. They proceeded back to the nurse's station, but this time to find out which room held their son. It was time to see him, and make the life and death decisions that no parent ever wants to make for their child.

They entered Dex's room, and what they saw made them feel weak and in disbelief as to the reality of it all. Several nurses stood around him, monitoring all that was happening. His arm had a catheter inserted in it, with fluids and medication running throughout his veins. A ventilator - with tubes and a mask – took over most of his face, making it possible for him to receive the necessary oxygen that was keeping him alive. A machine monitored all his vitals. His head was wrapped in bandages and his body was fully sheeted, as heated blankets kept him warm and his temperature regulated. He was black and blue and unconscious, with abrasions covering his entire face and arms.

Nancy began to cry and sob uncontrollably. "Mike, I cannot handle this…I just can't. I feel like I am going to pass out," she said as the room began to spin out of control.

"Nurse, please help my wife!" Mike yelled to the group attending their son, as Nancy slipped from his arms to the awaiting cold floor - leaving him to stand alone, helpless for all the members in his family.

CHAPTER 10

The day of the accident had come and gone and Dex was still alive the next morning. Mike and Nancy stayed in the room with him the majority of the evening, except for short breaks to use the bathroom or get coffee to help them stay awake.

Nancy was numb and resigned to it all now, having to accept this new normal for Dex. The emotional pain was great, but she and Mike knew they had to be strong for both of their children now.

They could not avoid going back to Sarah's room for much longer. They knew she would be emotional and seeking answers again about Dex. It was not anything they wanted to deal with, but unfortunately there was no other choice.

A new staff of nurses and physicians took to their morning rotation, checking in on Dex. It was time for Mike and Nancy to take a break and let the medical staff attend to their son.

They entered the hospital cafeteria, prepared to eat, realizing it was a forced effort as they pushed their trays passed the breakfast food in front of them. Each one chose bacon, eggs and toast, taking their seats amongst the other visitors who were busily eating breakfast also.

Some there for a happy event like the birth of a child or grandchild, and others there for the dying like they were -all together in a group, but going in different directions with their emotions.

They were only able to eat a few bits, as hunger was forgotten at a time like this. "I can barely eat, Mike," Nancy admitted as she looked up into her husband's tired face, just pushing her scrambled eggs around on the plate.

Mike glanced back at his wife with concern. "Try to eat a little. It will be another long day and you must keep your strength up."

"I know, Mike, but I am just so in shock over all of this."

"Me too," he sighed feeling depleted, looking up at Nancy with weary eyes and a day's worth of stubble on his face.

They finished their coffee and made their way to the elevator again, pushing the button to the 5th floor to find Sarah. It had been one less thing they had to deal with since Sarah's doctor had decided that she needed to stay in the hospital overnight. The thought of taking her to Dex's room the night before and asking her to keep a vigil was more than they knew she could deal with.

Mike and Nancy entered Sarah's room, finding her sitting up, watching TV and finishing her breakfast.

"Good morning, mom and dad. How is Dex?" she asked, as she scooped her last bite of strawberry yogurt into her mouth, looking surprisingly better after a good night's rest.

They joined her, sitting in the chairs that were still pushed up beside of her bed.

"I'm glad to see that you ate all of your breakfast, dear," Nancy mentioned sweetly with the best pretense of a smile that she could muster, trying to intentionally change the subject.

"Mom? Yes, I ate my breakfast, but what about Dex?" she asked irritably and to the point again.

Nancy looked to Mike for support, pleading with him silently for an answer for their daughter.

"Sarah, we do not want to upset you."

"Oh my word, Dad. I am 18 years old and I have a right to know about Dex!" she demanded, as she pressed the button to make her head raise up a little straighter in the bed.

"Yes, you do. But we want to make sure you are strong enough to handle this - after what you have been through yourself."

"I am strong enough," she said firmly. "The doctor was in a while ago and said I am being released today."

Nancy looked at Mike again, filled with worry and concern for her daughter's well being at the news that they must share.

Mike cleared his throat and shifted in the chair, grabbing the guardrail of the bed for support. "Sarah, Dex is in his room, but he is on life support and nothing has changed. He has had no improvement overnight. Things are not looking good for him."

Sarah already knew this was what her father was going to say. She had a premonition during the night about Dex. He came to her in a dream and was smiling and telling her he was going to be ok – even if they would be apart. She tried to tell him to stay with her, but he walked up a hill and waved goodbye, disappearing from her site. She tried to run after him, but her legs were in slow motion and would not move fast enough to catch up with him, as she cried and then woke up with actual tears running down her face.

"I want to see him... please. I need to tell him I love him."

"Of course, dear. But we should probably wait on your doctor and make sure you are checked out of the hospital first. Also, we need instructions on taking care of you," Nancy added gently, while patting her daughter's arm.

Dr. Reynolds made his way to Sarah's room during his morning rounds. He looked over her lacerations as her parents looked on.

"I would say everything looks pretty good, Sarah," he announced, as he assessed her bruises and scraps almost a day later. "Your stitches are not red, so the antibiotics are working."

Mike and Nancy stood by the window, trying to give the doctor his space to examine and speak with their daughter.

"Dr. Reynolds, is Sarah able to leave today?"

Dr. Reynolds turned his attention to Nancy who was anxiously waiting for an answer.

"I would think so, as long as she continues to take her medication and returns to the hospital in a week to have her stitches removed," he said over his glasses that were low on his nose.

Mike asked for a word alone with Dr. Reynolds, as they proceeded to the hallway to talk alone.

"As I am sure you are already aware, doctor, my son and daughter were together in the ocean when the riptide dragged them out to sea, causing this terrible accident."

"Yes, I have heard."

"Well, I am a little concerned for Sarah. She has been resting nicely here in her hospital room and seems to be on the mend, but that is not the case for my son. We are returning to intensive care to be with him shortly. You see, he is dying," he said sadly with downcast eyes, even though Dr. Reynolds had already been updated to the life-threatening circumstances.

"What would you like me to do?" Dr. Reynolds asked, knowing this sort of pain had no easy remedy for a family.

"I am not sure what the answer is to that question. You see, Sarah and Dex are twins. They are very close and she wants to be with her brother right now. I want that for her also, but not at the expense of her health suffering."

Dr. Reynolds paused, placing his finger against his face in contemplation. "I think you should let her have as much time with her brother as she would like. If she starts getting too emotional, you can have the nursing staff page me; and I, or my assistant on duty, will give her something to calm her down."

"Alright. Thank you, Dr. Reynolds," Mike replied with anxiety etched all over his face that was now his constant companion. He knew this situation was going to get tough on the whole family very soon, and he was going to have to be the strong one to control it.

Dr. Reynolds and Mike entered Sarah's room again, as she lay in bed relaxing with Nancy sitting nearby. A news report came on the TV about the accident that she and Dex had been involved in. The reporter said that the one teen had been rescued from a riptide and was fine, but the other, was pulled from the ocean by a lifeguard from Marlin Beach, and was now dying.

Sarah looked at her mother in shock and disbelief. "I cannot believe they are saying this!"

Dr. Reynolds intervened. "Sarah, the news sometimes can be cruel and misleading, but in this case there is some real truth to what they just reported. Your father and I have been discussing your release and how you may react to seeing your brother in the state he is in."

Sarah listened intently as the tears began to spill from her eyes. "Is Dex going to die?"

Dr. Reynolds glanced at Mike and Nancy and then at Sarah. "We are not God. Who can say, but the prognosis for your brother is not looking good. I would suggest you spend some time with him. If things start bothering you too badly, take a break, or we can give you some medication to calm you down. Does that work for you?"

"I guess so, Dr. Reynolds," she answered reluctantly, realizing she didn't have any other choice in the matter.

With that said, Dr. Reynolds had a nurse come into the room and the release papers were signed. Sarah was free to leave. She walked with her parents to the elevator, and pushed the button to the 10th floor – where her twin, friend and wonderful brother was waiting.

CHAPTER 11

As the elevator doors opened to the hustle and bustle of the nurse's station, Mike and Nancy felt the need to escort Sarah to the waiting room area not far from Dex's room.

"Why don't we sit here for a minute?" her father instructed, as they took a seat on the firm, but uncomfortable, institutionalized leather sofa.

A look of concern was etched all over their faces, but especially Sarah's. She looked at both of her parents and held out her hands to them both. "I know you think I can't handle this and you want to protect me, but Dex is my brother and I love him. I want to be there for him, no matter what."

"We know that, honey, but we want to prepare you for the shock of what you will see. Dex is unconscious, as you know. He has tubes leading from his arms, and he also has a mask on his face with more tubes leading to a ventilator. His head and chest are wrapped and he is badly bruised and hardly recognizable. Machines are all over the room just monitoring him and keeping him alive," Mike explained.

Sarah sat listening and shaking her head in disbelief. "Oh, if only we could go back to a couple days ago. It was so much easier then," she said forlornly with much regret.

Mike and Nancy silently agreed, knowing that reality was just a distant passing thought now, and things could not be changed.

"I guess what I am asking is, do you feel you can handle the emotional impact of seeing your brother like this after the trauma you just physically went through yourself?"

"Yes, dad, I can," Sarah said with new calm and resolve, wiping her wet, tear-filled eyes with the back of her hand. "Let's do this. I am ready to see Dex," she said stoically while rising, ready to go into his room.

The three made their way into Dex's room, trying to enter quietly. A nurse was charting his vitals and looking over his fluid levels, while a doctor was speaking softly to the nurse, trying to get the recent update on any changes to his condition.

Sarah's heart skipped a beat as she observed her brother who was so badly beaten up and broken. She breathed a silent prayer. *Dear God, give me the strength to be here for Dex right now.*

Her mother and father held on to her tightly, supporting her weight on either side, as she approached her brother's hospital bedside - still standing a distance away.

The medical staff stopped what they were doing as the family approached.

"Is it ok if we could just visit with our son for awhile?" Mike asked.

"Of course. We are just finishing up," the doctor whispered, giving a sympathetic smile to the three of them. "Take as much time as you need."

The nurse and doctor departed, allowing Mike, Nancy and Sarah some time to be alone with Dex. They approached his bed, being very careful not to touch any of the tubes or equipment attached to him, as per the nurse's instructions. The sound of the ventilator was constant, as they watched Dex's chest rise and fall to each beat.

The family stood for some time, just watching him, quietly closing their eyes and begging God for a miracle. Not a word was spoken and it was some time before anyone broke the spell of the silence between them.

Sarah looked at her parents in total despair and frustration. "Is it all right if I talk to him alone and by myself?"

"Yes, sweetie," Nancy answered sadly, looking to her husband for direction.

"We will leave you alone with Dex for a few minutes - if you feel up to it?"

"I am fine. I need this time," she said firmly, as they nodded and walked out of the room, leaving her alone with him.

She took the seat that was placed beside of the hospital bed, and just stared at her brother. Tears began to run down her face again as she remembered the joy of just riding the boogie boards together before the riptide tore them apart and changed everything.

"Dex, I am here. I hope you can hear me. It is Sarah, and I am so sorry this has happened. I want you to know that I have been praying and asking God to make you better. Please get better, Dex. I just don't know what I will do without you."

He lay motionless, with the ventilator continuing to make his chest expand and contract; giving her comfort that because of it he was still alive.

"I am so sorry, Dex," Sarah said, as she rose up from her chair to look over him. "I should have never insisted that we go to the beach house for a few days before mom and dad showed up for the weekend. I…. just…. wanted some time… alone with you. That's all," she said with a soft cry, feeling very frustrated that he could actually hear her.

She surveyed the room and found a magazine lying on a table between a couple of lounge chairs - on the opposite wall, where a bank of windows brought some much-needed filtered light through the half-drawn metal blinds. She looked out at the busy street below that was a scurry of activity with cars and patrons coming and going. The sun was shining brightly and she knew that the beach was only a short distance away, filled with happy vacationers unaware of the danger that could change a life forever - just by the changing of a tide. She sighed, knowing she needed to stay strong for Dex - more now, than ever in the past.

Sarah grabbed the ladies magazine and went back to her chair and began to read to Dex. "This may be boring brother, but I think I will read to you how to make a great summer meal. Does that sound like something you would like to hear?" she asked the non-responsive form of her twin, as she bravely began to recite the ingredients needed for making homemade macaroni salad.

It was some time later that Mike and Nancy reappeared. They had walked back to the cafeteria and gotten another coffee to go, as they tried to clear their heads as best they could. They entered Dex's room, surprised to find Sarah reading to her brother, but relieved that she seemed to be in control of her emotions under the circumstances.

"We're back, honey," her mother whispered.

Sarah turned with a start. "I don't think we need to whisper, Mom. I think Dex can handle it," she said with a realistic, eerie blank look and broken smile.

"Ok…" Nancy replied, surprised but her daughter's change in attitude since they were gone.

"I do feel that we should definitely be with him at all times. That is for certain. Maybe we can take shifts, but I do not plan to leave the hospital unless my brother goes with me," she added emphatically, laying out a plan of action for the family to follow.

Mike and Nancy were amazed by Sarah's newfound strength and determination. In some ways, she seemed to have more strength now than they were feeling.

The day, and the days to follow, were filled with a monotonous routine – nurses, doctors, checking on vitals and fluids, the ventilator, and the non-stop vigil of the family members by Dex's bedside. Mike, Nancy and Sarah would take turns sleeping in the chaise lounges in the room or out in the main waiting area on the 10th floor. It was a draining routine, and one that was exhausting to all involved.

One week to the day of the accident, Sarah had her stitches removed. Dr. Reynolds looked over her abrasions, bumps and bruises. "I feel you are recovering well, Sarah," Dr. Reynolds stated, as he placed a bandage over the area where the stitches had been previously. Do you have any concerns?"

"Not for me, but I do for my brother," she added, looking at Dr. Reynolds for guidance.

He paused, trying to be sensitive to the situation that he had been kept well informed of. "I know this is a very difficult time for you, Sarah. I would suggest that your family turns to Dr. Peterson for answers. *I can only address your medical needs.* I am sorry," he said matter-of-factly, somewhat cold to the endless pain and tragedy that surrounded his job.

As Sarah took the elevator back up to the 10th floor, the doors opened to a familiar face sitting in the waiting area. She stopped, dead in her tracks, staring at the person who had changed all of their worlds — the lifeguard, who was responsible for rescuing her brother, but in her opinion, had failed, because of the shape Dex was in.

"What are you doing here?" she gritted out, with her hands tightening by her sides in balls of rage.

"I wanted to check on you and your brother," Lance answered politely, caught off-guard by her apparent anger.

"No need for that! You have done enough damage. Please leave the hospital and let my family be alone!" she demanded, as she placed her hands on her hips in a defensive posture.

"I am very sorry you feel this way," Lance resigned in total surprise. I tried my best, and again, I am sorry," he repeated, while rising from his seat and walking towards the elevator.

Lance was in shorts and a t-shirt with Marlin Beach on the front of it. He was tan, shaven, and looked well groomed, ready to take on the day. Sarah, on the other hand, looked tired and disheveled, still in the sweat pants and a t-shirt her mother had bought for her from the hospital gift shop one week earlier.

For one moment their eyes locked, as they tried to read the mood and the thoughts of the other. Lance pressed the button and the elevator doors opened, as he entered it. He turned to look at Sarah one last time. "I just wanted you to know that I have been praying and hoping for the best. I truly mean that," he said sincerely, as the elevator doors closed in front of him, leaving her to stand alone with her thoughts.

CHAPTER 12

The presence of Lance had left Sarah quite shaken. She felt it best, not to mention it to her parents with all that was going on with Dex. Even though it totally unnerved her that Lance came to the hospital, she had handled it and hoped that he had gotten the message loud and clear that - there were no kind regards where he was concerned.

Dex's condition was obviously not improving, and she knew that Dr. Peterson seemed to be showing up more frequently now to his room. She entered Dex's room and found her mother and dad deep in conversation with the doctor. Nancy was crying and wiping her eyes, making it obvious to Sarah that something was terribly wrong as her mother signed off on a form that was presented to her.

"What is going on?" Sarah asked anxiously, as she approached her parents and Dr. Peterson.

They paused for a moment, before Dr. Peterson addressed Sarah directly. "Your brother is not improving, which in all reality, was what we had already anticipated on day one after his surgery. Not only is he not improving, but his condition has grown worse, with his organ function totally in decline."

Sarah looked at her parents and then to Dr. Peterson in disbelief, suddenly feeling nauseous. "Maybe there is a chance he will get better, doctor?"

"No, Sarah. That is not going to happen at this point. I am giving your brother only 24 hours to live."

"Oh my God, noooo!" she yelled out at the top of her lungs, looking very frightened and confused. "Just do something to save him! Please!"

Dr. Peterson grabbed Sarah's shoulder, trying to steady her. "I think you need some time alone with your family, young lady. I will be in the hospital and will check back within the hour," he stated firmly, looking to Mike and Nancy both as he departed from the room.

Sarah paced the floor in front of the windows, praying and hoping for a miracle. *Please, God, please. I will do anything if you heal my brother. Take me - not him. He deserves to live!*

Mike approached his daughter, deep in his own sorrow. "Honey, spend some time with Dex. Your brother needs you by his side right now," he added, giving her a caring hug.

Mike and Nancy left the room and closed the door behind them. Sarah gingerly approached Dex's bed, not wanting the bad movie to play out any further. She could not sit down. She placed her hands on the metal railing that was attached to the side of his bed for safety, steadying herself as she looked down over her brother.

She was silent for some time, just lingering and taking in every inch of him from head to toe. Just to look at him, Sarah felt Dex had not changed much in a week, even though the doctor had confirmed that he had. He lay still and quiet, while the respirator continuing to do its work. Warm blankets were constantly being placed on him, keeping his body temperature regulated. His head was still bandaged along with his abdomen, and most of his face was covered in tubes and a mask that held it all in place, which frustrated her that she couldn't see him without all of it.

Even though she was not to touch him, she reached out and lightly rested her hand on the blanket where she knew his hand was concealed. "I am sorry, Dex. I know I say this to you daily, but I really mean it now - more than ever. How can I say goodbye to you? It isn't fair we have only had 18 years together. What will I do without you in my life?"

She bent her head and began to cry over the railing, feeling a slight jump from underneath the covers. She looked up, and then at Dex for a sign, but he remained motionless. She ran from the room, hoping this was a positive sign.

"Mom and Dad, I just felt Dex's hand move!" Sarah said with excitement.

"What do you mean?" Nancy asked in disbelief.

"I know I wasn't to touch Dex, but I laid my hand on top of the blanket where I knew Dex's hand was, and I felt it jump after I spoke to him for awhile."

Mike immediately went to the nurses' station and had Dr. Peterson paged. Within minutes, he met them in Dex's room along with two nurses by his side. They asked for the family to give them some space - requesting that they move towards the bank of windows - so that they could accurately evaluate what was occurring with Dex.

Dr. Peterson turned back towards the family, after removing his stethoscope from Dex's heart, with a sad look on his face. "It is time to say goodbye. I am sorry to have to inform you of this, but the end is here."

The three began to cry, as the medical team folded back Dex's covers to his waist, exposing his ashen gray arms, wrapped chest and bruised and battered body, leaving them alone with Dex.

Each took their turn to say goodbye - to touch his arms, and hold and kiss his hands. Within minutes, the heart monitor had flat-lined and Dex was gone, leaving them alone – paralyzed with the reality of it all.

Mike, Nancy and Sarah – all three – stood in a line, shoulder to shoulder - holding on to the metal railing that overlooked their loved one. Dex was now gone, and a big part of each one of them went with him - never to be gotten again.

CHAPTER 13

The Miller's made their way from the hospital room after some time, giving the nursing staff a chance to remove all the tubes, mask and catheter from Dex's arm. The ventilator no longer made its racket and was silent for the first time in a week. Someone from the morgue had been contacted, being directed to quickly begin organ removal so that someone else could have life, as per the "signatures of release" that Mike and Nancy had just given.

Mike had to drag Sarah and Nancy away to a private room that Chaplin Roberts met them in once again.

"I am so sorry, folks, for your loss."

Sarah could not be consoled as she grieved and cried loudly as the Chaplin continued.

"When you feel ready, you need to contact a funeral parlor of your choice to pick up your loved one. If you do not know whom to contact, I can give you some excellent recommendations here locally."

"That is quite alright, Rev. Roberts. I will be contacting a funeral parlor in Baltimore, where we are from - to pick up my son."

An hour later, Rev. Roberts had done his best to provide comfort, words of wisdom, and a parting prayer to the grieving family. He left the family alone, suggesting that they stay for however long they needed.

Mike excused himself, leaving Nancy and Sarah alone, knowing he had to make the inevitable call he dreaded - for Dex to be picked up and taken away by hearse to Baltimore. When he returned, his face was very red and swollen from the private tears he had shed. He lost his only son - the one he had coached baseball for, and taught to swim in their backyard pool as well as the ocean. He looked stoic as he re-entered the room.

"I have made all preparations for Dex. Someone will be here within a few hours to pick him up. It is time for us to go home now and prepare for Dex's funeral. I know it has been a long week, but it is time to leave," he announced, looking wearily at Nancy and Sarah both.

Sarah stood, in disbelief by her father's words. *"We can't leave Dex here and go home! What if he isn't picked up, and something goes wrong?"*

"Sarah, Dr. Peterson and his staff assured me they would take care of all the necessary arrangements. They feel it is in our best interest to go home now and get some rest."

"I will not be resting any time soon, dad!" Sarah gritted out, feeling very angry at the world around her.

The drive back to Baltimore was strained with friction and quietness, as mother and daughter attempted to sleep - one in the front seat and one in the back, as Mike drove home in silence.

Sarah was stretched out in the back, and with everything that had happened in the past week she had totally forgotten that her car and other belongings were still at the beach house. She wondered if anyone had even gotten their things off of the beach that day, including her and Dex's cellphones.

She knew her dad had a good friend at Marlin Beach, by the name of John, that he played golf with regularly. Hopefully, he had been contacted and had taken care of things and she would never have to go back to the beach house again.

Sarah tried to sleep in the car while resting on her side, in a state of half-conscious sleep. Dex came to her in a dream and was smiling - with a glow around his face that was perfect without bruises and cuts – appearing to be totally happy. She awoke, sitting straight up in the back seat. "Dex!" she yelled, as her dad pulled the car off the road with a jerk, waking Nancy in the process from her slumber.

"Are you ok?" he asked as he looked behind in concern, taking a few deep breaths to regain his composure.

"Yes, daddy, I am. I just had a dream about Dex, and he looked so healthy again with a smile on his face."

Nancy yawned, looking at her husband and then to Sarah. "Consider that to be a sign from Dex - that he is ok."

"I guess so, mother," Sarah shook her head in sad resignation, knowing she would hear those same words from the many "well-wishers" in the next few days about her brother.

They made their way back to Baltimore, making all the arrangements for the viewing, funeral and reception to honor Dex. An obituary was placed in the local paper, as well as on the funeral parlor's website. Many friends of the family, and of Dex's – mainly from the high school he attended, along with his sports teams – were notified. Flowers were ordered, and a caterer was contacted to provide food and drinks for afterwards, to be held back at the family home for all who wanted to attend and visit.

The day of the funeral was sunny with low humidity - a perfect day to honor and say goodbye to Dex. A large number of friends, family and loved ones gathered at the community church where they regularly attended. The room was filled with the sweet sounds of the choir singing comforting hymns, providing encouragement to all those that heard - to be at peace without Dex.

The pastor gave his remarks that were filled with the unfairness of someone so young dying, but having the hope of going home to be in heaven and seeing departed relatives. Somehow, Sarah felt relief at knowing that, but angry - all the same, that he was gone. She had days to think about it, and she was numb and unwilling to accept what had happened.

Many cried, as they passed his coffin one last time. Dex's best friend, Zachary, whom he had grown up with from the time of youth, along with Dex's last girlfriend, Livia, that he had just broken up with a few weeks prior, paused to pay their final respects in front of the casket. Sarah chocked back her tears as she watched them, knowing how close they were to her brother.

"He was the best, Sarah," Zachary expressed, while wiping tears from his eyes. "I will never forget him," he added, as he hugged and comforted Mike and Nancy, and Sarah too.

Livia dabbed her eyes with a tissue as she approached the family. "I just got our prom pictures back. I can't believe he is gone," she said, while shaking her head sadly.

Few words were spoken, with only an occasional nod or hug given, as each on-looker paid their final respects to Mike, Nancy and Sarah.

The paw bearers carried Dex to his final resting place, on top of a hill, overlooking the city and the harbor. Sarah knew she would be stopping there often, just to have her time alone with Dex. She felt so empty now that he was gone, and had to will herself just to walk and function.

The black dress that her mother bought for her to wear to the funeral, made her feel depressed. She never wore black, and somehow she felt Dex would have been ok if she had just showed up in jeans and a t-shirt.

She watched the steady stream of loved ones file past Dex's coffin for the last time, dropping a long-stemmed white rose on top of it before saying a final goodbye. She lowered her head, not wanting to be next, but her mother handed one to her anyway.

"Here, Sarah, take this and say goodbye to Dex," she instructed.

Sarah stood, numbly staring at her mother, obliging her request but not really wanting to walk and do so. She knew it would be inappropriate to make a scene, but all she wanted to do was scream and cry, and hold on to the coffin, and yell no...no...no! But of course she couldn't do that. She had to be proper at a time like this, and say her final goodbyes while everyone was watching - just as her mother and father were ready to do - for Dexter William Miller, the most wonderful brother anyone could ever ask for!

The limousine drove the family back to the house; to the obligatory wake and reception that Sarah did not want to attend either. Her grandparents - on both sides - along with her aunts, uncles and cousins were there too. She felt responsible for Dex's death and she didn't want to answer their questions. She didn't care about meat trays, and cakes, and the casserole dishes that were given in great quantity so that the family didn't have to cook for a while. She had no appetite for food or fellowship. All was lost for her now, and life would never be the same. Dex was gone, and so was her heart.

Who could really understand what she was going through, other than maybe someone else who was a twin? To spend 9 months in the womb with her sibling, to come forth in birth, to suckle on her mother's breast by her brother's side, to sleep many times in the same crib, to throw food at each other in a high chair, to be dressed alike, and to play with her only brother until the time of daycare when her mother was teaching - was more than she could bare. And as the years went on and they got older, they would watch each other play baseball and soccer, cheering the other one on to victory. It was only natural to quiz the other when it was time for a test in school, or to lend an ear when a friend or even their parent wasn't being kind or fair. *It was now over and no more!* She was lost and totally alone.

Sarah's thoughts tormented her, and she was barely able to sleep most nights, with Dex constantly visiting her in her dreams. She knew that she no longer had the half that made her the whole. It was too soon to say goodbye - to her best friend and brother. Sarah never saw it coming before they made that final trip to the beach. It was not something one thought about. The accident had made her grow up overnight, whether she wanted to or not.

She made a vow that day, after the funeral and once her relatives finally departed, that she would never get that close to anyone again. The pain was just too great from losing Dex, and she would guard her heart from any future blow of loss – and unequivocally, she would make sure of that.

CHAPTER 14

10 years later…..

Sarah Miller was an accomplished, project manager and designer for her father's architectural firm. She had attended the University of Maryland, graduating with a dual degree in Architectural Design and Business Management, excelling to the top of her class and graduating with honors.

After the death of her brother, Dex, she decided to pour all of her heart and soul into college and then her career, not allowing anything or anyone to intrude upon her goals. An occasional boyfriend crossed her path, but she never kept them around for longer than a few months, when her emotions started feeling vulnerable.

The beach house was rarely used after Dex's death. The family tried to go to it on several occasions, but the pain and memories were just too great. Even when they went there, if they attempted to sit on the beach with their chairs and umbrella, or even get in the ocean like they had done many times before, it created an emotional break down in Sarah that could not be remedied. She would run from the beach, with an anxiety attack that left her in a panic. Her parents knew that it was a problem, but Sarah insisted that she was all right and just avoided the beach.

They even considered renting it, but somehow that wasn't an option either. The house had become almost a shrine and memorial to Dex. The thought of strangers coming to the beach house and allowing their children to jump up and down on Dex's bed, or the possibility that anything in his room could be destroyed, was incomprehensible. So the house remained empty - and sadly so.

Sarah's parents insisted on family counseling right after Dex's death, feeling this would soften the blow if they all attended. She seemed to be making some progress - as were they, but college began and Sarah felt she would be all right, claiming her studies would keep her mind occupied.

When summer unfolded, almost a year to Dex's death, they chose to take their family vacation back to The Dancing Seahorse. That was when Mike and Nancy realized Sarah was not past her brother's death, as much as she pretended.

The anxiety attack that she had experienced, was so severe that they ended up in the Emergency Room, and Sarah had to be medicated just to calm her down. The doctor suggested therapy, after her parents explained the situation; but even with Sarah's renewed promises to do so, it never happened.

She never saw Lance again during the infrequent early visits to the beach house after Dex's death, and she was grateful for that. If he was a lifeguard still, he was not watching the waters in front of their place any longer.

She often wondered what happened to him, as she still remembered the sad look on his face the very day of her brother's death - before he got on the elevator at the hospital. She had no ill will towards him really, since he was a non-factor in her life after so many years; but she hated how fate was cruel and unfair. He was a part of the past that left her without her brother Dex, along with any chance of hope for her own personal happiness.

Now, her parents had decided it was time to sell the beach house. Sarah offered to go to Marlin Beach and see what condition the house was in after several years of non-use. Mike and Nancy had a concern that she couldn't handle things, but since her father had just suffered a heart attack a few months prior, she knew she had to be the strong one and deal with things in their place.

She packed a few things, planning to stay for a long weekend through Monday. Whatever needed to be done, she would assess and review with the realtor. Once she was gone and back in Baltimore, the real estate company could coordinate any necessary repairs before listing the property. It would be a simple ending to the beach house lifestyle the Miller's knew and loved - over thirty years of memories for her mother and father. It would not be easy to go back, but she had learned to build an icy protection around herself that most could not penetrate through.

Sarah placed her several bags in the car, along with a cooler filled with food and drinks, and headed out of the city. She had been working passionately on several large projects for Miller's Architecture, which was her family's business, taking on more work since her father's illness. She considering hiring someone new in a management role, to take some of the load off of her shoulders, but decided against it in the end. *A few less hours sleep*, she concluded, *would suffice in keeping up with the extra busy workload.*

Her father insisted he was not ready to retire yet, but she worried about him and his health. A few stints to his heart later, Mike claimed he felt as good as new; but with the blockages of his arteries, his doctor suggested a major change to his diet and his exercise routine. Nancy had her hands full trying to keep him focused on the required changes, but they would take walks together in the evening and cut out the red meat - as some vital first steps to improving his health.

Sarah was happy for a few days' break, and her co-workers had promised to take over any work responsibilities while she was gone. It was hard for her to relax. Work was her constant companion that demanded much out of her. She had considered from time to time, getting a cat to keep her company once she moved from her parents' home; but she couldn't handle the extra responsibility when it came right down to it, even if it meant that she was alone.

With her over-sized sunglasses in place, and her hair pulled back into a tight ponytail, she drove across the Bay Bridge with her windows rolled down, breathing in the fresh, salty sea air that smelled of seafood. She glanced down at several fishing boats and a large container ship that was dragging a triangular-shaped, white-foam tail from behind its motor. A few seagulls soared lazily through the air, rising and falling to the currents that pulled them along the way. It was a beautiful day and she felt at peace with her pilgrimage.

Maybe I should stop at Mom and Pop's? She thought, as she approached a familiar produce stand and shop her family traditionally visited every chance they got on their way back and forth to the beach. As she pulled into the sandy soiled driveway area, she realized she was only one of two patrons. She approached the stand, overflowing with watermelons and cantaloupe, smelling the heady aroma of the fruit and vegetables in front of her. It was early summer, and she doubted the melons were local, but she could pretend. She thumped the watermelon, hearing the hollow sound that gained her approval.

"I'll take this and this one too," she smiled at the young female clerk, who rang up her purchase.

"That will be $7.00, please," she announced, while looking at Sarah for the money.

Sarah placed a ten on the counter, as she grabbed the melons and thanked her and walked away.

"Your change, miss?"

Sarah turned with the melons in each hand. "It's fine. It's your tip," she said with a sweet smile. "Enjoy your day!" she added, making her way merrily back to her car. She placed the melons in the back seat, and turned on the radio. She turned the channels until she found a favorite, local beach station – a mix of today's hits, but with oldies and beach tunes sprinkled in from time to time. She sang to many of the songs, her one joy that never left her.

Her cellphone rang as she drove the remaining distance to Marlin Beach. "Hello, it's Sarah," she answered over her Bluetooth speaker.

"Sarah, it's dad. How are things going so far?"

"So far, so good. I stopped at Mom and Pops," she chirped, knowing her father would appreciate that. "I will bring you a couple of melons once I return."

"Great!" he answered. "I am calling to let you know that I contacted my old friend, John Snyder, who owns Snyder's Beach Dreams Real Estate – in Marlin Beach - about the beach house. I am not sure if you remember him. I used to play golf with him from time to time, and he has a key to our place just in case of emergencies or to check up on things - which he has done in the past.

"No, dad, I can't say I remember him," she answered, trying to place him after so many years.

"I let him know that we want to sell the beach house, and he agreed to stop by today and talk to you about listing it."

"Ok…?" she said with some hesitation, wanting some time to

unwind first. "Did he say what time he would arrive?"

"2 o'clock, if that is ok with you?"

"Sure, dad. I will make it work."

"Great! Keep me updated as to what John says."

"I will. Take care, and give mom my love," she added fondly, as she disconnected the call.

Sarah knew the task at hand, but when it came right down to it, she didn't expect the realtor to show up that very day. As she drove off the short expanse of a bridge entering the town, she noticed the jet skiers making paths back forth throughout the bay. She could see the rows of newly built townhouses, with cheerful bright aqua and yellow metal roofs, and an assortment of restaurants that lined the way. Life was busy this time of the year at the beach, and also the time when the town made the necessary income to sustain itself before the cold weather hit again in the late fall.

Several blocks later, Sarah approached the beach house, pulling into the paved parking lot area that was oversized for guests. She sat in her car, just staring at the house and its surroundings. *It looked almost untouched - frozen in time - from ten years earlier*, she realized.

The side entrance to the house with its door, windows, walls, decks and stilts - that sturdily held the house in place - was magnificent in style and structural design. She was impressed and proud of her dad and his abilities to build such a strong fortress, that withstood the hurricane force winds that occasionally ripped through the town. Her schooling taught her on an educational standpoint about architecture, but it was her father who was her real teacher and mentor to the art of their trade.

She could hear children at play, a short distance away on the beach, but could not see them from the sea grass and dunes that were positioned between the beach and the house. Even in this detail, her father had intentionally maintained the dunes for privacy, but also for protection against the strong storms that could bring the beach right up to the house's foundation if this barrier was not there. The dunes had become an added delight, as birds and other water fowl would nest and take refuge between the reeds. Her parents would spend many hours on the deck, just taking in the simple joy of watching and observing nature at its best.

Sarah finally opened the door of her car and had to will herself just to leave its safe confines. She rested on the closed driver's door of her automobile, breathing in deeply of the humid sultry air that was so characteristic of being by the ocean. She could hear the strong waves roaring in the background, making her shudder at what they were capable of.

"I got to do this," she forcefully willed herself, knowing that walking into The Dancing Seahorse was going to be a challenge that she thought she had moved past, but obviously hadn't.

CHAPTER 15

Sarah entered the beach house, minus her suitcases and other things, just wanting a moment alone with the inside smells and feels of all that she remembered. She had to steady herself for a moment, grabbing hold of the sofa as she took in the closed blinds that were in front of her. She tugged on the ribbed metal cording, pulling back the blinds to the glass patio doors that were closed and securely locked. Beyond, were the hurricane shutters that were still in place, and she knew they needed to be pushed back and opened also. After some effort, she accomplished the task, as she paused to look out over the deck and the large expanse of the ocean in front of her.

It was noon and the beach was quite busy already. Many brightly colored umbrellas of blues, reds, greens and yellows dotted the beach at a variety of angles. Chairs and coolers were being dragged by beachgoers and set in place, along with random beach towels laid out here and there. Children played with footballs and flew kites. Sandcastles were being built and boogie boards floated on the water, as the riders waited and rode in the large waves.

Sarah paused, finding her hand reaching for her mouth. Her brain cried out – danger! Watching anxiously the young children and teenagers catching the next wave, she felt her heart racing and her pulse begin to quicken. The lifeguards seemed clueless to the danger that the ocean could hold, as she knew only too well that the tide could change without warning. *What is wrong with them?* She thought irritably, as she watched one looking down from his tall stand, flirting with a pretty girl in a bikini instead of watching the boogie boarders.

She retreated to the inside, unable to watch any longer. Shutting the patio glass doors and locking them in place securely, before reclosing the blinds, made her feel a lot safer. "This is ridiculous," she reasoned, trying to catch her wits about her.

Sarah went from room to room, attempting to give it a professional overview for the sake of the upcoming sale, but finding it hard to get past the personal. Most everything was in good shape, she felt, as she turned on the water to the sinks and flushed the toilets along the way. She concluded that maybe the place could use a coat or two of fresh paint, but beyond that - nothing seemed to have any real issues.

She paused, as she walked into Dex's room. Nothing had changed - as if his room was still that of an 18-year-old. His queen-sized bed still held its original comforter with the red, white and blue stripes. She wasn't even sure if her mother had ever washed his sheets after the accident. She walked around the room and opened the doors to his closet. She shook her head sadly, as she noticed a few of his golf shirts, khaki pants, along with several pairs of his jeans still hanging from hangers. As she glanced down, she noticed a barely used pair of his sneakers and several sets of Dex's favorite flip-flops. She bent to pick up one of the thongs, noticing a few grains of sand still clinging to where the top met the sole. She touched the sand, rubbing it around between her two fingers, before replacing it - making sure it was laid straight by its match, before closing the closet door to her discovery.

Sarah walked towards his bed and the nightstand beside of it. She tugged open the top drawer, seeing a scattering of papers, carnival ticket stubs, receipts and pictures that were a part of its contents. She sat on the bed and emptied the drawer on the top of the comforter;

curious as to what else it held. As she picked up each piece, she turned it over, realizing many of the things were events that she had attended along with Dex. She thumbed through each picture, finding several of their family when they were kids, the prom picture of him and Livia, along with the picture that caused her to stop dead in her tracks – the selfie of her and Dex right before the riptide accident! *How can it be?* She pondered, as she stared blankly at his happy, smiling face before she burst into tears. *"Oh my God, Dex. I am so sorry!"* she cried.

Sarah stuffed the memorabilia back in the drawer, shutting it firmly in place, as she lay on the bed curled in a fetal position, just crying softly to herself of all that was lost.

Some time later, she left his room; realizing time was getting away from her. The question of the picture stuck with her, as she made her way to back to the main part of the beach house. "It must have been mom," she surmised; assuming her mother had placed his special things there, as she had done also, back in his bedroom at the family home in Baltimore.

Sarah washed and dried her face and re-combed her hair back into a tight ponytail, knowing John Snyder would be there soon to meet her. She straightened her top back in place over her blue jeans, wanting to look more presentable than she had just been a few minutes prior from her tears. Several trips later, she had the car unloaded and had turned on the refrigerator and air conditioning.

She opened a bottle of water and made a turkey and cheese sandwich on whole-wheat bread with mustard. As she sat at the glass kitchen table with its four chairs that used to hold her loved ones, she remembered the many happy family meals that they had shared together. Her mother and father would lovingly grill and prepare many homemade dishes and salads that they would enjoy, along with the fresh produce from Mom and Pops.

She remembered the last Scrabble Game and how Dex and her

ended playing after only three games, and that he was the winner. The boxes of several games sat on a shelf nearby, and she knew if she opened the Scrabble Game, the score pad would still be there from the last game with Dex.

Sarah continued to survey the room, realizing the realtor would want to see out over the ocean. She willed herself to open the blinds again, along with the patio doors that brought in a nice southerly breeze. She sighed, looking out over the ocean once more with her arms crossed in front of her, resting on the metal railing. *It's just beautiful,* she heard whispered in her ear, as she turned to leave the patio with a start. She stopped, unable to move, remembering Dex's poignant words the last time they were together at the beach house.

"Yes, Dex, it is..." she sighed, as she turned to the ringing of the doorbell, chasing away her thoughts and bringing her back to the present.

CHAPTER 16

Sarah hurried to the door, opening it after the second ring. A much younger man stood in the doorway that she had not anticipated seeing, based on the fact that John Snyder was her father's age.

"Hello?" she asked in confusion.

"Yes, I am here about your house. I am with Snyder's Beach Dreams Real Estate," he explained with a warm friendly smile, extending his hand to shake Sarah's.

Sarah offered her hand and motioned for him to come into the beach house.

He entered the room, just taking a quick perusal of the scene directly in front of him, walking towards the patio without invitation. "Great view of the ocean," he commented casually, as she watched his athletic form move in that direction.

"Yes, it is," she answered in confusion, as he turned back to face her. She noticed how handsome he looked with his brown curly hair and his kind brown eyes. He looked familiar somehow, but she couldn't place him. He wore a long sleeve, white golf shirt - with a Beach Dreams emblem, along with tan khakis; holding a brief case in his hand.

"Maybe we should sit and talk and I will go over the contract with you, before we take a tour of the place?" he suggested, moving towards the table. "We already know the specs on your house, and it should be no time until we have a contract," he said matter-of-factly.

Sarah paused, not joining him at the table, while crossing her arms again and addressing him from a distance. "Forgive me for being so blunt, but I was expecting John Snyder - the owner of the company – who was suppose to have come here for this meeting."

"I'm sorry for my rudeness," he said with a bright smile that displayed his straight white teeth. "I just left another house and I apologize for running late for yours and not calling. I sometimes have a hard time slowing down," he admitted with a grin. "Forgive me for the lack of introduction – I'm Lance Snyder - John's son. He got detained and asked me to stop by in his place."

"I see…" she replied suspiciously while eyeing him, still uncertain of her apprehensions. "Could I interest you in a water or coffee?" she offered, as she made her way towards the refrigerator trying to regroup and be professional.

"Water, would be great."

Sarah brought two, making her way to the table.

Lance had already opened his brief case, placing the standard real estate contract on the table in front of her for her review. As he paged through the contract, something was unnerving Sarah as she took in his side profile. She knew him… her instincts told her that *she knew him*, but that was impossible.

And then it happened…. Lance pushed back on his sleeves, and the tattoo was revealed that Sarah had not seen in 10 years - on the beach, the day of the accident. There was no mistaking that it was the same tattoo with the life preserver with the initials "JW" on the inside of it that she could now clearly see. It was the same lifeguard who had failed at his job, of not saving her brother ultimately from death!

Sarah looked at Lance in shock, as if she had just seen a ghost. "I *now know who you are...*" she said with dawning awareness. "Please leave my house immediately!" she demanded firmly, while walking and opening the front door, insisting that he leave.

Lance looked up at Sarah in bewilderment, totally baffled and drawing a blank at what he had done wrong. "Did I say something wrong?" he questioned, as he gathered the contract, placing it back in his briefcase.

Sarah stood at the door, shaking her head in utter frustration. *"Did you say something wrong?* She gritted out. "The better question is - *Did you do something wrong?*" she added bitingly, as he approached her.

He studied her face as he joined her by the door, stopping in front of her before leaving. "I apologize if my abrupt entrance has made you feel uncomfortable."

"Goodbye, Mr. Snyder," Sarah said with loathing, as she slammed the door in Lance's face.

Lance stood in the driveway, briefcase still in hand, staring at the door that was just loudly slammed shut in front of him. "What the hell did I just walk into?" he said aloud as he shook his head in total bafflement and got back in his car. Not one to be rejected, he sat for a some time just looking at his cellphone and his current messages, not wanting to leave the property without an explanation.

Sarah paced the living room floor with her arms crossed defensively, trying to calm down and figure out what to do next. She considered calling her father about what had just happened, but did not want to upset him in the process. She could not believe her misfortune that Lance Snyder had actually shown up at the beach house. *Either he is very insensitive to the past or just doesn't care about anything or anyone other than making money*, she thought as she continued pacing.

Fifteen minutes later, Sarah sat on the sofa knowing she needed to contact another real estate company - and to do so quickly, so that she could go back to Baltimore and back to her job and career. She put down her laptop on the coffee table in front of her, having chosen another realtor based on client feedback and reviews - ready to make the call.

With that decision reached, the doorbell ran again. *"Now who can that be?"* she pondered, as she walked to the door.

She opened it, amazed at the unabashed boldness of Lance who was standing in front of her once again. *"Did you forget something?"* she asked, glaring at him as he stared back, unfazed by her intimidating manner.

"I would like an explanation as to what I did?" he asked directly, as he held her light blue eyes captive with his own. "I deserve that. My father will want to know…"

Sarah gulped, not sure what to do and say, as she hesitated to respond.

"It's obvious you do not want me to be your realtor, but can I just come back in for a moment so I can understand what is going on?"

Sarah looked at him, realizing he was being sincere. Most likely, their fathers had been close friends at one point, even though she was having a hard time remembering the connection.

"Yes, come in," she offered, motioning for him to go back to the kitchen table. She noticed he was without his briefcase this time. So she knew he wasn't going to insist upon the contract being signed, which gave her peace of mind.

Lance took a seat and glanced over at Sarah who was still standing across the room. "If you would join me, this may make things easier," he suggested, as Sarah hesitantly made her way back to the table, taking the furthest seat away from Lance.

"So tell me what has made you feel so uneasy?" he asked curiously, as he stared at her, just waiting for her response.

"You don't remember me, do you?" she asked, with her lips pursed tightly with tense agitation.

"Should I?"

"Ha!" she bit out nervously, realizing she had made a mistake allowing him back in the beach house. *"Ten years ago…. do you remember what happened right outside on this beach?"*

Lance sat quietly, searching his memory of ten years earlier. "Much has happened on this beach, to be honest," he said with distant stormy eyes.

"Maybe to you, but not to me, and not to my family," she hissed, rising again and resuming her pacing. "I lost my brother ten years ago - from that ocean and by your hands," she pointed towards the patio doors, looking out over the crystal sea in front of her and then back at Lance.

Lance's eyes opened wide with the memory of what she was referring to, as if a light bulb suddenly went on inside his head. He had not knowingly been insensitive to the memory, but much had happened during his 6 years as a lifeguard. Not only had others died immediately by drowning or within days like Dex, but some survived and were disfigured or paralyzed. Many were rescued though, and went on in life just as Sarah had done – healthy and well. He carried this weight, not only from what he had experienced, but also for his friends and fellow lifeguards that had been through it too.

Lance breathed deeply and rose from the kitchen chair, running his hands through his hair. "Oh my god, I didn't realize it was you. It's been a long time, and to be perfectly honest – you look totally different than what I remember," he admitted, feeling badly of his oversight. "My father never told me that it was *you* I was meeting up with," he confessed, as he made the connection.

Sarah stopped to boldly stare at Lance. "*Well, now you know. Nothing has changed concerning my opinion of you!*" she blurted out. "I know you attempted to save my brother, Dex, but you failed in the long run. Our family has never been the same. *Do you understand that?*" she demanded adamantly.

Lance exhaled, at a loss as to how to handle the situation any further. He made his way again to the door, stopping to look at her one last time. "I know I can't change your mind about me or what has happened, but I did try to rescue your brother that day. That riptide was stronger than anything I had ever seen before or after it. You just have to know that I risked my life that day too, for your brother. I am so sorry for all that you and your family has been through, but more than that - I am sorry that you just can't get past the pain."

Lance didn't wait for her response as he opened the front door and left her to stand alone - looking at a closed, steel door that had been shut in her face this time.

"No one slams a door in my face!" she stammered out in frustration, finding him impossible to deal with.

As Lance drove away, making his way back to Beach Dreams, the scene of that tragic day flooded his mind once again. The memory of the horrific event may have faded over time, but it was now front and center in his mind again - reminding him of Dex, unconscious in his arms, and Sarah pleading on the beach for her brother to be rescued.

CHAPTER 17

The couch pillow was wet from the tears where Sarah had been crying for way too long until her eyes were red and swollen. "The nerve of him to say that I just can't get past this!" she yelled aloud, sitting up in a daze. "Just do this, Sarah," she said to herself, rising to wash her face off for another time at the bathroom sink that day.

Even though she wanted to get another real estate company involved, she knew her parents wouldn't understand. So it was time to call home another time.

"Hi, Dad, it's me again."

"Sarah, papers signed?"

Sarah paused, not wanting to continue. "No, Dad, that's why I am calling you. We do not have an agreement with the Snyder's at this point."

"And why not?" Mike asked in surprised. "Didn't John show up?"

"No, Dad, he didn't."

Mike rubbed his face, taken back by his friend's apparent lack of concern and for not showing up as he had promised. "Well, I am sorry,

Sarah. Maybe something came up. Why don't you let me give John a call and see if he can still meet you at the beach house yet today."

Sarah hesitated, not wanting to open up "Pandora's Box" again for another time. "Dad, about that...you may *not* want to call him. Maybe we should just call another real estate company and get another realtor to help us?"

"Sarah, you are talking in riddles. What is going on?"

Sarah took a seat at the kitchen table, holding her hand to her brow. "Your friend John did not show up, and he sent his son instead with the contract."

"Ok... and what is the problem with that?"

"Do you not know who his son is, Dad?"

Mike shook his head silently to himself, unsure where Sarah was going with it all. "No, enlighten me."

"Lance Snyder. The same guy who was the lifeguard who tried to rescue Dex."

Mike sighed, looking towards Nancy with concern. "I am sorry, Sarah. I didn't know, and I never put two and two together. *He is John's son?*"

"It seems impossible, Dad, but Lance Snyder is the one responsible for Dex not being here today with us."

Mike shook his head again in exasperation. He had been through this one too many times with Sarah. He and Nancy had chosen to go forward in life and be happy, in spite of the misfortune of losing their precious son so many years before; but Sarah, on the hand, could not let go of the past.

Mike realized his daughter was Dex's twin sister - that linked them together in almost a mystical way - and Sarah was there to witness and experience the horrific events of that horrible day; but she was sadly locked in the past.

When Dex was put in the ground, Sarah's heart and soul went there with him. She would not allow herself to go forward and be happy. Somehow it felt unfair to her, that she could have a fulfilled life and Dex would never experience the same.

"Sarah, we have gone over this many times before. That young man did his best trying to save your brother. He brought him out of the ocean and did his job that day. He kept him alive until the ambulance picked him up."

Sarah began to cry again. *"I am here dealing with this dad, and it suddenly feels like yesterday*. I had to walk through this entire house, and I looked in Dex's room and it broke my heart. Can you understand that? And now you are telling me to get past all of this and use Lance as our real estate agent too?" she said in utter hurt and despair.

Nancy saw the look of concern on her husband's face as she walked over to sit by his side, holding his hand in support. Mike bent towards her, giving her a kiss on the cheek, feeling just as much in love with her as he had felt 32 years prior when he married her, knowing her comfort was always what he needed at times like this.

"Sarah, does your mother and I need to come there and take care of this situation with the beach house ourselves?"

"No, dad. You do not," she said with new resolve. "I will contact Beach Dreams and set up a new appointment with John Snyder. You need to continue to relax and I will take care of this."

"Take as much time as you need."

"I plan to be back in the office on Tuesday."

"Don't rush things, Sarah. We are relying on you to get the place in shape and sold. You haven't taken a vacation in a few years, even though I have encouraged you to do so. Take the time to say goodbye to the beach house, and please try to work through the past."

"Dad...?"

"Sarah. Just do this - for all our sakes."

"Remember, it hasn't been that long since you had a heart attack. You can't run the company without me."

"Yes, I can, and I will! The doctor has released me to go back to work, as you already know, and that is my intention. Do you think I sent you to Marlin Beach just to deal with the selling of the beach house?"

Sarah was stunned by her father's words. *"What are you saying?"*

"I am saying, that your mother and I could have been there doing what we requested of you, but we wanted you there - hoping it would bring you some much needed closure."

Sarah sighed, realizing her parents had an ulterior motive behind all this now. "I'm not sure how long I can stay here. I feel Dex here... you know," she said sadly.

"Maybe that's a good thing, dear," Nancy replied, hearing her daughter's words over the speaker of the cellphone that Mike had turned on for his wife to hear also.

"Mother, is that you?"

"Yes, dear. I have heard the conversation and I agree with your father. If you sense Dex being there, then talk to your brother. Don't run away from what you have been avoiding. It is time to be at peace with everything the beach house has been for you – be it good or bad. We love you, Sarah."

"I love you guys too."

CHAPTER 18

It was already three-thirty on Friday, and things were still up in the air concerning the selling of the beach house. Something had to be done, and Sarah promised her parents she would accomplish the goal and do what they had requested.

"Good afternoon, Snyder's Beach Dreams Real Estate," was the cheery greeting that Sarah heard as she made her call.

"Is John Snyder in, please?"

"May I say who is calling?"

"Yes, tell him it is Sarah Miller - Mike Miller's daughter."

Sarah was going to be succinct in explaining that point to Mr. Snyder. If she had to work with him, she would remind him of who her father was, along with the fragileness of the situation where his son was concerned. She would be polite and professional, but the lines would not be crossed again for Lance to show up unannounced to her home. John Snyder would be her realtor, and no one else, and she would make sure of that!

Alison Snyder had been in the real estate business for over 20 years and knew Marlin Beach like the back of her hand. She was her husband's partner in life and in business, and was now bringing her son Lance into real estate as well - grooming him to take over in time. She was trim and beautiful, with a chin-length blonde bob and a great wardrobe that every female wanted. Her makeup was well applied, and she always kept her nails polished and well groomed. She was the envy of many women in the town for her professionalism as well as her great looks. Everyone in Marlin Beach, as well as the surrounding area, liked her. She was not only personable, but she truly loved and cared for her community.

Patti, the receptionist, paged Alison. "There's a call on line two, Mrs. Snyder."

"Alison Snyder. How may I help you?"

Sarah was caught off guard that once again it wasn't John Snyder. "Ms. Snyder, my name is Sarah Miller, and my dad is a friend of John Snyder."

"Yes, Sarah, we are aware of that. I am Alison Snyder - John's wife, and he is still out of the office."

"I was calling to speak with your husband and set up an appointment - so that he could come to my family's beach house and start the process of listing our property."

Alison was somewhat confused. "Didn't my son, Lance, show up to do that very thing at two o'clock today?"

"Yes... he did, but I prefer to work with your husband instead - if you don't mind."

"What seems to be the problem?" Alison asked, just as Lance was entering her office, unaware of what had happened.

"It is personal - to say the least," she replied curtly. "And…. since my father requested that your husband do the listing, I think it would be best if he handles this," she added, trying to resolve the issue without any further discussion or questions.

Alison looked at her son as she scribbled a note, letting him know that it was Sarah Miller on the phone.

Lance looked back at his mother and just shrugged his shoulders and shook his head in disbelief, pacing around the room until she was finished with the call.

"I will have my husband contact you when he gets back in, but he is playing golf right now and he never has his phone turned on when he is getting in a round," she said with a smile, as she continued to look at her handsome son, still seeking an answer.

"Well the problem is, Mrs. Snyder. I wanted the house listed before the day was up."

"I understand that, but in all fairness, Lance was ready to do that for you today," she said diplomatically, wanting to please her, but ready to defend her son all at the same time.

Sarah fumed in frustration, knowing she was getting nowhere. "I am on a very tight schedule, Mrs. Snyder. I have to get back to my job in Baltimore in a few days."

"That is totally understandable. We are open tomorrow, if you don't hear back from us today. Will that do?" she added pleasantly, as she continued to watch Lance pace the floor.

"Do I really have a choice in the matter?" Sarah answered back in frustration.

"Things will all work out," Alison promised. "I will have John call you as soon as I speak with him."

"Thank you," Sarah politely offered, hanging up her cellphone, anxious to have the situation remedied.

Alison Snyder returned the receiver to its cradle, as she paused and stared at her son who was now sitting directly across from her desk. "For heaven's sakes, what in the world is going on with this lady?" she asked in bewilderment.

"I don't even know where to begin, mom," Lance said with a sigh. "I went to the Miller's beach house around two – yeah, I was running a tad late from another appointment – but I did get there only a couple minutes late."

"Is that her problem?" she asked irritably, knowing her son had to work on punctuality when it came to over-booking one too many appointments, and then running over into someone else's appointment time.

"No, that's not her problem! That would be easy compared to what is eating at her," he answered, as he rose from his seat again.

Alison continued to listen, waiting for Lance to explain to her what was going on with Sarah.

"She got very angry with me when she realized who I was."

"Lance, how do you know her? She is from Baltimore and not Marlin Beach."

"Yes mom, I know that. But, she vacationed here with her family as she was growing up. I was a lifeguard then and she remembers me."

Alison raised her eyebrow, looking at her son with a smirk. "Ok... you didn't have a fling or something with her back then, did you?" she asked, not sure as to where he was going with his story.

"No, it wasn't romance – to say the least. I was the lifeguard who rescued her brother ten years ago, or should I say - tried to rescue him - according to her," he added sadly with downcast eyes.

Alison looked at her son trying to read his thoughts. "Obviously, something ended badly?"

"Yes, mom. Don't you remember? Dad used to play golf with Mike Miller quite regularly years ago. His son, Dex, got caught up in a riptide and died from the accident. Not right away, but he still died shortly thereafter. He never came to and was in a coma and died a week later. His sister Sarah is lucky to be alive since she was rescued from that same riptide. It was on the local news and in the papers after it happened, if I recall."

"Oh my… Lance. I remember now. We sent flowers and a sympathy card to their home in Baltimore. Your dad had to retrieve their items off of the beach that day, and placed them back in the beach house after Mike had called and asked him to do so. Then a few days after the funeral, he contacted your father again and asked him to arrange to have Sarah's car shipped back to their home in Baltimore. After that, they barely came back to the beach, and when they did - they kept to themselves. I never thought there was an issue though, since your dad and Mike were always close friends. No one ever told us they were holding you responsible," Alison said with a look of regret and despair in her eyes.

"Mother, I hope you realize I tried my best to rescue him," Lance replied, feeling somewhat hurt that he had to defend himself.

"I am sorry, Lance. I didn't mean to upset you, but all these years later and this girl is still wrestling with this?"

"She is far from a girl…" Lance mentioned in a far-off distant way, remembering the beautiful, fetching picture Sarah had made without even trying to do so.

Alison looked knowingly at her son, understanding what he was implying. "Lance, I don't think this is the time or place to be attracted to someone under the circumstances."

Lance paused, looking back at Alison in amazement. "I know it has been awhile since I've had a steady girlfriend, but seriously mother, I am not *that* desperate! She is attractive and apparently successful, but emotionally I can not be around someone who won't deal with her past, and then turns around and blames me."

Alison studied her son, sensing his protest was a little over-stated. "Lance, your father *will deal* with Sarah Miller. You have plenty of other clients to keep you busy with this summer," she said while rising from her desk chair, coming around to link her arm through her son's. "Let's grab a sandwich and an iced tea across the street before dad gets back. I have several contracts to go over with you. We close the beginning of next week on two, and I want to make sure all the inspections are done and in order."

Lance and Alison headed across the street to the Old Bay Café, sitting down to a leisurely early dinner when her cellphone rang.

"Yes, honey?"

"I'm done and on my way," John Snyder informed his wife, driving back to Beach Dreams after winning his round of golf. "Are you in the office?"

"Actually, no. Lance and I are at Old Bay having an early dinner. Do you want me to order you something?"

"Sure, the *usual*," John replied, meaning his two crab cakes, fries and a cold beer.

"Before you get here, I need to tell you that things have been a little unusual today," Alison continued, as she sipped on her sweet tea and lemon.

"How so?"

"Lance never closed the deal with Sarah Miller."

"Oh?"

"It's a long story and I will give you the details once you get here, but the bottom line is - she will *only* deal with you as the listing agent. She does *not* want to deal with Lance."

John shook his head in irritation as he drove towards the restaurant. He was relaxed and didn't feel like dealing with any drama. He knew how difficult clients were being anymore. Mike Miller had been a friend from his past that he truly liked, and he wanted to do him a favor by listing his house; but he didn't feel like dealing with his high maintenance daughter, if she was now having a problem with his son.

As he pulled into Beach Dreams, he parked his Mercedes and put up the roof, adjusting his ball cap and shorts to look more presentable. He crossed the street, walking the short distance to his favorite hangout, ready to meet his wife and son who were waiting on him.

Lance and Alison would have to shed some light on what had occurred, and why he had to be her agent of choice. If the situation presented more issues than it was worth, Sarah Miller may have to look elsewhere for a real estate agent in Marlin Beach.

CHAPTER 19

After John was filled in by Lance and Alison as to the dilemma at hand concerning Sarah Miller, he looked at things quite differently as he ate his dinner - pondering what to do next. Of course he was sympathetic, remembering that tragic event and the death of Dex. Mike was never the same after that. He not only lost a golfing buddy, but a friend who feigned getting together after that point.

Everyone in Marlin Beach knew of the accident when it first occurred, even though the memory of that event may have now faded after so many years. John knew he had to return the call and be sensitive to Sarah's wishes, but he also wanted to be supportive of his son's innocence. The situation presented a challenge as to how he would deal with the listing and selling of the Miller's beach house, since Lance usually was the one directly involved with the majority of clients these days. He was determined that he would not choose between Lance and a potential sale if she became unreasonable, whether Sarah Miller liked it or not.

John Snyder was just as well known and respected as his wife, Alison, not only in business but also in regards to being a part of every fundraiser or social event thrown in the area. He grew up in a small town named Logan, which was across the bay from Marlin Beach, being the high school football star and class president. John's family had an established and successful real estate company, so he felt it was only natural to gravitate towards the beach and start a real estate business there of his own. His primary focus was beach properties only, which avoided his parent's turf of Logan. It had paid off, and his company was the number one producer in real estate sales for Marlin Beach and other nearby beach communities.

He was in his mid-fifties, still good-looking with a devilish grin, with the same brown hair and kind eyes of his son. He displayed a slight bulge of a stomach that extended over his belt from one too many beers, was slightly balding with graying at the temples, and was known for smoking cigars with his friends. He was always in golf clothes, choosing to wear his real estate's company logo on his baseball cap that he was rarely without.

It was John's time, after so many years of working, to start taking it easy and relax more since he was dealing with high blood pressure issues that required medication. Golf was his passion and he played locally whenever the weather permitted; but when winter made it impossible, he would take his golfing buddies and head south to the Carolinas or Florida for a few days.

Alison, always gave her blessing for him to do so because she was still very much involved in Beach Dreams, working over 50 hours most weeks, keeping the business well-organized, running, and successful, with the help of her son and other staff.

Lance, was their only child, and the third generation of Snyder's to be in the real estate business. It had taken some time for him to transition into the job, preferring and enjoying the outdoors and lifeguarding more. His mother and father had basically given him an ultimatum several years before, that it was time to stop playing and to take up the family business.

John rarely took appointments anymore, but would still do so for a close friend under special circumstances – that was, if it was easy listing and without complications. The situation with the Miller's qualified as one of those times, even though he thought Lance could have handled it just as well on his own. If bad blood still lingered from the death of Dex, then he would have to smooth things over and deal with it as best he could.

"Hello, is Sarah there?" John inquired.

"Yes, this is she," she answered, taking a seat on the couch.

"Sarah, this is John Snyder. I am calling to set up an appointment with you concerning your beach house."

"Oh, yes, Mr. Snyder, I have been waiting for your call," she said cheerfully, feeling a sense of relief that the beach house was finally going to be listed and he was on board.

John shifted back in his desk chair, still overly full from his dinner. "Would it be asking too much for you to come to my agency in the morning – say around ten o'clock - to go over the paperwork?"

Sarah rose to pace the floor again. "Mr. Snyder...?"

"Call me John."

"John..." she said awkwardly. "Is there any way we can still meet tonight? My schedule in very tight at work and I was hoping to finalize things quickly."

He chuckled, looking at his desk clock, realizing it was almost 7 o'clock. "I would like to say yes, but I am not a late night person any longer," he admitted, knowing by 9 p.m. he was usually fast asleep on the couch.

Sarah sighed, realizing another day's delay was eating at her, and she couldn't do anything about it. "Could I ask then that we just meet here at the beach house in the morning?"

"I typically ask that my clients meet me first at my office initially. It is easier that way - in case changes have to be made to the contract and we need to reprint things."

She wondered why Lance could make it work to come to the house as he had, but for some reason his father couldn't. It was her father's wish though for her to work with Beach Dreams and John Snyder, so she would do whatever needed to be done to get the ball rolling.

"That is fine," she resigned. "I will see you tomorrow at ten."

"See you then. Have a good night," John added, as he ended the call. He already had a keen sense of what was ahead with Sarah Miller, and he really didn't want to deal with it.

Alison poked her head around the corner, curious to the call. "Was that Sarah Miller?"

"Yes, it was. She hesitated about coming in here... you know. Probably worried about running into Lance," he said nonchalantly, rising from his chair to grab his jacket.

"Hmm, maybe one of us should call Lance and tell him to avoid getting here until after she leaves."

John looked at his wife, kissing her on the cheek. "Now when has Lance ever listened to us, dear? I think he will know what to do if he runs into her tomorrow."

Alison smiled. "He listens, John. That is... when he wants to," she added with a wink and a smile. "Takes after someone I know," she teased, pinching him playfully in the side of his overly full stomach.

John laughed, smacking her backside. "Whatever you say, dear.

Let's get out of here and get this place locked up. Gotta catch some of the Orioles yet on TV. They are playing tonight - you know."

Alison rolled her eyes, walking hand in hand from Breach Dreams with her friend and beloved husband. She knew his baseball viewing would last for all of 30 minutes once he was home, and then he would be passed out on the couch, fast asleep and snoring loudly.

CHAPTER 20

Sarah Miller sat in her car, in front of Snyder's Beach Dreams Real Estate, arriving early by 9:30 a.m. before it was even open. Not a single car was there yet as she waited impatiently, drinking from her carafe of coffee, that she had acquired a taste for over the years since Dex had passed.

She had a very restless night sleeping, back in her old bedroom in the beach house. The shrieking noise of the wind through the open window, stirred her from her slumber. Her thoughts kept racing back to the past and Dex who used to sleep in the room right beside of hers. She had slept at her parents' house many times over the years since her brother's death, but it felt so different now – here at the beach – by herself, and without anyone to keep her company. She felt childish for being afraid, allowing her imagination to run wild – almost feeling like she could sense Dex's presence right beside of her. Being alone in the house had brought back too many memories that she didn't want to deal with.

If Sarah had her doubts before arriving, she was now resolved that selling the beach house was the right thing to do. It was time to close this chapter – not only for her, but for her parents also. To never see The Dancing Seahorse again, or even be involved in Marlin Beach and all its activities - would end the pain of the past. At least that was what she was hoping for.

The Mercedes convertible pulled into the parking space adjacent to hers, as the casually dressed, smiling gentleman waved and walked up to her car, motioning for her to roll down the window.

"Are you Sarah?" John Snyder asked, as his ball cap tipped in her direction.

"I am," she smiled, assuming it to be John.

"John Snyder," he nodded, as he made his way towards the building. "Take you time and I will be in here waiting," he offered, as he walked past her car, opening the door and disappearing.

Sarah closed her eyes and breathed, trying to focus at the task at hand. She gave herself one last appraising look in the rearview mirror before exiting the car. *"I hope I don't run into Lance. Please...God...don't let me run into Lance,"* she said aloud anxiously, as she entered the brightly colored, pink and green painted structure, shutting the door a little too loudly behind her.

She jarred a picture near the front door, making it rattle on the wall to her embarrassment. She turned around to look, but no one was present in the empty waiting area as John called her name loudly from his office.

"Sarah, no one is here yet. I am the first door on the left," he yelled, as she made her way back to his office. "Can I interest you in a cup of coffee?" he offered with a warm smile, as he turned from his personal coffee maker with his cup already in hand.

"No thank you. I already had some."

John took a seat at his desk, as he sipped on his hot brew, studying her from afar. She was dressed in slim-fitting white capris slacks, and had a black short-sleeve spandex top, which hugged her curves. Her legs and calves were trim and well defined, and she wore matching black sandals that displayed her perfectly polished toenails. Her hair was pulled back into a tight ponytail, with a touch of mascara and pink lip-gloss on her lips. Her fingernails were manicured short with clear nail polish completing the look. She wasn't a girly girl, but more tomboyish with a simple beauty that was understated. She appeared restless, as she crossed and uncrossed her legs several times, trying to break the few moment's of silence between them. He concluded that she was pretty, but her nervous energy could make any man run.

He smiled, trying to put her at ease. "I'd like to go over the standard listing contract and explain everything, if that would be alright?" he said over his readers. "If you have any questions or concerns after that, now is the time to discuss them and we can modify the contract and take it from there."

"That works for me," she agreed willingly, realizing John Snyder was no threat to her after all, like his son was.

"When we finalize things, I will be happy to stop by the beach house today and do a walk through with you. That way if I feel any repairs, painting or updates should be made, I will give you my opinion. You are in charge of this though. You do not have to agree to any changes to your property," he added, with a reassuring smile.

Sarah shifted in her chair, feeling like the house was perfect just as it was and required no changes. If she did agree to do some upgrades, it would just be another issue she would have to tackle before leaving town.

"Can we list the house before any work is done to the property?" she inquired.

"Of course," John said with a smile, trying to ease her worries. "We will list what is to be done, and any potential buyers will know of our agreement to have it all completed before settlement."

Sarah and John continued to talk as he thumbed through every page of the contract, finishing with the starting and ending date of the listing, and where Sarah's signatures and initials where needed.

"We will add the listing price once I assess and appraise the property today, if that is all right with you?" he concluded, as he gathered up all the paperwork placing it neatly on a pile to the right side of his desk.

"Of course," Sarah agreed, feeling confident in John's thoroughness, and realizing her father had made a wise decision in choosing him as their agent.

Alison pulled to the back of Beach Dreams by 10:30 a.m., entering the building and walking past her husband's office, as she did everyday.

"Hello," she greeted pleasantly, as she stopped in John's doorway, hoping to put Sarah at ease.

"Sarah, this is my wife, Alison," John mentioned casually.

"Oh, hello," Sarah answered in surprise, not expecting the intrusion and looking around from her chair.

"It is nice to meet you. Please get back to what you were doing," she smiled, excusing herself as she closed the door to John's office.

The normal hours of operation for Beach Dreams began at 11 a.m. on Saturdays. By 10:45 a.m., Lance pulled into the parking lot, realizing Sarah's car was parked out front. He drove his Jeep behind the building, parking beside of his mother's BMW.

"Shit, now what?" he thought irritably, forgetting Sarah was meeting his father there first, instead of at the beach house. He leaned on the outside of his car and dialed his cellphone. "Mom, I'm out here, and I forgot dad was meeting with Sarah Miller this morning."

"The door is shut to his office, Lance. I got it covered!" she replied reassuringly, already being a step ahead of him in thought.

"Oh, great! Thanks, Mom," Lance said in relief.

"Did you expect any less?" she quipped, knowing Lance was on the way and she needed to intervene.

Lance quietly entered the front door, hoping Patti the receptionist didn't acknowledge him, as she did most mornings.

"Good morning... La..." she started to say, before Lance put his finger to his lips to silence her. She looked at him in confusion, just shaking her head as he walked by. He tiptoed towards his dad's office door, stopping to pause as he heard Sarah speaking. She sounded intense, as he assumed she would be.

Alison opened her door slightly, motioning for Lance to come in. She whispered in his ear. "Be quiet, since I have the speaker on to your dad's office. I want to hear what Sarah is saying to him." Lance just looked at his mother in amused surprise. She was always trying to protect him. They made their way quietly towards the desk, not even sitting for fear they would be heard.

"How is your mom and dad doing, Sarah?"

"They are fine. Just fine," she added, knowing John had been sincerely nice to her from the time they had first spoken.

"I would like to clear something up with you. I am sorry that you felt uncomfortable working with my son, Lance. I know you felt uneasy under the circumstances, but he truly would have been nothing but professional if you would have given him the chance," John mentioned with sincerity and kindness in his eyes.

Sarah shifted, knowing she had to meet the situation head on now, since John was being so honest and direct. If they couldn't talk about this and clear the air, then what chance would they have at a civil working relationship? "Mr. Snyder, I mean… John," she began, clearing her throat and standing up to pace the floor, "I am sure your son does a fine job for you, but I can't get past what happened to my brother and your son's involvement in that."

John observed her actions as he watched her intently. "Sarah, have you shared you feelings about this with your parents? After all, this is their beach house too," he added tactfully.

Sarah began to fume, seeing where Lance inherited his persistence. *"My parents have nothing to do with this!* They have given me the responsibility of *selling the beach house*. My father had a heart attack a few months ago, and no - I will *not* be bringing your son into the conversation with them, if I can help it!" she remarked plainly, placing her hands on her slim hips in open defiance.

John rose and met Sarah where she stood. "I understand your feelings, and I am sorry to hear the news about your father. Please give him my best," he added warmly, but continued. "Lance is my son and *I won't* have you treating him like he is a monster! Either we get past this thing, or you can find another realtor!" he demanded with a stone-faced glare, as he removed his ball cap waiting for her response.

Sarah's eyes began to water in disbelief as she made her way back to the chair. "I am sorry, sir," she said with downcast eyes. "My parents have requested that I use you, and I promise - I am done speaking baldly about your son," she said softly.

John sighed, studying the emotional female, feeling conflicted by her obvious pain. "All right," he agreed reluctantly, sensing his upcoming golf games could be cancelled because of her. "I will be at your house by today at 2, if that is all right with you?"

"That is perfect!" Sarah agreed, finding her mood suddenly perking back up, rising to shake John's hand. "I will see you then, and thank you for taking me on as a client."

"You are welcome, my dear," he answered, shaking her hand in return. "I will see you soon."

Sarah gathered her things and made her way to the front entrance area again, ready to leave. Patti looked up from filing her nails, still confused by Lance and his actions "Have a good day!" she offered questionably, as Sarah closed the door behind her - a little less firmly than when she first entered.

Lance looked at his mother and shook his head, as Alison released the speaker button to John's office, giving them the ability to speak freely again.

"I told you mother, this was going to be a problem."

"Not for your father, Lance. Not for your father."

CHAPTER 21

Sarah grabbed a quick salad and headed home to enjoy it from the view of her deck. The day was beautiful again, and she realized that the more she took in the scenes in front of her on the beach, the more relaxed she was becoming. Her anxiousness was easing and it was good to be away from the office, as much as she didn't want to admit it.

Her cellphone rang and she grabbed for it halfway across the patio table.

"Hello?"

"Sarah, it is John Snyder."

"Yes."

"I am on my way, but it has been awhile – your home is The Dancing Seahorse - correct?"

"Oh, yes!" she answered, rising to take her empty salad container with her, before throwing it in the trash.

"Great! I am on my way. I will be there in a few minutes."

"I'll will be here waiting," Sarah, replied anxiously, wanting to get the walk-through done and the listing started, so that she could return to Baltimore. *Maybe if I'm lucky, I will be home this evening*, she thought, as she hurried to her room to change her clothes.

Sarah slipped into a pair of blue jean shorts with an aqua sleeveless tank top pulled over them, along with her white flip-flops that were her favorite pair. She preferred being casual when she was not working, and as much as she wanted to get back to routine in Baltimore, she was enjoying her day and the time on the deck eating her lunch and getting some sun.

As promised, John Snyder was there within fifteen minutes, as he knocked on the door instead of using the doorbell.

Sarah walked at a brisk pace from her bedroom to the front door, not wanting to keep John waiting.

"Come in," she greeted with a sweet smile, surprising John at the change in her demeanor.

"You look relaxed," he mentioned indifferently, as he immediately began walking around the place, looking over each detail as he talked, writing things down in a notebook and taking pictures.

Barely a questioned was asked, as he continued walking from room to room, looking from floor to ceiling, opening and closing drawers and closets, flushing toilets and taking measurements. He was trying to keep the conversation light, as he did the job that was second nature to him.

"Shall we go outside?" he asked Sarah, as he proceeded to the deck. "Your father is a fine architect, Sarah, do you know that?" he complimented, as he grabbed hold of the deck railing that was overlooking the dunes and the beach.

"Yes, he sure is," she beamed with admiration. "And I am not sure if you know this or not, but I am an architect too - with his firm," she added, proud of her accomplishments.

John cleared his throat as he straightened his ball cap. "I think I heard rumors to that affect that you were in the family business," he grinned, giving her a wink.

Sarah liked John and he put her at ease. He was laid back and she felt she could trust him. She understood why her father and him had been friends over the years. They proceeded to walk down the side steps of the house and circled around the outside - taking in the roofline, windows, hurricane shutters, decking and siding. John gave his approval that all appeared to be in good shape and without damage. He continued to walk a distance away, taking pictures of the property from numerous angles, focusing in on the house's close proximity to the beach. Sarah hung back, allowing him to go to the beach on his own. Even the thought of walking there, set her pulse to racing.

"I think I have what I need now, Sarah," he mentioned, being out of breath from his walk back up to the beach house to meet her again. "Why don't we go back inside and I will tell you my thoughts; but first, I need to grab my briefcase from the car."

"Of course," Sarah agreed, as they made their way back into the house where they took a seat at the kitchen table, ready to discuss business.

John proceeded to open his brief case, extracting out the signed contract that he had gone over earlier with Sarah at his office along with his laptop. He sat quietly, drinking the water she offered, as he typed in the data from his notes and uploaded each photo.

As he finished, he turned the laptop in her direction, ready to begin his presentation. "Young lady, your parents have maintained The Dancing Seahorse very well," he begun, sitting back on his chair with his hands strung together behind his head. "I realize the beach house has not been used that often in the past 10 years, which has helped to maintain it pristinely beyond my initial expectations. I see no evidence of rotting on the outside, and surprisingly the plumbing and appliances appear to be in excellent condition and working order."

"So all is in good shape and ready to go?" Sarah questioned optimistically.

"Hmmm... yes and no," he replied, knowing she was anxious to get things over and done with. "I must be honest," he said, facing her directly to gain her attention. "The house has a dated look and I feel the color of the paint needs to be changed."

"Really?" Sarah answered in surprise, being subjective in her opinion about the beach house.

John chuckled; knowing how sensitive people could be about their properties, and then taking it to heart. "Well, that is half of it."

"There is more?" Sarah asked in surprise, rising from her seat to get another bottle of water before leaning against the kitchen counter to prepare for his additional remarks.

John stood too, making his way to the dishwasher, opening it since he had missed it on his first inspection. "To be honest, Sarah, the furniture needs replacing. It is outdated by today's standards."

Sarah stood quietly, shaking her head side to side - *no.* "Mr. Snyder, that is where I draw the line. Let someone else buy furniture for the place."

"I'm not suggesting you buy new furniture. I am suggesting you stage the place through a staging company with modern, up-to-date furniture, and it will definitely help to sell it more quickly. They can help you store it or assist in selling the old, if that would help."

Sarah grimaced, pacing nervously into the living room, picking up a sofa pillow and holding it to her chest. *"The furniture is fine and I won't be staging it,"* she insisted adamantly. "We can paint it, but again - I don't even see the point in that, to be honest," she conceded, while looking around at the walls that clearly didn't need to be changed at least in her mind.

John shook his head, resigned to do whatever she wished. "Sarah, it is your choice. It may just take a little longer to sell the place or get your price – but that is fine."

After some discussion, they sat at the kitchen table again as John showed Sarah the specs on his computer. "I think a fair listing price would be Nine Hundred and Fifty Thousand Dollars - based on the neighborhood, size, and beachfront location of The Dancing Seahorse. That is what I would suggest," he mentioned straightforwardly, looking to her for insight.

"I would agree," she replied. "But I do feel like I need to run it by my mom and dad before I give you the final answer."

"Take all the time you need," John replied, as he rose from the kitchen table, repacking up his briefcase with a copy of the contract and his computer. "But we do have an issue."

"And what would that be?"

John paused, looking at her with his briefcase in hand. "I know you are on a tight schedule and want to get back to Baltimore, but it is Saturday and its 5 o'clock already. I cannot proceed forward until I hear back from you. Once we confirm the price, then I need to put the information into the MLS network to make the sale of your beach house live. I stop working after 5 on a Saturday, and I do not work on Sundays. So things will not proceed forward on my end until Monday," he stated adamantly, waiting for her answer.

Sarah shifted her weight, crossing her arms and looking to the ceiling in frustration. "I had hoped we could have worked this all out before the end of today, and now you are telling me it won't be until

Monday?"

"That is correct, young lady," he said firmly. "Not to bring up a sore subject with you again, but Lance would have made that happen by your deadline. I am semi-retired and Saturday evening is date night with my lovely wife, and Sunday is my time for playing golf."

Sarah began pacing again, feeling impatient with the news. "I guess I have no choice in the matter, now do I? I will call my father and confirm the listing price, and leave a message on your cellphone with the answer."

"That will work," John answered with a wink, making his way to the door.

"And the paint?" she yelled, as he opened the door ready to leave.

"He turned, looking at her with a smile. "I guess you need a painter and I doubt that will be happening by Monday when you want to leave."

"Sarah shook her head in total aggravation. "You win, Mr. Snyder. I guess I won't be leaving now on Monday either," she stammered. "When you get a chance, I would appreciate the name of a good painter that you would recommend?" she shouted.

"Absolutely," he said with a big grin, shutting the door behind him.

Sarah sat on the couch for some time, hugging the throw pillow again, knowing it was time to call her parents with the news. "Dad, it's me. I met with John Snyder and he feels that a fair asking price for the beach house is Nine Hundred and Fifty Thousand Dollars."

"That sounds about right," he answered, as he sat relaxing on his sofa with Nancy, snuggled up against her and watching a movie.

"What I didn't plan on - was the house needing to be painted. I will have to stay here awhile longer to get things organized past Monday," she said, feeling defeated.

Mike smiled, giving a nod to Nancy. "Things are fine here, honey. Just do what needs to be done."

Sarah grabbed the throw pillow, clutching it a little bit tighter to her chest for comfort. "Do I really have a choice in the matter, dad?"

"I guess not, sweetie. Just try to relax and enjoy the beach house, and make the most of it. Soon enough The Dancing Seahorse will be sold - and a distant memory for all of us."

CHAPTER 22

After leaving a voicemail for John Snyder with the go ahead on the list price, Sarah ordered a small pepperoni pizza and had a glass a wine. The deck called her name again, as she ventured out onto the patio, lighting a citronella candle she found packed away in a closet. The air was balmy and the sun was setting with a huge orange glow already on the horizon. She knew this was a sign of another beautiful day to follow. Children played, while numerous groups of people sat in semi-circles enjoying food and beverages spread out on large beach blankets in front of them. The last rays of the sun dipped below the horizon, as Sarah watched it retreat where the glistening waters met it.

"What am I to do, Dex?" she said aloud, as she sipped on her wine, placing her bare feet against the railing for support.

Sarah wrestled with the thought of changing The Dancing Seahorse in any way. In her mind, it was perfect - just the way it was and had always been. She could not even mention to her parents that John Snyder thought the furniture should be changed. *Nothing is wrong with the furniture or the paint - for that matter!* She stammered, being unsure what was the best thing to do.

It was not only the changes to the beach house that she had to deal with, but the actual sale of the property too. *If only Dex was here to help me with this…* she pondered as she poured herself another glass of wine. Too many memories of the family were resurfacing, along with the happy times they had shared.

She walked from the rattan patio chair to the deck railing, looking out over the darkened ocean that had a beam of light shining a path across it - as far as the eye could see from the moon above. *"Dex, if you can hear me, I need your help. Should I even sell the beach house?"* she spoke aloud, hoping the moon could somehow magically transport the message to her brother above.

As she lay in her bed with the windows open, the breeze blew softly against the shades making them rattle. She fell asleep and for once she slept soundly. Dex visited her again in her dreams, as he did so many times before, but this time the dream was different – he sat perched high on top of the deck railing, with a paint brush in hand - painting the path that led to the beautiful moon.

Sarah awoke, feeling well rested and hungry, all at the same time. She pondered the crazy dream that she remembered with Dex and the paintbrush. "Too much wine," she said aloud with a shake of her head, making her way to the shower. She had packed a floral sundress with a low-cut back and spaghetti straps that barely held it in place, and slipped into it along with her white flip-flops again. With her hair pulled tightly back in her signature ponytail and a swipe of lip-gloss, she decided to walk to The Seabreeze Diner for breakfast.

The diner was busy with a full house of Sunday morning breakfast goers. She had forgotten that it was the busiest time to eat at the beach, with the weekend vacationers visiting. Sarah looked around, trying to find a table, but opted for the counter instead after the hostess told her to seat herself. She ordered bacon, eggs, toast and coffee while she looked over her emails on her cellphone.

Lance sat at a far-off table of the diner taking it all in. Sarah had not noticed him, as he kept his head safely from view behind his Sunday paper that he enjoyed reading leisurely one day out of the week. He placed it on the table, once she was seated with her back to him, as he admired her from behind. He had not noticed from his brief encounter with her 2 days prior, how much she had changed in 10 years since he had last saw her. No more the girl, but a woman with soft curves. Her backside was tight, with the sundress dipping low, and her calves were muscular with slim ankles. She was slightly tan, but not overly so. He liked her hair pulled up, exposing the soft curve of her beautiful neck. He felt foolish staring at her, knowing how she detested him.

The waitress reappeared, offering him more coffee that he gladly accepted. She knew him because he was a regular that showed up every Sunday – being John and Alison's son, and also an active part of the community.

"Lance, is there anything else you would like?" Janet asked with a smile, ready to lay his bill on the table.

"That will do it, hon," he answered, looking up at her warmly; ready to pay before she walked away. He glanced at Sarah again as a thought crossed his mind. "Janet, you see that woman sitting there at the counter?" he whispered, pointing in Sarah's direction.

"Yes, I see her."

"I want to pay her tab too. How much?"

"Six Dollars."

"Here you go," Lance replied with a sexy grin, as he handed her a twenty, walking from The Seabreeze Diner with his newspaper still tucked under his arm.

Sarah glanced up just as Lance was leaving, recognizing him as he turned and smiled at her. She lowered her head, not sure what to do or say. *"The nerve of him,"* she hissed madly, nervously fumbling for her credit card in her wallet, and desiring to leave after that.

"May I have my bill?" she asked irritably of Janet, as she walked quickly past her.

"Honey, its been paid," she announced with a stack of dirty dishes piled high up to her nose.

"By whom?" Sarah demanded.

"The good-looking guy who just left," Janet mentioned, nodding her head towards the entrance, while making her way through the swinging doors back to the kitchen.

Sarah fumed as she grabbed her purse, making her way quickly out of the restaurant, looking both ways for any sign of Lance. To her surprise, he was right behind her, having made a trip to the men's room before leaving.

"Did you lose something?" Lance asked with a sarcastic tone, noticing Sarah's actions.

"Did I lose something? She replied. "No, I *didn't* lose something!"

"Well, that's good to know," Lance answered flippantly, making his way to his Jeep.

Sarah followed right on his heels. "Mr. Snyder, I cannot *accept* you paying for my breakfast!" she bellowed.

"No big deal," he smiled, shrugging his shoulders.

She sieved in frustration at the man's apparent insensitivity that she wanted no contact with him. "I insist you take...you take the money...back once I get change," she stammered in embarrassment, after realizing she had only a credit card and a couple ones in her wallet.

Lance began to laugh, totally unnerving her further.

"I *do not* find this funny at all, Mr. Snyder."

"I can see that," he added, as he stared at her brazenly. "You just look so darn cute when you are frustrated," he teased, as he got in his Jeep, looking at her from his open window. "I think I owe you for coming to your house instead of my dad initially, and setting you back a couple of days. Don't think nothing of it," he winked, pulling away from the driveway – leaving Sarah to star in astonishment at his retreating vehicle.

She walked back to the beach house in a daze, sitting on the steps that lead up to the front door, wondering what had just happened. *Lance was flirting*, Sarah realized, and she didn't know why. *Is John putting him up to this so I soften and allow Lance to take over again with the listing?* She shook her head, brushing aside her irrational thoughts. "This is silliness. Just coincidence – nothing more," she concluded, as she dismissed her apprehensions, making her way back inside, ready to enjoy the rest of her day.

CHAPTER 23

Lance Snyder had complied with the wishes of his parents to be in the family business of real estate, but his heart was always somewhere else. As a lifeguard in his late teens and early twenties, he felt a sense of pride for protecting the waters and rescuing people. He had more successes than failures in way of water rescues, but even one life that was lost was more than Lance or any lifeguard wanted to deal with.

He attended community college in the local area, choosing to devote some of his free time to volunteer for emergency EMT work once his summer lifeguarding job was done for the season.

Lifeguarding did come to an end as a job for Lance, but he continued to be on call as a volunteer with the EMT ambulance crew in Marlin Beach. John and Alison admired their son for his efforts to assist whenever needed in the town with emergency calls, proudly displaying his "years of service" plaques on the walls in the waiting area of Snyder's Beach Dreams Real Estate.

It was Monday, and Sarah was anxious to hear from John Snyder, ready to get the listing started and on her way back to Baltimore and her busy career. She was putting the final touches on a design project that was time consuming, and it needed to be finalized so it could go out to bid.

"Good morning, John," Sarah greeted, as her phone rang from his incoming call.

"Good morning to you too, Sarah. I have given our meeting some thought from Saturday, and I wanted to give you my opinion on the matter."

"Oh?" Sarah replied, taking a seat at the kitchen table while sipping on her coffee.

"I do feel your beach house needs to be painted throughout, as I already mentioned before, and you may want to avoid listing it until that work is completed."

Sarah fumed, shaking her head in disbelief by John's obvious disregard for her busy life. "I do not have the time to spare. I need to get back to Baltimore."

John sat back in his chair, knowing she would block his suggestion. "I understand, but a place does not present well with paint cans and drop cloths in the way, when someone is trying to walk through it. Honestly, its not even safe."

Sarah breathed deeply, knowing what John was saying made perfect sense. "Ok, so let's think this out," she answered, rising and pacing to gather her thoughts. "The painter is hired, and then what?"

"Who I use to do painting is excellent, but he likes the customer to select and buy the paint themselves. He will call in the quantity needed, and then you can go to the hardware store in Logan and order and pay for it. He will pick up the paint there, along with the other supplies that he will need, before showing up at your property to begin painting."

"Why Logan? Isn't there a store here in Marlin Beach that he works with?"

"It is only fifteen minutes - out of town - and he gets an excellent discount there for his customers."

Sarah sighed, feeling it was more than she anticipated going through just to have the beach house painted. "Do I need to stick around once the paint is picked out or am I free to leave after that?"

"You are free to go back to Baltimore once you pick out the paint. The man I use for painting is in business for himself. His name is Andrew Scott, and he is expecting your call today. I spoke with him already this morning, and he said he could stop by your place because he is in the area already working. He will go over everything with you, including the price for labor," John outlined, trying to put Sarah's mind at ease.

"Ok, sounds like a plan. How long does the painting usually take on a place this size?"

"That is something you will need to go over with Andrew, but typically about 2-3 days."

"That long?"

John just shook his head with her endless debate, getting up to pour himself another cup of coffee. He looked out the window, noticing the rain that had just begun. It would interfere with his golf game if the weatherman was true to his word about the amount expected.

"Sarah, once the house is painted, the listing will begin. Pack your things and go back to Baltimore, after you have your meeting with Andrew. Stop by Logan's Hardware and make your paint selection on your way home. I will coordinate everything else for you. Just leave a key under the mat by the deck doors on the upper level."

"Ok..." she paused, realizing John Snyder was very capable of handling things.

With her things packed, Sarah emptied the top drawer of Dex's nightstand into her large suitcase, along with his shoes and clothes still left in his closet. The kitchen cookware and dishes remained, along with the sheets, comforters and towels in the closet. One last beach trip would be in order to get the last of the items, before turning The Dancing Seahorse over to the new owners, but for now this would suffice.

The doorbell rang just as Sarah finished loading the rest of the water into her cooler. "Coming," she yelled, running to the door to greet the painter.

"Andrew Scott," he announced, not reaching out a hand in her direction. "Sorry, I'm a little messy. Been painting down the street," the older man announced, with flecks of paint still clinging to his glasses and clothes. He wiped his feet carefully on the outside mat before entering the beach house.

Sarah crossed her arms, watching his inspecting eye as he glanced at the walls in front of him. They walked from room to room as he made some notes on a small piece of paper from a spiral notebook that he removed from his painter pants' pocket.

"I think this should be a fairly easy job," he concluded. "I will contact Logan Hardware with the amount of paint you will need. Just pick out your color, which should probably be an eggshell throughout," he suggested. "I will pick it up tomorrow and get started shortly thereafter."

Sarah looked at the list with pricing and quantities that Mr. Scott presented to her. "How would you like me to pay you for your labor?" she questioned, feeling $1,000.00 was more than reasonable.

"John Snyder will take care of that. You can settle up with him at closing," he stated matter-of-factly.

"Well, thank you. That makes things easy."

"Do you have any questions?" he asked, ready to be on his way back to the project at hand that was waiting on him.

"No… I would just ask that you cover the beds and furniture," she answered distantly, thinking again of Dex's room.

"Don't worry. I always take care of that," Mr. Scott reassured, making his way out of the front door as quietly as when he first arrived.

Sarah finished packing her car and then started the engine, but turned it off again. "Nuts, I forgot to leave the extra key," she realized, retreating back inside of the beach house through the steady rain that was beginning to fall. She opened the kitchen drawer where the silverware was, extracting the key and placing it under the outside deck mat.

The rain was continuing to come down fairly heavy as her wipers had a hard time keeping up with the constant pounding that was leaving her visibility impaired. She made her way out of Marlin Beach, crossing the bridge onto the mainland, seeing only a few people with bending umbrellas brave enough to walk in the deluge of rain.

Sarah had only driven a short distance and even considered going back until the rain had eased, but decided to go on against her better judgment. It had definitely become unbearable, and she knew many others had pulled off the side of the road to wait out the storm. She trudged ahead with her four-way flashers on, being determined to get the paint selection over with so that she could return to Baltimore and Miller's Architecture.

Sarah leaned forward, close to her steering wheel with her defroster on, hoping that the rain would settle down some - but to no avail. She turned on her radio and found a local station announcing that the rain would not let up for several hours yet. "I can not believe this," she sighed in frustration, as she looked down and turned the radio off again.

And then it happened…. as she looked up in fright, crossing her face with her hands to protect herself from the ongoing car that was coming straight at her from the wrong direction.

Squeal, boom and then silence….

Her car had been hit by a car crossing into her pathway, and she was off the road with her car turning over several times before landing on it's side with a crash into an adjacent field – with her last thoughts being before she passed out - as she hung upside down still buckled in her seat with the airbag in her face and blood dripping down - *this can't be happening to me…*

Lance received the call for EMT help, as he lite up the lights that were installed on the top of his roof for emergency purposes. He was only a short distance away from the accident, racing to assist whoever was in need.

He was first to arrive at the scene at hand, being followed shortly behind by an approaching ambulance from Marlin Beach. A car - with its front end smashed in - was off the center median, with a disoriented man walking towards the road, holding his head in confusion. The EMT's ran from the ambulance and proceeded in his direction, as they yelled to Lance to go to the overturned Mazda on the other side of the road in the field.

Lance jumped from his Jeep, grabbing his emergency medical bag and running to the field, as the rain poured down over his face and clothes, soaking him immediately through to the skin. He realized the female was unconscious and her face was stained with dirt, with a slow drizzle of blood leading from her forehead, as he gazed at her through the foggy car window.

He quickly opened the medical bag, extracting a hammer and a knife – breaking the window and cutting the seatbelt free. He then reached in and lifted her lifeless body from the wreckage of the overturned car.

As he laid her down, still cradling her in his arms a safe distance away, the rain continued to pour – washing the blood from her face and making her stir. Lance opened his mouth in disbelief as a fellow EMT worker met him on the side of the road.

"I know her," he breathed in disbelief, looking up at his friend who looked back at him in surprise. "It is Sarah Miller," he said, while wiping the hair from her face and shielding her from the rain. "We got to get her to the hospital, stat."

The gurney was brought and Sarah was placed on it, as she was loaded into the oncoming second ambulance that had just showed up - racing her away to the hospital in Channel Ridge. Lance sat by her side, keeping a steadying hand on her, not caring about his Jeep or when he would pick it back up again.

"Where am I?" she asked in dazed confusion, as she looked up into the kind face that was still blurry in detail.
"You are going to be ok now, Sarah," Lance reassured holding her hand; suddenly realizing history was repeating itself again.

CHAPTER 24

The deluge of torrential rain made the ambulance drive difficult, as they navigated towards the hospital. The siren blared the entire way, making it reminiscent of the sad events from ten years prior. Even though Lance was not there in the ambulance with Dex or Sarah the first time, it was a painful reminder of the past - he realized, as they pulled into the back entrance of the same hospital.

The gurney was unloaded and rolled through the doors, as Lance continued holding on to Sarah's weak hand – lending his support as she mentioned that her head was hurting, still being far off in a distant daze.
She was placed in a sterile room, as a medical team arrived to exam her. Lance reluctantly left after they asked if he was family, before they stripped her down, washing and placing her in a gown, and finishing up with a shot for pain. He stood in the hallway, as he watched them push her from the room, leading Sarah away to an awaiting CAT scan.

Lance speedily walked to the waiting room of the emergency part of the hospital, knowing he had to place a call to his father. Sarah's cell phone was obviously still in her car, so it was unlikely that the hospital would even know whom they should call or notify for her.

"Hello?"

"Dad, it's me," Lance stated anxiously.

"Everything ok?"

"No, Dad. It's not."

John Snyder walked from his office and joined his wife in hers, sensing something serious was about to be said. "What's going on Lance?"

"Sarah Miller."

John began to laugh. "Don't worry, son. She is out of your hair. Andrew Scott stopped by her place earlier and gave her the details for the painting that needs to be done. She is on her way back to Baltimore as we speak."

Lance sighed. "No, dad, that is *not* the case. She was in a car accident. A guy hit her as she was driving, just outside of Marlin Beach. I got the emergency call after the accident, and responded - not even realizing it was Sarah. It was raining badly and I had to bust her car window in and cut her from her over-turned car. She's pretty beat up, dad," Lance said in despair, running his hand through his still-wet hair.

John plopped down in Alison's upholstered chair across from her desk, suddenly turning white and looking like he was going to pass out. *"You can't be serious?"*

"I am very serious, dad," Lance said, while walking through the automatic doors to the awaiting covered patio area outside. The rain was still falling, but now at a lighter pace. "I rode with her on the ambulance and she is here now at Channel Ridge Regional. I can't believe this is happening again - what is the likelihood?" he asked of his father, feeling in total disbelief by the irony of it all.

John stood back up, looking at Alison as he turned the speaker to his phone on for her to hear. "Your mother is with me and we are going to join you at the hospital. Has her family been notified?" John asked, as he grabbed Alison's purse, handing it to her as he led her out to the car.

"Doubtful," Lance answered, running his hand through his brown locks again, realizing he was wet and cold. "I was hoping you would call her parents under the circumstances."

Alison and John jumped into Alison's BMW, as she drove towards the hospital and John continued to talk to Lance. "How is she, son?" he asked cautiously.

"I don't think anything is life threatening - if that is what you mean. But she got pretty banged up, and when I found her she was bleeding and unconscious. She is in x-ray now being evaluated. God help us all, if this is a repeat of ten years ago!" Lance added in exasperation.

"It will be ok. Let's hang up now so I can contact Mike."

"Yes, dad. Do that. I got to get back inside anyway and see how Sarah is doing. And then I must fill the hospital in about her family in Baltimore."

"Take care and we will see you soon, son. And hey – don't take this personally. You rescued her. Remember that."

"Yeah, I know," Lance, breathed, not sure anyone but his parents would realize that or even care.

Mike Miller was just finishing up from a meeting when his phone rang. He was surprised to see that it was a call from his old friend, John Snyder. He had hoped Sarah wasn't being too difficult, and he didn't have to talk some sense into her again.

"Hi John," he greeted, knowing it had been too long since he had last sat down and had a beer with his golfing buddy. "Everything ok with the beach house listing?"

"About that - yes, that is proceeding as planned, but there is something else," he said hesitantly, not wanting to give Mike the alarming horrible news. "It's about Sarah."

"What about Sarah?" he asked, closing his briefcase, knowing he had to leave early for the day for his follow-up doctor's appointment.

He looked to Alison for support as she drove, reaching out to touch her shoulder. "Sarah has been in a car accident."

Mike grabbed his chest, sitting down firmly - fearing another heart attack. "Is she ok?" he asked, trying to hold on to the table edge for support.

"I think so, my friend. Alison and I are on our way to the hospital now to check on her."

"How did you find out about this?" Mike asked, trying to calm himself down with some deep breathing and a swig of water.

"My son Lance rescued her."

"Your son Lance rescued Sarah?" Mike asked in disbelief.

'Yes, he did. He does volunteer EMT work, and he just so happened to be on the scene when the call for help came through. It was raining badly and someone hit her."

"Oh my God!" Mike expressed in shock, grabbing his head with his free hand. "I got to call Nancy and let her know. She will be so upset."

"Don't think the worst. Lance doesn't think anything is life threatening, but I am sure you will want to get to the hospital as quickly as possible for Sarah's sake."

"Where is she?"

"Channel Ridge Regional Medical Center."

"My word... what are the chances of that?" Mike replied forlornly, remembering that was the very same hospital he had lost his son in.

"I know, my friend. But everything is going to be alright this time."

Mike contacted Nancy as to the unfortunate series of events, and she packed a bag quickly for the both of them, knowing how this went down ten years earlier. She shed a few tears, but knew she needed to stay strong not only for Sarah but for Mike with his current health issues. The helicopter was called and they boarded it together, on their way to the same place that held both of their children – one in death, but also one in life.

Lance made his way back inside the hospital after receiving the call back from his dad that the Miller's had been contacted and were on their way. He paced the room, waiting his turn for the admission's desk to call him, after taking his ticket from the machine. "Number 62," the secretary announced, as Lance approached the counter, taking a seat in front of the over-worked, dark-eyed hospital employee. "Are you checking in?" she asked irritably.

"No, I'm not. But I have some information for you that you may find helpful for someone who just did - a short while ago," he offered.

"And whom might that be?" she asked in frustration, not sure his information was prevalent due to HIPPA regulations.

"I am a volunteer EMT worker," Lance explained, pulling his EMT identification card out of his wallet as proof. "I was on the ambulance that brought in Sarah Miller. I know her and her family. I doubt she has any identification on her that would give you her information."

The irate worker looked at Lance differently now, realizing he was on her same team – dealing with the public and all the affairs of the hospital.

"Please just write down her emergency contact information and I will pass it on. Thank you."

Lance did as she requested and slid the paper in her direction. "Sarah's parents live in Baltimore and have already been contacted. They are on their way to the hospital."

The admission's clerk looked at him and shrugged. "Number 66," she bellowed loudly, already excusing him - knowing her fellow workers sitting near her - had already admitted several other people while she took too much time speaking to him about Sarah Miller.

Lance continued to pace around the front of the emergency room entrance, waiting for his parents to arrive. He knew he could not go back to be with Sarah since he wasn't a part of her family, but he was still very concerned about her condition and prognosis.

His mom and dad rushed through the automatic doors after parking the BMW nearby, finding Lance who had worry etched all over his face.

"How is she?" Alison asked.

"I wish I knew," Lance answered in frustration.

"My God, Lance, you are soaked," his mother commented, placing an arm around his shoulder.

"Let's go buy you some clothes and get you a cup of hot coffee to warm you up," John offered, while walking with Alison and Lance to the gift shop.

The helicopter blades beat out the same reminiscent rhythm of an earlier tragic time when the Miller's flew to the same hospital ten years earlier. The rain had made the flight an unforgettable bumpy experience, and they were happy to land - departing into Channel Ridge Regional in a fine mist of rain and fog.

"Where is my daughter?" Nancy hurriedly asked in despair, as she and Mike swiftly made their way through the back of the hospital emergency area.

"She is in there resting," a nurse advised, walking with them in the direction of Sarah's room. They found her with a bandaged forehead and a swollen black and blue face, sleeping peacefully with the covers pulled up under her chin. Relief flooded them, as they realized their daughter was breathing naturally without the aid of a ventilator like Dex had been hooked up to.

Nancy cried into Mike shirt, as she broke down with the sight of her daughter. "I am sorry, Mike, but how is this happening again?" she asked of her husband with frightened pleading eyes, no longer the strong pillar of support she wanted to be.

"Shhh," he whispered quietly against her hair. I am sure the doctor will be in soon. Let's not think the worst."

They took a seat by Sarah's bed, waiting for some time before the doctor appeared in the hospital room.

"Hello, folks," Dr. Owens greeted with a bright smile, extending her hand to shake Mike and Nancy's.

Mike and Nancy rose and walked a short distance away, speaking to the doctor with lowered voices.

"What is going on with our daughter?" Mike asked, anxiously awaiting her answer.

"Can we walk outside? It may be easier to talk," Dr. Owens

suggested, pushing the door open for the Miller's to walk through.

They walked into the hallway and Dr. Owens escorted them into her office, offering them both a seat in front of her desk. "As I am sure you already know, your daughter was in a car accident. She was leaving Marlin Beach and it was raining very badly. An oncoming car crossed the median strip and hit her car - rolling it over into a field."

"Oh no," Nancy yelled, bringing her hand up to her mouth. Mike patted Nancy's arm, silently asking her to calm down.

"Mrs. Miller, things will be fine," she explained, looking at Nancy and then to Mike in a caring way. "Your daughter did suffer some minor cuts and bruises, but she will heal. We did a CAT scan and it did confirm that she has a major concussion, which made her pass out before she was rescued. Beyond that, she has several bruised ribs and a broken arm."

Nancy began to cry again, relief and fear flooding over her all at the same time, as her hands covered her face to block out what was happening.

Dr. Owens looked at Nancy with concern as she rose from her desk chair. "Mrs. Miller, if you feel you would like something to calm you down, please let me know. Otherwise, I will be going. We plan to keep your daughter here for a few days for observation, since she has a severe concussion and is still suffering from shock after what has just happened to her."

Mike and Nancy shook Dr. Owen's hand one last time before she departed, telling them to stay for however long they needed to.

Mike's phone began to ring, as he looked at the familiar number. "Hello?"

"Hi Mike, it's me - John Snyder. Alison, Lance, and I are here at the hospital wanting to check in on Sarah. Can we meet in the cafeteria for coffee and a bite to eat?"

"Sure," Mike agreed, as he grabbed Nancy's hand guiding her towards the cafeteria as Sarah slept.

It had been some time since the two couples had seen each other, and Mike and Nancy were not even sure if they had ever met Lance.

"Thank you for rescuing Sarah," Mike said appreciatively, looking at Lance over a bowl of steaming hot, Maryland crab soup.

"I am so sorry, Mr. Miller," Lance replied sincerely, looking at Mike and then to Nancy with concern etched all over his face.

"Will she be ok?" Alison asked.

"The doctor thinks so, as long as she can get past the concussion that she has," Mike interjected.

"A concussion?"

"Yes, Lance, *she has a concussion*," Nancy remarked curtly, still in shock with the unfolding chain of events, and knowing how Sarah felt about him. "And a broken arm and bruised ribs too."

Lance looked down at the table, his heart breaking with the news. "I am so sorry Mr. and Mrs. Miller. I truly am," he answered sadly, looking up at each one again with pain etched all over his face.

"Under the circumstances, do you still want to proceed forward with the sale of the beach house at this time?" John asked gently, knowing the business arrangement between them was still on the table.

"I think not," Mike replied firmly. "Let's get through this with Sarah first."

"I think that is a good idea," John answered, as he looked to the group at the table who mutually agreed with the decision.

They made their way back to the emergency waiting room after leaving the cafeteria.

"We think we should get back to Sarah. We want to be there when she wakes up," Mike explained to the Snyder's.

"We will be here waiting," John answered.

"That is *not* necessary," Mike responded with a warm smile, taken back by the dedication of his old friend.

"We will be here waiting," Lance interjected soundly, looking to all concerned and giving the final word.

Mike and Nancy walked down the hall and back into Sarah's room. The nurse was finished taking her blood pressure, and speaking to her as she rolled the blood pressure cuff back up. "I'm sorry your head hurts. It is to be expected with a concussion."

"A concussion?" Sarah asked sleepily, still trying to acclimate to her surroundings and to what was going on.

"Yes, honey, a concussion," her father added, making his way back to her bedside.

"Dad? You're here?" she asked, looking at her father and then to her mother. "Why are you here?"

Mike and Sarah took a seat again by her hospital bed. "You were in a car accident. Do you remember that happening?" Mike asked.

"Sorta...it happened so quickly. It was raining really hard...I remember that. And the noise of a crash," Sarah said in a far-off distant way.

"Well, you are in the hospital. You have a concussion, some bruised ribs and a broken arm."

"I do?" Sarah asked, still sedated with pain medication.

"Yes, honey, you do," Nancy replied sadly, looking at her daughter with concern.

"You will be fine, sweetheart. We will be here for you."

Sarah looked at both of her parents. "Where is my car?"

They looked at each other, not sure what to say. "I would guess somewhere safe. There is no need to worry about that right now," her father reassured, knowing he had to locate her vehicle and her other personal items when the opportunity presented itself.

CHAPTER 25

Sarah slept through the night, being awakened by a nurse every few hours, which was the standard practice with a concussion. Mike and Nancy sat in the waiting room with the Snyder's, periodically checking on their daughter, and staying awake by drinking very strong coffee from the snack bar.

"You guys have been great, but seriously, we will call you with any news on Sarah. Go home and get some rest," Mike urged.

John looked at Alison. "Why don't we wait until the doctor shows up this morning and gives you the update?"

"If that is what you would like," Mike resigned, feeling guilty for their lack of sleep.

Lance reappeared, having walked outside for a spell just to clear his head. "Any word on Sarah, yet?" he asked, hoping for an answer from the weary group.

"Not a thing," Nancy added, looking at her watch. "But the nurse said that Dr. Owens will be here soon doing her rounds, and then maybe we will get an update."

Within the hour, Dr. Owens appeared in the waiting room, addressing all that was present. "Mr. and Mrs. Miller, would you like to go somewhere private to speak?" she asked, looking to them for guidance.

"No, that is quite all right," Mike, answered. "These are friends of ours and you can speak openly about Sarah in front of them."

Dr. Owens smiled, looking to each one. "Sarah is awake and has actually drank some ginger ale and has eaten some crackers. She is in a lot of pain and it will take some time for her to recover. She is not out of the woods quite yet from the concussion. I would like to keep her here for several more days for testing and observation."

Lance looked at his parents, realizing how exhausted they were. "Mom and dad, please go home. I am not leaving, but you definitely need to. Go get some rest and I will keep you updated."

"I agree with Lance," Mike interjected, rising with the group to say their goodbyes. "But you, Lance, should go with your parents also. Sarah is our responsibility now. You have been so kind to not only rescue her, but to stay throughout this whole ordeal."

Lance shook his head no, as he firmly disagreed. "I will *not* leave."

"Call us, Lance," Alison requested, knowing it was impossible to change her son's mind once he had decided on something.

John and Alison made their way back to Marlin Beach, getting a few hours of sleep before going back to work at Beach Dreams, keeping their ringers on just in case Lance called with any updates.

Mike and Nancy kept a constant watch by Sarah's bedside, as she slept and woke in two-hour intervals, at the nurse's urging. They prayed silently to themselves, asking God for no setbacks and for her speedy recovery. At four p.m., she finally awoke fully on her own, being more coherent than she had been since the accident occurred.

"You guys are still here?" she asked drowsily, looking at each one of her parents.

"Yes, darling," Nancy answered softly, casting a worried glance at her daughter's beat up face, that was very swollen with only slits for eyes that were barely open.

Mike got up, gazing over Sarah who looked so fragile and vulnerable to him now. "Sarah, I have something to tell you."

"Yes, dad?"

"It's about the accident and who rescued you."

Nancy looked at Mike with concern. "Should we really be discussing this with Sarah now?"

"Yes, Nancy, we should," he said firmly, turning his attention again to his daughter.

"When you were driving in the rain, a driver hit you and your car flipped. An EMT found you – he had to bust out your window and remove you through it - by cutting your seatbelt first."

"Oh my... I did not know," she said with dawning awareness.

"Why I am mentioning all this to you, Sarah, is because it was someone you already know who rescued you from the accident," her father continued.

"I am totally lost, dad," she said, while touching her sore head. "Just tell me who that person is," she moaned, knowing her pain was affecting her from head to toe.

"It was Lance."

Sarah rolled her eyes to the ceiling, trying to focus on her father's words, thinking she did not hear him right. *"Who did you say?"*

"Lance," Mike repeated again.

"That's what I thought you said," she answered in disbelief. *"How could that possibly be?"*

"He volunteers as an EMT, and he got the call as soon as your accident occurred," Nancy added, trying to put some logic behind her daughter's questions.

She sat quietly, just looking at her father and mother. "What do you want me to say? You know how I feel about him... This changes nothing."

Mike looked at his daughter, feeling total relief that she was alive, but irritated with her all at the same time. She lost Dex - her twin brother - he knew, but they lost Dex – their beloved son - also. "Sarah, Lance has been in the waiting room now for over 24 hours. Are you telling me that you do not have it in your heart to thank the man who saved your life, and has not left this hospital and is still here?"

Sarah felt tears welling up in her eyes. "You're right, dad. Why don't you ask him to come to my room, and I will thank him personally."

"Are you sure, Sarah?" Nancy asked in concern.

"Yes, mother. I am sure."

Mike went back to the waiting room and found Lance reading a magazine. He looked up in surprise as Mike approached him. "Lance, Sarah would like to see you now," he said plainly, as Lance rose off his seat, adjusting his newly purchased gift shop shirt and jeans.

"Thank God..." he replied in relief, walking side by side with Mike to her room. "Is she doing ok?"

"Why don't you ask her yourself?" Mike answered, looking meaningfully at Lance.

They proceeded to Sarah's room where Nancy was sitting by her bed, concerned about Mike's decision to force Sarah's hand where Lance was concerned.

Lance looked at Sarah, still in disbelief by her changed appearance. She no longer held the beauty of what he had seen that day at the diner, just a few days prior - with her trim athletic body, sexy outfit and her hair pulled back in a tight ponytail. She was broken and bruised, with a swollen face and a wrapped forehead – almost unrecognizable and in a daze.

"Hello, Sarah," he said softly, trying to respect the distance of approaching her and getting too close.

"Would you like us to stay, Sarah?" her mother asked in concern, being over-protective of her daughter.

"No, it is ok. You guys can leave," Sarah replied, looking at Lance with a look of helplessness.

"We will be right down the hall, Sarah," Mike reassured.

"Call us, if you need us, Lance," he added, as they left the two of them alone in the room.

Lance approached the hospital bed, looking at her for some time without saying a word.

"It's ok to sit," she offered, as she turned her head in his direction and Lance wearily took a seat from his lack of sleep. "My parents said that you stayed here all night. That was not necessary," she added, as she closed her eyes for a few moments, feeling the twinges of pain return.

Lance continued to look at her with uneasiness. "I felt it was *very* necessary. I am concerned for your well-being, Sarah."

"That is very nice of you," she admitted, finding it hard to accept his graciousness. "My parents have informed me that you were the one that rescued me from the car accident. Is that true?" she questioned, as she gazed up at him, still not sure if it were so.

"Yes, Sarah. It is true. I was there on the scene after the accident, and I have been here ever since. I just needed to know you were ok."

Sarah considered his words, not sure of his motivation, but *probably having something to do with guilt over Dex*, she surmised.

"Thank you," she breathed, barley above a whisper, with her eyes glistening with tears.

Lance stood again, reaching over the railing, while lightly touching the blanket that covered her. He closed his eyes, breathing a sigh of relief. "Please let me know if I can do anything at all to help you or your family," he offered sincerely.

"You have done enough, Lance, but I am very grateful," she said as she drifted back off to sleep, with Lance just standing by her bedside for some time before he left.

"Sarah is sleeping," Lance announced, as he made his way back to the lounge area where Mike and Nancy were anxiously waiting. "I think I am going to go now. My car is somewhere on the side of the road between here and Marlin Beach, and I need a shower and some clean clothes - but I will be back."

Mike was astonished by Lance's loyalty to his daughter. "We appreciate your efforts, but you definitely need to get some rest. No one can keep up your pace. It isn't healthy, you know."

"I'll be fine. Let Sarah know that I will return tomorrow," Lance added, as he waved goodbye to Mike and Nancy, and a day that finally gave him some much-needed closure.

CHAPTER 26

Lance was able to get his car, after calling a cab that drove him back to the very spot of the accident where his Jeep was still sitting. The deep tire marks were still etched in the field, as well as in the median strip between the two roads. It was a vivid memory and reminder again to Lance, how quickly things could change. He noticed that Sarah's car, along with the other driver's car that had hit her, were no longer there. He hoped that whoever picked them up had Sarah's belongings somewhere safe.

He made his way back to his house, calling his parents along the way - giving them the update on Sarah. They were relieved to know that she was doing better and that Lance and Sarah had spoken. John and Alison were not the only ones concerned – he was too.

Most people wanted to be friends with Lance. He was not only handsome, but also very easygoing. It was not part of his nature to hold grudges or have a person mad at him - that was, the exception being Sarah Miller. Hearing her words of thanks made him feel suddenly better. Maybe if he could make things right with her, even with her misconceptions about Dex, they could be friends.

He took a shower and ate some leftover spaghetti that he still had in the refrigerator, before climbing into bed for the night. He thought of Sarah again in the diner with her backside turned towards him. She was definitely a turn-on. He felt guilty putting her in that context, as she lay in the hospital in a fragile state, trying to heal. As hard as he tried, he couldn't shake the image. She was having an affect on him – and his genitals were telling him so.

Lance rolled over and looked at his alarm clock. "Seven a.m., damn, I wanted to be up by now!" he yelled, getting up and grabbing a shower quickly. He brushed his teeth, shaved and combed his brown curly locks into place. He grabbed a pair of faded jeans and a white golf shirt that his father had given him for his last birthday. He looked better than he had in the last couple of days from getting some rest.

On the way, he stopped at The Seabreeze Diner, grabbing a cup of coffee to go with a dash of French vanilla creamer, and a bagel with cream cheese. The goal was to get back to the hospital in a timely fashion, maybe giving Sarah's parents a much-needed break.

Lance parked his Jeep and made his way to the gift shop, selecting a dozen yellow roses in a clear vase, hoping he could present them to Sarah in person. He walked to the waiting area, but her parents were nowhere to be found. He then turned his attention to the receptionist, wanting to get a visitor's pass.

"I am here to see Sarah Miller?" he requested, looking to the senior gentleman volunteer for assistance.

He looked up her name on the computer, and then over his glasses at Lance. "She's been moved. Room 210 – second floor. Here... put this on your shirt," he requested, handing him a sticker with the identification that Lance would need.

"Thank you, sir," Lance said with a kind smile, placing the sticker on his shirt.

He pressed the elevator button, making his way to the second floor with the flowers still in his hand. "Whew, I hope she is going to be ok with me showing up again," he breathed, knowing he was treading on thin ice with Sarah.

Lance made his way down the hall, past the nurses' desk, without anyone stopping him to ask where he was going. He passed the visitor's lounge that had only one man waiting, who was busy reading a magazine. And then he was there – room 210 – on the right side of the hallway. He could hear Sarah's parents talking to her. *Should I enter?* He thought, as he hesitated in the hallway.

Lance walked through the half-opened doorway, pausing to knock. "Is it ok to come in?" he asked inquisitively, smiling at all three, as they looked back at him in surprise.

"Of course!" Mike answered cheerfully, pleased to see that Lance had returned as promised.

Sarah looked at Lance, in disbelief that he returned, as he made his way to the other side of her bed.

"I brought these for you," he said with a friendly cheerful smile, placing the flowers on a shelf nearby so that she could see them.

"Lance, thank you. That was *not* necessary," Sarah said with some hesitation, but was genuinely pleased by his thoughtfulness.

"You look well-rested," Nancy interjected, realizing she was lacking in the sleep that Lance so obviously had just had.

"Yes, I did go home. I needed to do a few things, and yes, I did sleep - but I'm back now," he said with firmness. "I thought maybe I could sit with Sarah for awhile, and you guys could take a break and maybe get some rest yourselves."

Sarah looked at her parents and then at Lance in amazement.

"We wouldn't want to put you out," Mike answered, not sure how Sarah would feel about leaving her alone for a lengthy period of time with Lance.

"No problem at all, if Sarah is ok with it?"

"I...guess that would be all right," Sarah replied with some hesitation, adjusting herself upward in the bed with her free arm that wasn't in a cast, with a pain-filled grimace.

Lance looked at her in concern. "Don't worry, Sarah. I won't leave your side. Whatever you need, I will be here to help you."

Sarah looked at her parents again, finding the whole situation with Lance hard to believe that he would even offer such a kindness, but accepting of it nonetheless. "Mom and Dad, it is ok. Lance is right. You should go get some rest. I will be fine."

"Where would you like us to go?" Nancy asked in confusion, not sure if she meant the waiting area.

"I mean, go check in a hotel; or better yet, go to the beach house. I am eating now and starting to feel somewhat better," Sarah added half-heartedly, still very bruised and aching from the accident.

"Can I have a word with you, Lance, in the hallway?" Mike requested.

"Sure," Lance agreed, following Mike as they walked together towards the patient lounge.

"Have a seat," Mike requested, patting the seat beside of him. "Look, it is very nice of you to come back to the hospital to visit Sarah. I cannot climb into that head of hers, but she has held a grudge towards you for way too long over the loss of her brother. We greatly appreciate all that you have done from the time you rescued Sarah from her car accident, but you do not have to feel obligated any longer," he said succinctly. "It is her mother and my responsibility now to watch over her during her time of recovery."

Lance just looked at Mike, pausing for a moment before he answered. "I understand your feelings, but I want to do this. Plain and simple – I just want to be here for her. You and Nancy need the break. Sarah had an excellent idea that I hadn't thought about. Go back to the beach house. You haven't been there in awhile. Maybe it is time to see the place again, especially since you are selling it."

"You may be right about that. We haven't actually said goodbye to The Dancing Seahorse," Mike said regrettably, with a distant look in his eyes.

"Well, now is the perfect time," Lance replied sympathetically, while patting Mike's shoulder. "And by the way, I did some research as I drove here this morning. Here is where Sarah's car is located and the phone number of the business who is holding it," he said, handing Mike the paper with the necessary information.

"Thanks, Lance," Mike answered sincerely, studying the paper in front of him.

"I would look her car over closely, and take pictures inside and out with your cell phone for insurance purposes, and then remove any items of value. I am sure her luggage is still in the car, along with her purse, cellphone and laptop. Not sure if those things made it in one piece or not, but it wouldn't hurt to figure that out for the insurance adjuster."

They left the lounge and continued to walk down the hall, looking out over the large expanse of windows that showcased the cityscape of the street below them.

"I hope you won't find this presumptuous, but I took it upon myself to rent you a car for a couple days. I know you are without your vehicle and it is the least I can do to help," he added kindly, looking at Mike as they continued to walk. "Also, if you are up to it, my parents would like to treat you and Nancy to lunch or dinner tonight in Marlin Beach.

Mike's mouth dropped open in pleasant surprise. "Well, I gotta tell you, Lance, that I never thought you or your parents would do so much for us. Thank you. I am truly touched," he said sincerely, reaching out to shake his hand warmly.

Mike and Lance made their way to the outside where the rental car agent had dropped off the car and had left the keys in the glove box.

"Let me know what I owe you, and I will pay you back for this, Lance," Mike offered, genuinely moved by his thoughtfulness.

"Think nothing of it! The rental information is lying on the passenger's seat. If you want to extend the time for a while or switch out the car, I rented it from A-1 Rentals in Marlin Beach. And remember, my dad will call you soon to see if you and Nancy would like to meet up with them," he added, hoping that they would take the time to do so.

After getting the keys, Mike and Lance took the elevator to the second floor, walking back to Sarah's hospital room. Nancy was still sitting by her daughter's side - just where they had left her.

"Nancy, it's time to go. We have things to do and we need some rest!" Mike announced matter-of-factly, as he approached his wife and grabbed her hand, ready to leave.

She paused to look at Lance worriedly, before departing. "Please call us if you need us."

"I will, Mrs. Miller."

"Call me, Nancy. Please..." she said, getting up to give Lance a hug. "Take good care of Sarah, until we get back."

Sarah looked quietly at the group, realizing her parents' were actually leaving the hospital and she would be alone with Lance.

"Goodbye, honey. We will be back after we get some rest," her father promised. "I'm leaving you in good hands, so just relax and get better," he added, as they walked from the room and closed the door behind them.

CHAPTER 27

Lance had been in and out of Sarah's room periodically throughout the day, trying to give her time alone to rest. He walked from the hospital and followed up on a few phone calls and emails related to Beach Dreams that he had neglected and needed to respond to.

As Lance returned to her room, he found her sleeping soundly. He stood by her bedside, taking in the scene at hand. She was still very swollen, with the bandage that had been wrapped around her head when she first arrived at the hospital, still in place. Her right arm had a cast on it that wrapped around her hand, with only the tips of her fingers exposed as it ran up and covered the top of her elbow. He was not sure where her bruised ribs were located, but he knew that it must be painful based on his EMT training. Overall, she was a pitiful sight, but he still saw the raw beauty in her being. Her lips were full and moved slightly as she breathed, while her pulled back hair was a delicate shade of blonde with natural highlights of lighter blonde hues running throughout it. He liked her natural look, which was the thing that caught his eye even when he first saw her at age eighteen so many years before.

He sat in the chair as she slept, half dosing off himself for a while.

"Sarah?" came a voice that made Lance and Sarah both wake up at the same time. "It's Dr. Owens. I am here to check on you today," she announced, as Lance stood up with a yawn, making his way out of the room so that Sarah could have some privacy alone with her doctor.

He paced outside in the hallway, until Dr. Owens approached him after her exam. "Are you a friend of Sarah's?" she asked.

"Yes, I am," Lance confessed, realizing that those were words never spoken before.

"I wanted to let you know that even though Sarah has made some improvement, she has a long road ahead of her in way of healing. I still would like to keep her in the hospital for a day or two, and then she will need someone to be with her at all times for several weeks. It will take awhile for her ribs to heal, and I still want to keep watch on her concussion. I will be taking more tests tomorrow, just to make sure no blood clots have formed in her head."

"That sounds serious, doctor."

"It's just a precaution – that's all."

"I will inform her parents of what you just shared."

"Please do. The nurse will be in soon to get her up and out of bed. It's time for her to start walking - as painful as that may be."

Lance returned to Sarah's room, as she looked at him in misery. "I wish I felt better," she sighed. "My head won't stop hurting."

"It will be ok," he promised, patting her good arm and taking his seat again by her side.

He opened a magazine that he found on a small table nearby, paging absentmindedly through each page. "You know the doctor wants you to get up and try to walk today?"

"Yeah, I know…but I really don't think I am up for it quite yet," she moaned, feeling her resolve crumbling at the thought of it all.

Lance looked at her with concern. "Sarah, I will help you. Don't worry, I can walk with you if you would like."

Sarah glanced back, studying his handsome face that seemed sincere in intent. "Why do you want to do so much for me and my family? *What's in it for you? It isn't necessary - you realize that?*" she gritted out, still angry over the past and his constant presence now reminding her of it again.

Lance sighed in exasperation, rising from his seat. "Do me a favor and go back to being mad at me once this all behind you. Okay? Right now, *accept* my gift – *it is sincere and I care!*"

She stared at him with tears beginning to puddle in her eyes. "You make it so hard to say no, don't you?"

He walked to her side table and reached for a tissue, handing it to her before turning to leave. *"What's in it for me?"* Lance repeated back to her, looking deeply into her pain-filled eyes. "Seeing you well again and smiling. That's worth more than you could know."

Mike and Nancy arrived at Parker's Towing, requesting to see the car of their daughter - Sarah Miller.

"Over this way," the attendant directed, pointing towards the mangled car that caused them both to look on in disbelief.

"Oh my word," Nancy gasped in shock, her hand finding its way to her mouth again.

"We knew it would be bad, dear, after hearing that she rolled it,"

Mike stated realistically, looking at his wife with concern from the look on her face.

Mike drove the rental car up beside of Sarah's wrecked one, getting out and taking the necessary pictures inside and out, as Lance had suggested. He retrieved her suitcases out of the trunk that were partially broken, that still held her clothes and other items safely inside – which included Dex's things that appeared untouched. He opened the glove box and found a stack of papers and booklets related to the Mazda that he took. Luckily, her purse was found on the floor of the passenger's seat, with Sarah's cellphone tucked safely inside of it. Her laptop didn't fare so well, as he found it smashed up against the back seat that had met the front, with a cracked and broken screen that was now unusable. Beyond that, the cooler was unrecognizable - distorted and crushed, with its contents spilled out on the floor of the trunk. Mike realized his daughter had been lucky and could have lost her life in the accident, as badly damaged as everything was.

Sarah's insurance company had been notified and they agreed that Mike and Nancy seeing the car first, taking pictures and then removing Sarah's possessions was a good first step, since the claims adjuster was running behind and unable to evaluate and access the damage for awhile yet. A settlement check would be issued, after the vehicle was deemed "totaled". Then an additional check would be forthcoming from the other party's insurance company, once the hospital bills and other expenses were calculated. If not provided freely, a lawyer would need to be hired. No one liked to go through the process – but it was the way of a car accident – and unfortunately so.

The drive to The Dancing Seahorse was bittersweet for Mike and Nancy, realizing that neither one of their children was with them now, but thankfully, Sarah was still alive.

They parked the rental car, looking at the familiar structure that

Mike had designed and built. He sat in the car just staring at the house that he treasured, looking in pride at his workmanship that he was so proud of. Nancy broke the silence, reaching out to touch her husband's hand. "Why don't we go inside, dear? I really could use some rest before we return to the hospital to be with Sarah again."

Mike looked at his wife understandably, equally weary and needing of sleep. "I know. Just needed a moment to look at the ole gal for a minute. That's all," he said with a sentimental smile.

"Who are you calling an old gal?" Nancy teased, grabbing out to squeeze Mike's hand firmly.

"Definitely, not you, my beautiful lady. Definitely not you."

After some well-deserved rest, Mike made his way out on the deck, just to sit and watch the beachgoers that were still enjoying their activities in the lingering final hours of the late afternoon sun. Nancy continued to sleep, giving Mike some well-deserved time alone, remembering all those quiet moments that he spent in that same spot many years earlier. He breathed deeply of the fresh salty air and felt the breeze blowing gently over his face. *It has been too long*, he thought to himself, as he enjoyed the feel of the sun warming him.

Mike grabbed his ringing cellphone off of the patio table, realizing that it was John Snyder trying to reach him again.

"Hi, John," he greeted. "Sorry I haven't gotten back to you. So much has been going on with Sarah, and I was just grabbing some much needed shuteye."

"Totally understand, my friend," John replied as he drove in his car, after finishing up another round of golf. "How is Sarah doing?"

"She is making some slow progress, and of course she is still in the hospital. Do you realize that Lance is with her?" Mike asked, as he walked down the deck steps and made a visual inspection around his property on all sides.

John shook his head silently and bit his lip, not surprised by his son's compassion to help her. He had always been one to give of his time since he was a young boy, and he was proud of him for doing so now - even with her bitterness towards him. "Lance is a good man, Mike. I am glad he can be there for Sarah."

"We greatly appreciate all of your family's kind gestures. It means a lot to Nancy and I that you and Alison showed up at the hospital on that first day."

John pulled his Mercedes into Beach Dreams, walking and talking quickly past the receptionist, stopping in the hallway in front of his wife's office that was still with a client. "Mike - Alison and I would like to take you and Nancy out to dinner tonight," he said simply, while eyeing Alison and giving her the hint to finish up.

"Hmmm... we thought we should get back to Sarah."

"You got to eat, man," John continued in his brash way, walking into his office and grabbing a water from his mini fridge.

Mike began to laugh. His friend hadn't changed in all the years of being apart. "Ok. Let me get Nancy up and we will meet you. What time is good for you guys?"

"How about 6 at the Old Bay Café?"

"You still going there?" Mike teased, knowing it was John's favorite hangout - being only across the street from his real estate company.

"Best crab cakes in town, Mike. You know that! And of course they take care of me and the family wonderfully."

"Yeah, I know. Nancy and I like the place too," he admitted with a knowing grin. "We will see you at 6."

The four met and dined by a table overlooking the bay, that was always reserved for the Snyder's. Crab cakes with Old Bay seasoning, peanut oil fries with the skins still on them, and Maryland coleslaw completed the fare. The sunset was magnificent, as the group enjoyed the two-man band that was set up near the bar, playing a variety of beach themed tunes.

"It's been too long. You know that?" John mentioned with a sincere smile, looking at his friends across the table while drinking a Natty Boh that he encouraged them to have also.

Nancy smiled with some hesitation, as she looked at Mike with worry, realizing it was almost 8 p.m. "Poor Sarah, she must think we have forgotten her."

Mike glanced at his watch. "Oh, boy... maybe it's too late to go back to the hospital now. Time has gotten away from us."

"Don't worry," John said with a gruff boisterous laugh. "Let me call Lance and see if he is still there. It wouldn't hurt you to stay one more night before going back to be with her. We can talk about all the details about the upcoming listing of your property."

"No business tonight, John," Alison insisted firmly, patting her husband on the hand. "That is for another day," she reminded him kindly, looking at Mike and then to Nancy with an understanding smile.

John excused himself to use the bathroom, stopping to call Lance along the way. His phone rang, going straight to voicemail. "Call me, son," was the message, as he slipped off to make another one of his all-too-frequent pit stops.

Lance walked out of Sarah's room, taking a break again while she slept. He had gone to the hospital cafeteria and had picked up a sandwich and another coffee, which was helping to keep him awake from his lack of sleep. She had been civil, but mostly quiet for most of the day. He read cooking articles to her while quoting the ingredients for award winning meals. Sarah's head turned slightly towards him, as she remembered doing the same for Dex many years before as he lay dying. Lance continued to bore her with his endless chanting of the measurement sizes, even speaking in a falsetto voice just to lighten the mood.

He turned on his phone as he sat in the Jeep, listening to several voicemails - his father's being the last.

"Call me, son."

"Dad?"

"Hello, Lance. Been trying to reach you," John yelled loudly over the blare of the music that was playing in the background.

"Where are you?"

"Old Bay Café. Where else?" he laughed, making Lance grin. "We are with the Miller's and time has gotten away from us. They are concerned about Sarah and getting back to hospital tonight."

Lance took a bite from his sandwich and washed it down with a final swig of his coffee. "Tell them not to worry. Sarah is fine. I will stay with her throughout the night and then they can come back in the morning. Were they able to get her things out of the car?"

"I think so. They said something about that," John replied, not remembering the details. "They are staying at the beach house and I know they got a little rest today."

"That's great," Lance said in relief, knowing the vigil at the hospital without rest - was a lot to bear for anyone, including him. "Tell them I will stay here until they get back in the morning."

"Will do, Lance. And son, I'm proud of you for doing what you are doing."

"Thanks, dad. It's the least I can do," he replied, knowing he needed to hear that about now with Sarah's icy response.

John joined the others back at the table, having a hard time talking over the music. He leaned in and spoke loudly for all to hear. "I talked with Lance. He is with Sarah and will stay with her throughout the night. He said to tell you that he will see you in the morning."

Nancy looked again at Mike with concern, knowing how Sarah felt about Lance. "Maybe that isn't such a good idea," Nancy interjected.

"Nonsense! Lance said she is sleeping," John insisted, rising from the table and snapping his fingers in the direction of the waiter for another round. "I'm sure she was given some medicine to relax her for the night. Why not hang with us for awhile longer, get a good night's rest, and then head back to the hospital in the morning?"

"I agree, Nancy. She will be fine until we get back there in the morning. We haven't had a decent night's rest now in a few days," Mike realized, trying to ease his wife's apprehensions.

"Very good," John announced, standing and ordering four more beers for "ole times' sake" for the table.

Lance returned to Sarah's room, and found her being escorted from the bathroom by a nurse, with pain etched all over her face. She looked at Lance, as she was being helped into the bed and tucked back in safely.

"Do you know where my parents are?" she asked, looking at him with questioning eyes of concern.

"They are out to dinner with my parents in Marlin Beach," he replied with a warm smile.

"Hmmm," she answered. "That's nice."

The nurse charted her vitals and took her blood pressure one last time for the evening, before giving her a dose of pain medication in her IV before walking towards the door. "Would you like some sherbet?" she asked pleasantly, as Sarah shook her head- *yes* - and smiled.

Lance returned to his seat and watched Sarah raise the head of the bed with the remote, before she smoothed the blanket back in place over her. "I promised to stay with you tonight. Your parents need some rest and they will return first thing in the morning."

Sarah sighed, knowing there was no use in debating him. The fight was out of her and Lance was determined to get his way. In the short time she had spent with him, she had figured that much out about him. "You can go, Lance. I will be fine…. honestly," she said with slurred speech, already feeling the affects of the sedative kicking in.

The nurse returned a short time later with the promised sherbet and a cup of fresh water and ice. "I see our patient is asleep?" she mentioned casually, looking at Lance in a slightly flirtatious way.

"Umm… yes," he answered, surprised at her outward show of cleavage and a saucy smile, as she bent over to place the items on Sarah's tray before moving and adjusting it over the bed.

She left again, returning with a blanket and pillow, pointing to the recliner on the opposite side of the room. "That folds back for sleeping. Feel free to use it along with these," she offered, handing Lance the items she held in her hands.

"Thanks," he answered simply, not wanting to continue the conversation with her.

"I will check on Sarah throughout the night and you can have her sherbet if she doesn't wake," she mentioned with one last playful, toothy smile before pulling the door shut and lowering the lights.

Lance walked to the recliner and placed the pillow and blanket on the chair, before sliding it closer beside of Sarah's bed. He pushed back and reclined, continuing to watch her as she slept peacefully, feeling groggy himself. Sleep came easily for him, as he felt content - knowing that this was where he wanted to be.

CHAPTER 28

Morning arrived and with it a flurry of activity. Lance was awakened by the early morning shift of nurses and doctors who were now on duty for the day. As he brought the recliner back up in its sitting position, Sarah was surprised to see him by her side. She was helped from her bed and walked to the bathroom once more, while Lance pushed the recliner back across the room, folding the blanket and placing the pillow on top of it. He straightened his shirt and rubbed his hands over his face. He needed to use the bathroom also, and get some food and a shower.

Sarah was helped back to bed, just as her breakfast was placed on her tray, finally beyond the mostly liquid diet that she detested. Eggs, toast and tea sat in front of her, as she was put in an upright position, causing her ribs to ache. The nurse was staunch in her approach, saying it was time for Sarah to start moving more and eating solid food again, which was the main goal for the day.

Sarah looked at Lance, feeling half-embarrassed, knowing he was seeing her at her worst. "You are *still* here?" she remarked, reaching with her good arm for the fork.

"Yeah, for a little while yet... until your parents arrive," he smiled understandably, trying to give her some peace of mind.

Lance excused himself, finding a bathroom and some food of his own, along with another cup of coffee. His phone rang, to an unknown number, but he answered it anyway.

"Hello?"

"Lance, its Mike Miller. I'm calling you from my wife's cellphone, in case you didn't recognize the number. We are on our way and should be there within thirty minutes."

"Oh, Mr. Miller, no worries – take you time," Lance replied, making his way back to Sarah's room.

"Is Sarah ok?"

"As far as I know, yes. I was with her throughout the night and she slept soundly. I just slipped out of her room while she was eating her breakfast."

Mike smiled happily, looking as his wife, as they listened together on the speakerphone. "Well that is great news! Let her know we will be there soon, and Lance – we can't thank you enough for all you have done."

"Yes, Lance, thank you," Nancy, added, agreeing with her husband.

Lance walked back into Sarah's room, finding her alone with her food tray gone, watching television and looking more alert.

"Breakfast seems to have agreed with you."

Sarah smiled. "Really? Why do you say that?"

Lance returned the smile. "You just seem like your are turning the corner today – breakfast, feeding yourself, watching TV – that's all."

"Yes, I do feel slightly better. The doctor says I may be going home tomorrow."

"That's great Sarah!" Lance exclaimed happily, while patting her covers. "I just spoke with your parents and they should be here shortly."

Sarah looked at Lance knowing he would be leaving her soon, and for some reason she didn't want him to go. "Mom and Dad went beyond the call of duty by coming here, but so have you, Lance," she confessed with guarded, vulnerable eyes. "I am so grateful for you being here," she added hesitantly, finding his brown eyes again that she held with her own.

"You are welcome, Sarah..." Lance answered, wanting to say so much more, but having his thoughts interrupted by the door opening behind him. He turned to see Nancy and Mike smiling happily at the site of their daughter who was looking much better than when they last saw her.

Nancy approached the bed, gently kissing Sarah's still bruised cheek. "My dear, I am here now," she consoled, feeling guilty for being away from her, as tears of relief filled her eyes.

"It's ok, Mom. I am all right," she reassured, looking lovingly at her mother, and then to her father who was standing beside of Lance on the opposite side of the bed.

Mike reached out and patted his daughter; just happy she was on her way to recovery. "Has the doctor been in to see you today yet?"

"Yes, dad, he has. He says I may be going home tomorrow."

"Excellent!" Mike replied.

Nancy looked in her husband's direction. "I guess we will all leave for Baltimore tomorrow?"

"I can't leave just yet, Mom. The doctor will want to see me back here in a week or so, and I think I may want to stay in the area at the beach house."

"Then we will stay too!" Mike replied enthusiastically, looking at his wife and then to his daughter for their approval. "We are selling the beach house, so why not spend one last time together for a few weeks enjoying the place?"

"What about work?" Sarah asked, feeling suddenly concerned about the business and the lack of them not being there.

"I got my computer and my phone. What more do I need?" he smiled, giving her a gentle look of understanding. "You don't need to worry your pretty head about such things, Sarah. We have a good team in place, and the business will be fine."

Sarah just sighed, glancing at the three of them in total helplessness, knowing there was nothing she could do to change the situation. "I guess it will all work out," she whispered, suddenly feeling very sleepy again.

Lance looked at Sarah as her eyes were beginning to close. "I'm going to leave now, Sarah," he said to her softly, as she turned to focus on what he was saying. "If you need anything, don't hesitate to let me know."

Sarah paused to consider his words, realizing at that moment how wrong she had been about him. "Thank you..." she breathed, as she closed her eyes and drifted back to sleep.

Mike and Lance walked from Sarah's room, stopping in the second floor lounge. "We can't thank you enough for all you have done, and for being with Sarah last night."

"I wanted too," Lance answered, ready to push the elevator button and leave. "I am glad you guys have decided to stay awhile longer in Marlin Beach. I think it may be a good thing."

"I hope so..." Mike answered, looking a little uncertain. "You know Sarah has had her anxieties about the place. It hasn't been easy."

Lance glanced at Mike, not knowing what to say, but sharing in his concern. "Keep me updated. I do care," he added sincerely, before walking into the elevator and saying goodbye before the doors shut.

The drive back to Marlin Beach was filled with much reflection. Lance knew his feelings for Sarah were growing, but he wasn't sure if it was happening out of a sense of guilt over Dex, or maybe from the car accident that she just had - or if it was something more. He knew though, that he had felt a sense of relief wash over him when he realized the family was not returning to Baltimore just yet. *Why do I even care?* He thought, as he made his way back over the bridge, knowing that she only felt disdain and loathing towards him for the most part.

He pulled into his driveway, sitting and contemplating the situation for several minutes more. "Gotta get to work," he spoke determinedly, knowing it was time to get back to Beach Dreams and selling some real estate.

Mike and Nancy stayed in the hospital throughout the day, helping Sarah walk down the hall, as much as they knew she would debate not needing to do so.

"Mom, I just feel so weak and my ribs continue to hurt," she grimaced with pain.

"At least your IV is out now and your head is un-bandaged. You will get through this, Sarah. Dad and I will be with you every step of way," Nancy promised with a smile, holding onto Sarah's good arm as she leaned on her mother for support.

"I feel badly about work," she confessed, as they made their way back to her room. "After what dad has just been through with his heart, now this has happened!"

Nancy helped her daughter back into bed, smoothing the blankets over her in the process. "Sarah, you and dad are both alive. That is all we care about. Stop worrying about the business. Your dad is in contact with his staff throughout the day. Matter of fact, he is in the car right now going over a few things with them, as we speak," she added, bringing the table that held Sarah's water back over the bed so that she could sip it through a straw.

"I understand that, mom, but maybe it's time that I sit in on some of those phone calls too."

Nancy looked at her daughter with a shake of her head, admiring her drive, but realizing how hard it was for her to just take a break and slow down. "Sarah, you *just* had a car accident on Monday, and it is only Thursday. You have a broken arm, bruised ribs and a severe concussion. Who wants to go back to work right after that? I think you need to give yourself some time to heal, as hard as it is for you," she added tenderly with motherly wisdom.

Sarah looked at her, knowing that all she said was true. "I just can't believe my luck, that's all. And to think Lance - of all people – was the one to rescue me."

"Is that such a bad thing? Maybe this is fate's way of showing you he isn't such a bad guy after all."

Sarah breathed out heavily while she looked at the ceiling, considering what her mother was saying. *"Whatever he is doing now, does not bring Dex back. You know that."*

Nancy grabbed her daughter's hand, looking sincerely into her sky blue eyes that echoed her own. "Darling, base life on today and the kindnesses showed today. The past cannot be changed. Dex would want you happy."

"Happy with the man who didn't save Dex?" she gritted out in frustration.

"Maybe so…" Nancy answered softly, getting up and standing by her bed. "Life has a way of turning things around full circle at times. Just let it go…."

Mike opened the door to Sarah's room, with an x-ray technician coming in behind him.

"Sarah, I am here to take you for one last CAT scan. We want to make sure things are improving before you are released," he explained, as he began to push her from the room.

"See you soon, mom and dad. Get some lunch," she smiled, feeling suddenly hungry and ready to eat once she was brought back from her test.

With her testing done, and another night spent with Mike and Nancy both on recliners, the day of Sarah's release was finally there.

Dr. Owens placed the stethoscope back around her neck, after listening to Sarah' heart and lungs. "I think it is safe to say that you are able to leave today and go home. Remember, you need to take it easy for a few weeks," she reminded her gently.

"How about going back to work?" Sarah asked inquisitively, desiring only to do so.

"Not now, Sarah," Dr. Owens advised, already being warned by her parents in the hallway that this would be her desire. "I know you will be staying in Marlin Beach at your beach house, and I think that is an excellent idea. Enjoy the time and take it easy for a while," she encouraged, as she signed her release papers, allowing her to leave.

A wheelchair was brought for Sarah, as Mike went to get the car. "Don't forget the flowers, mom," she reminded over her shoulder, as she was escorted from the room. Nancy grabbed the ones from Lance and the office, catching up with the group as they made their way down to the first floor.

Mike was at the front of the hospital waiting, as the orderly assisted Sarah into the front seat, as she grimaced again in pain while he fastened her in the seatbelt. Nancy climbed in the back seat and then they drove away, finally saying goodbye to Channel Ridge Regional Medical Center.

They passed by the site where the accident had occurred. Sarah looked out, surprised that she could still see the tire marks that were still obviously visible.

"That is where it happened..." she said in a far-off distant way to her parents, as her mind drifted back to that rainy, terrible day.

They crossed the bridge with its many boats, making it back to Marlin Beach. Sarah turned to stare out the car window at the numerous houses, hotels and restaurants that were quickly passing them by. "Boy, am I hungry," she confessed, as she looked at her dad with a hinting grin.

"Well, that's a good thing, and we can fix that problem quite easily," Mike smiled, making his way home to The Dancing Seahorse, that would be their destination for the next few weeks together.

CHAPTER 29

The trunk of the rental car was stuffed to the brim with an assortment of bags of groceries that Mike had purchased from the Super Fresh, before stopping at Tommy's to pick up several subs on his way back to the beach house. Sarah was already comfortable and resting on the couch - watching TV and drinking a cup of hot tea with honey, as he rang the doorbell, with an abundance of "take out" food in his arms.

Nancy ran to the door to assist her husband, making numerous trips back and forth from the car until everything was unloaded and put away. Mike had purchased several weeks' worth of food, beverage and other necessary items, so that the beach house could be restocked and comfortable for their time there together. They knew it was going to be awhile until Sarah was recovered, so it made sense to have the cabinets full and overflowing with food and drinks once more.

Mike opened the patio doors allowing the fresh air to blow in from the ocean. The wind chimes tinkled on the deck, making an inviting melodic sound for all to hear. He was happy to be back, even if it was for a short time, in his home and the place he had built and loved.

Sarah greedily bit into her turkey sub, realizing her appetite was very much back. "Dad, this is sooo good. No one makes a sub like Tommy's!"

Mike laughed, knowing Sarah was absolutely right. "Subs and fries and so much more! Yes, we do have good food here at the beach," he agreed, enjoying his Italian cold cut sub and Birch Beer.

They spent the afternoon snuggled together – Sarah on the couch, and Mike and Nancy on recliners - watching an old DVD movie that Mike had found in one of the drawers. Laughter filled the room as the comedy with Chevy Chase unfolded. It was good to be home, back with the laughter and the sweet smells of the sea permeating throughout the room.

Nancy made a pitcher of iced tea, handing a glass to her husband and one to Sarah, with a lemon wedge placed on the rim of each one. "What should we have for dinner?" she questioned, only a few hours after lunch.

Sarah shook her head and grinned, knowing her mother was always planning the next meal a few hours after they had just eaten. "Don't go to any trouble, mom. I am still full from my turkey and cheese sub," she groaned, placing her hands on her over-extended abdomen.

"Nonsense," Mike interjected, rising from the recliner to turn off the TV after the movie had finished. "We have the grill and I bought some charcoal. I want to fire it up and throw on a couple of burgers - just like the good old days!"

The three laughed in agreement, as they continued to talk and share pleasant family time together. It was rare that they took the time to do so, after Sarah had moved out and had gotten a place of her own.

"Whatever you say, dad. You have always been the grill master around here."

"Glad you remember that, my dear!"

Nancy laughed and got up and went back into the kitchen, pulling open her custom-made vegetable bin that Mike had designed especially for her.

"I can make some potato salad to go with those burgers. Does that work?"

"Yes, mom, but how about we give it a rest so that I can get hungry again?" Sarah joked with a sarcastic edge, giving her mother a fond grin.

The remainder of the afternoon was spent relaxing, as Sarah napped, Nancy read a novel out on the deck, and Mike took a long walk several blocks away. His doctor had encouraged him to exercise and the beach was the best place to make sure that happened.

While he was gone, Nancy made her potato salad and then retreated back to the deck to enjoy another iced tea with her book that she just couldn't put down. They were happy and content, and the plan to be back at the beach house was suddenly unfolding as being the right decision for all concerned.

Mike returned, winded and sweating from his long walk, but feeling rejuvenated from the experience. His phone rang, as he walked from the bathroom, wiping sweat from his brow. "Hello, Lance. Yes, Sarah is fine and she was released today. Yes, we are here at the beach house now."

Sarah came out of her bedroom, still groggy from her nap, realizing whom her dad was speaking with.

"Of course, you may stop by," he smiled, looking at Sarah who was shaking her head no. "Tomorrow would be fine. Say hi to your folks for me," Mike added, before hanging up.

Sarah sat at the table just looking at her dad in disbelief. *"Seriously, you had to invite him here? Wasn't the time I spent with him at the hospital enough of a thank you?"*

Mike sighed, taking a seat next to his daughter. "Sarah, your are not being fair. Lance is honestly a decent, nice guy. Can't you see that?"

She paused, resting her cast to her side and lowering her gaze. "I guess so... It's just so hard for me to see him in a different light – that's all."

Nancy joined them at the table, trying to change the subject. "Are you hungry yet?" she asked Sarah, knowing that question always brought out a funny reaction in her, and they could go back to enjoying their day together.

Sarah laughed. "Yes mother, I am *finally* hungry."

"Then let me get that grill fired up!" Mike chimed in, changing his direction and jumping up, ready to go and get started outside.

Nancy's grinned silently, realizing her intuition was right – she lightened the mood and made the group laugh, and it felt good to do that again.

They dined on the burgers and potato salad, and even convinced Sarah to eat with them on the deck. The evening was beautiful, just as they had remembered from so many years earlier, what it was like to have dinner together outside at the patio table, as they watched the children at play with their kites flying in the sultry breeze.

Nancy lit a few citronella candles, and Mike replaced the nautical themed flag on the deck that he found still hiding in the shed below. It was as if time had stood still with the beauty of it all – except Dex wasn't there - at least not in body, but in spirit with the family unit.

The sky broke into streaks of red and orange, leading to a magnificent sunset, letting them know that the day to follow would be beautiful - just as their pleasant time spent together was becoming also. The sun finally set and the moon rose to a crystal clear night that showed off the stars. There was no reason for conversation, as they quietly watched and listened to the waves lapping up on the shoreline.

It was some time until they made their way back into the beach house, with Sarah going in first. She was tired and the first day home had worn her out. Nancy and Mike lingered for a while longer, leaning in close on their rattan chairs, holding hands and sipping of Tanqueray, tonic and lime – just like they had done so many years before.

"It's beautiful – you know that," Mike mentioned almost in a trance, while looking lovingly at his wife.

"Are you speaking of the ocean or me?" she teased, enjoying the evening just as much as her husband was.

"Both, my love. But if had to choose, of course it would be you," he confessed sweetly, leaning over to give her a kiss on the cheek.

"Mike, I am so glad we are here, even if for a short time. I wasn't sure this was a smart decision at first, with all of the anxieties that Sarah has had in the past from being back here. I thought the place would be sold and we would never be here at the beach house again."

"Maybe it was meant to be, even under the bad circumstances that we came back."

Nancy stopped to look seriously at Mike as he took a sip of his favorite drink. "I think you are right. It may sound silly, but I feel as if Dex brought us all back here one last time to be together."

Mike smiled at Nancy. Our son is *always with us, Nancy.* Maybe we can feel him more here, but I *always* sense his presence no matter where I am at."

"Yes… I know," Nancy breathed, with tears filling her eyes. "I miss him like it was yesterday, Mike. It still doesn't seem possible that he is gone."

Mike grabbed Nancy's hand again, giving it a firm yet understanding squeeze, as they gazed out to sea and listened to the ocean's waves lap against the shoreline.

A dolphin jumped high in the air, outlined by the bright and shining silver moon, splashing as it swooped down again and disappeared from their site. A shooting star flashed quickly across the sky, making them both stop and stare with awe. They were participants in nature's finest display – and they marveled at the beauty of if all – wishing for the moment not to end.

CHAPTER 30

Lance was up at 6 and took a shower, stretching his arms high over his head - bending side to side to clear the cobwebs from his mind. He looked at his stubble in the bathroom mirror, knowing he needed a shave. His reflection showed weary bloodshot eyes, from restless sleep that he was lacking in. He still was thinking of Sarah and the hospital from only one-day prior, and as hard he tried, he couldn't get her off his mind.

He planned to see her today. For some reason, he missed Sarah, and he didn't quite know why. He dressed in khaki shorts and wore a teal colored golf shirt that he allowed to hang loose. Tan duck shoes with no socks, completed the look. He would go into the office for a few hours, but he had already gotten his work caught back up the day before. His mother would want him to show property throughout the morning and afternoon, but later on, he would see Sarah whether she had other work for him or not.

The time went by quickly with several showings, with one signed contract on a condo.

"Lance, can you come to my office?" Alison asked of him over the speaker, breaking into her son's concentration as he entered a new listing into his computer.

"Sure, mom, be there in a sec," he answered, pressing the save button before closing his laptop.

Lance walked into his mother's office, as she smiled sweetly at the face she adored. "Would you like to join your father and I for dinner tonight? We were going to try a new restaurant in Delaware that just opened recently."

"Got other plans, mom."

"Really?" Alison answered in surprise, as Lance took a seat across from her desk.

Lance laughed, giving his mother the eye. "You do know mom, I have a life outside of Beach Dreams and hanging out with you and dad all of the time - don't you?"

"I'm sorry, Lance. I know that," she giggled, shaking her head and flipping a page of a contract in front of her. "It is just so hard to get your dad to try out a new restaurant, since he is so attached at the hip to Old Bay Café. I just thought if you rode along, he would feel more comfortable trying a different place to eat."

"You'll be fine. Just drag him to your car and drive. I'm seeing Sarah tonight. She and her folks are back at the beach house, and I wanted to see how she was doing."

Alison looked up from her papers in amazement to concentrate on her son. *"What's going on Lance?"*

"What do you mean?" he asked, switching his weight and throwing his leg over the arm of her over-stuffed chair.

"She survived the accident and is obviously well enough to leave the hospital. Why continue to see her and be around her family since Sarah doesn't seem to like you? Has something changed?"

Alison did not mince words with her family or in business. She was straightforward when she suspected there was more to know, and would pry and get to the bottom of things whether those around her wanted to hear it or not.

Lance pushed out of the chair and walked around to the other side of his mother's office and stood. "Well, the listing of The Dancing Seahorse is part of it."

Alison laughed. "I think we got that part covered, Lance. The contract is signed and your dad feels we should just give them some time before opening that topic up again, since Sarah is at the place recuperating. As you know, they just got there and the house should be painted first before showing it anyway."

Lance paced back and forth, realizing his mother was right. "I don't know…I guess it goes beyond that."

Alison laid her papers aside and continued to study her son. "Tell me this isn't guilt still over Dex."

"That will always be there," Lance replied, looking reflectively at his mother. "But no, it's more. I think I am beginning to like her."

Alison rose from her desk chair, walking across the room to meet Lance and look him square in the eyes. "Do you realize what you are saying? You surely do like a challenge now, don't you?"

Lance smiled as he looked back at her, being lost in thought. "I know… I know. But dad says you were a challenge to him too - when he first tried to date you."

"Well, maybe… but you know your father – he is very hard to say no too! Then, and now still!" she laughed.

Lance and Alison left the building arm in arm, as they continued to talk. "I wish you the best, son. Always be kind and gentle to her and maybe she will come around," Alison added from her open car window, as she pulled out of Beach Dreams, ready to pick up John and drive to Delaware for the evening.

Sarah knew Lance was coming to dinner, after her dad had filled her in to his invite. She was nervous, but anxious to see him again. She looked through her clothes that were few, from only packing several outfits a little over a week ago.

Her parents had returned the damaged suitcases to her room, and had removed the salvageable items, placing them back in her closet and dresser drawers - after her clothes were washed. Dex's items were placed back in his room also - the clothes and shoes to his closet, and the memorabilia to his nightstand.

Sarah showered, after having her mother wrap her arm in a trash bag so that her cast didn't get wet, and attempted to wash her hair with one hand. After some frustration, she called for her mother who helped her finish. She put on the sundress she had worn at the diner, after which, Nancy combed her hair back into the tight ponytail she preferred.

Sarah looked at her reflection, as her mother combed the final strands of hair back in place. "Do I look okay?"

Nancy grabbed Sarah's shoulders, while kissing her on the cheek. "You look very pretty!"

Sarah stared back at her mother's reflection, seeing it in the mirror in front of her. "You're just saying that to make me feel better."

Nancy paused, leaning in as she whispered. "You have just been through a car accident, but you are very beautiful, Sarah. Believe that!"

Sarah turned to look at her mother. "Thank you. And so are you, mom," she gushed, reaching forward to kiss and hug her mother in return.

Lance stopped at Seaside Florals, picking up the flowers he had ordered for Sarah.

"Well hello, Lance," came the cheerful greeting, from his elderly babysitter from so many years prior.

"Hello, Miss Marie. It's so good to see you!" he replied, reaching over to hug her warmly. "It has been too long," Lance smiled, remembering how loyal she had been to him and his family when he was a child and his father and mother worked.

"Are the flowers for anyone special?" Marie asked with a wink to her eye, as she reached into the glassed refrigerator behind her for the pink roses, handing them to Lance.

Lance grinned, knowing she was prying, always hoping he would marry one day and she would be invited to the wedding. *"Maybe – we will see,"* he stated matter-of-factly, adding to the mystery.

"Is she someone from the area?"

"At one time. Her name is Sarah Miller and her parents have a beach house near here."

Marie placed her elbow on the counter with her hand to her chin, trying to recollect the name. "Her dad is an architect, right?"

"That would be the one!" Lance replied with a beam in his eye, giving her a kiss on the cheek. "I must get going. I am invited for dinner and I don't want to be late!"

Marie smiled, pinching Lance's cheek. "Don't be a stranger! It has been too long since I have last seen you. And remember, when you get married, I want an invite!" she yelled, as he walked out the door.

Mike was finishing up the steaks, with the charcoal smoke swirling around his head, as Lance pulled into the driveway. He grabbed the flowers, before shutting the Jeep door, and walked over to where Mike was cooking.

"Something smells amazing," he said, dipping his head in the direction of the grill for a whiff of the beef.

"Hope you like New York Strips," Mike beamed proudly, placing each steak on a large silver platter along with some grilled portabella mushrooms.

"Love them!" Lance answered, as they walked together up the steps and into the beach house.

Nancy was busy in the kitchen boiling corn and slicing some fresh tomatoes. She had already cut up the cantaloupe that Mike had gotten at the produce stand along with a few other items.

"Well, it's nice to see you again, Lance," Nancy greeted, wiping her hands on a paper towel, as Mike placed the tray with the steaks and mushrooms on the granite countertop.

The dining table had been set with Coral colored dinner plates in the shape of fish, with matching salad plates nestled on the top of each one – being hand-painted, in an array of tropical sea life that appeared to be swimming.

A large lime-colored candle sat in the middle of the table, which Nancy lit - filling the room with hues of citrus. Off to one side, she placed a pitcher of homemade lemonade with lemon slices floating within; ready to be poured into the aqua-colored glasses that each held ice.

The patio doors were open again and the breeze gently moved throughout the room, creating an inviting mood. Sarah appeared, having just left her bedroom, with dinner being ready to be served. Lance turned with the flowers in hand, realizing Sarah had the sundress on again that he had seen her in that day at the diner.

"Wow, Sarah, you look great!" was all he could say, as she walked towards him with a pleased smile on her face.

"Well thank you, Lance," she replied awkwardly, knowing her parents were taking it all in too. Sarah felt he was just being polite since it was obvious she was still bruised from the car accident and not looking her best.

"These are for you," he offered, placing the flowers on the counter as she took a seat at the dining table.

Lance joined her, being asked by Nancy to sit on the other side of the table, directly across from Sarah, before he placed the dinner napkin on his lap.

Sarah glanced cautiously at him, noticing that he looked very handsome in his teal shirt with the lights lowered and the candle playfully casting a romantic glow around him. "You didn't have to bring me more flowers," she said pragmatically, looking up at him quickly and then back to the plate in front of her.

He smiled slightly, sending shivers down her spine. "I knew the others from the hospital would need replacing," he replied softly, finding her irresistible in the candlelight also.

They ate the steak and sides, after which, Nancy went to the refrigerator bringing forth a beautiful trifle filled with cake, fruit, pudding and whipped cream that she had layered in a large glass pedestal bowl.

"Who wants desert?" she offered, as she placed the show-stopping desert on the counter nearby for all to see.

The dinner dishes were cleared and the desert was served in matching clear crystal bowls that went along with the glass pedestal container that the trifle was in.

"Anyone for seconds?" Nancy offered, as they finished their first helping.

"I would like to say yes, Mrs. Miller, but I am stuffed!" Lance admitted with a contented smile.

"Please, call me Nancy," she reminded, knowing it was hard for him to break from formality.

Lance shifted as he turned towards Sarah. She was studying his face and waiting for his response. "Of course, Nancy. If that is your wish," he said with a broad grin.

Sarah sighed, looking away towards the open patio doors, knowing her parents really liked Lance whether she resisted him or not. She had barely spoken to him throughout dinner, only answering his questions and not asking any of her own.

As Mike helped Nancy with the dishes, she suggested that Sarah and Lance should sit in the living room and relax. Sarah sat on the sofa and Lance chose one of the recliners, keeping a safe and yet comfortable distance away from her. Each drank another glass of the lemonade, finding conversation difficult and strained.

"So are you beginning to feel somewhat better?" he asked with genuine concern, looking at her legs that still displayed the bruises from the accident.

"Yes," Sarah replied, after sipping some of the citrus beverage, placing it on a coaster on the teak table in front of her. "Everyday, I am feeling a little better."

"Well, that is great to hear," Lance answered, smiling sincerely at her in return.

Nancy and Mike joined Sarah and Lance, with Nancy sitting on the sofa by her daughter, and Mike claiming the other recliner.

"We could play Scrabble, if anyone is interested? Nancy offered sweetly, looking to the group for the answer.

"No, mother!" Sarah yelled out hysterically, struggling to get up off of the sofa in a fit of rage.

The others looked at her in confusion, as Lance rose to help her off the sofa and Sarah slapped his hand away. She walked quickly to her bedroom, slamming and locking the door behind her.

Lance was dumbfounded, turning his gaze towards Nancy and Mike who were too stunned and embarrassed to talk.

"Did I say or do something wrong?" Lance asked, looking to each one of them for the answer.

"No son, you did not," Mike confessed sadly. "We played a lot of Scrabble when Dex was alive. Maybe it brought back a painful memory for Sarah – that's all."

Lance shook his head in disbelief, being at a loss for words after enjoying such a nice evening with the Miller's. "I think it is time for me to leave," he added regrettably, as Mike and Nancy got up to follow him to the door.

"I am so sorry, Lance, that things ended up this way. Sarah has just been through a lot - so please don't take it personally," Nancy soothed, trying to make him feel better.

Lance stared sadly at them both, knowing he had sacrificially given so much of himself in the last few days to her, and yet she wasn't coming around - as hard as he had tried. "Give Sarah my best, and thanks again for a wonderful meal. It was delicious!"

Lance drove away feeling totally defeated. Whatever he had hoped was developing in a positive way between him and Sarah - was now not in the cards. He could see that now. She just had too much deep-rooted, unresolved pain that she would not allow herself to get past. He shook his head, breathing in the sea air from his rolled down Jeep windows, as he made his way to Old Bay Café. He needed a drink - after all that drama - and hopefully a pretty female to talk with too.

Sarah lay in her bed, crying softly to herself. *"It was only Scrabble..."* she whispered quietly. She thought of Lance and how handsome he looked in his teal shirt, as he sat across the table from her at dinner. He had even brought her flowers again. *My parents didn't even go to that trouble*, she realized.

The window was open and the shade tapped lightly against the screen, causing her to turn and look at the ceiling. *"I sent him away. What was I thinking?"* she moaned, suddenly realizing Lance was someone that she very much wanted in her life, and now he was gone.

CHAPTER 31

A week had passed and Sarah was rather quiet with her parents, which had caused Nancy and Mike great concern. They drove back to Channel Ridge for her recheck with Dr. Owens, who was very pleased with her progress. Her ribs were healing and almost all the bruising had left her face and limbs. Her broken arm held the only real evidence remaining of the car accident. The cast would have to stay on for another month, but she was free to do some simple tasks, even though she was advised not to drive for a while yet.

It was decided that the beach house was the ideal place for her to continue to stay. Sarah resisted initially, but Mike and Nancy convinced her that the beach, with it salt air and balmy breezes, was the idea place for anyone to recuperate. Once back in Baltimore, she would not slow down, and she knew what her parents were saying was true.

John had given Mike a courtesy call, just to see how things were going, and if they wanted to proceed forward with the beach house listing. But under the circumstances, Mike felt it was better to put things on hold for a while. John agreed, after hearing the details of the dinner debacle that Lance filled him in on.

Lance kept his distance from Sarah and her parents. He stayed busy with real estate, trying to avoid the barfly that he had met at Old Bay Café, who kept calling him now on a daily basis since their one night together after dinner at the Miller's. He knew it was a mistake to have slept with her, but he felt rejected by Sarah. *She was a warm and willing body, and he was way overdue for some female affection*! He rationalized. The barfly didn't know where he lived or worked, but giving her his cellphone number was a bad decision – being made after having one drink too many.

As hard as Lance tried, he couldn't get Sarah Miller out of his mind. How something as insignificant as her body in that low-cut sundress, kept haunting his thoughts - was beyond him. He felt the dress was just made for her – as he remembered her face, neck, shoulders and legs - as she moved in it. He could see the shapely outline of her hips and ass replaying in his mind for another time, and it really turned him on. He snapped too, realizing he was daydreaming about her again.

With work done for the day, Lance decided to stop at the Crab Shack for dinner. He walked into the over-crowded restaurant, choosing to sit at the bar instead of a table.

"Having a drink or dinner?" the overly tanned bartender asked, as he waited for Lance's response.

"Both," he answered, getting a cold beer and an order of crab dip with chips to start. He felt a slight tapping on his shoulder, thinking that the barfly had found him, and he didn't want to turn around - just in case.

"Lance?" Mike asked in pleasant surprise, as he walked by him on the way to the bathroom.

Lance turned, realizing it was Mike, and stood to shake his hand. "How are things?" he asked with a heart-felt smile.

"Pretty good! Nancy and Sarah are at a table in the next room if you would like to say hi to them."

"Ok... sure," he answered awkwardly, not seeing that one coming.

"Would you care to join us for dinner?" Mike suggested, surprising Lance even further with his request.

"I'm not sure Sarah would like that," he said with laugh and a realistic shake of his head.

"Nonsense! I will be right back, and I will lead the way."

Mike reappeared and motioned for Lance to follow, as the dawning reality hit him that he couldn't escape from what was happening. He quickly downed his beer and left the chips and dip - throwing a twenty on the counter. Mike led him through the maze of other diners, as they made their way to the other room - right up to the table where Nancy and Sarah were sitting.

"Look who I found on the way to the bathroom!" Mike announced proudly, grabbing Lance in a squeeze to his shoulder.

Sarah glanced up in surprise, after sipping from her sweet tea, looking as if she saw a ghost. *"Lance..."* she could only say, not able to follow with another word.

"How are you?" he replied with a broad, handsome smile and eyes that were only gazing at her, causing Sarah's heart to skip a beat.

"Have a seat, Lance," Mike motioned, pointing towards the empty seat beside of Sarah's.

She looked at her dad in disbelief, not knowing what say or do next as he walked in her direction.

Lance grabbed the chair and slid it towards her - a tad too close for Sarah's liking - hoping to talk over the loud noise of the room. "You are looking well," he said loudly, as she could smell the beer on his breath.

She looked at him, honestly thinking she would never see him again, but thrilled that he was there all the same. "I feel so much better. I will be getting my cast off in a few weeks," she said, raising her arm to remind him of it.

"That's great!" he grinned enthusiastically.

Nancy and Mike sat close by, just watching as their daughter and Lance talked. Mike told the waitress to bring them all the "house specialty" which was a seafood platter with a crab cake, haddock, fried oysters and scallops - even though Sarah and Lance insisted it was too much to eat.

"That was some meal, Mike" Lance yelled, as he tried to talk over the band that was nearby, already playing another tune.

"It sure was!" he yelled back, as the waitress boxed up all the leftovers for them, writing their names on each, and placing them back on the table.

Mike looked affectionately at Nancy and asked her to dance. They got up and held each other close, as they swayed to a slow ballad. Sarah sat with her hands in her lap, awkwardly not knowing what to do as she gazed out at her parents. Lance watched them too, along with the other dancers, as he sat quietly with Sarah - only desiring to do the same. He boldly moved his hand towards her lap, grabbing her hand in earnest, as she looked up into his searching brown eyes.

"Dance with me, Sarah," he beckoned, not wanting her to say no.

She nodded her head – yes - as Lance led her to the dance floor a short distance away from her parents, holding her close and breathing in the sweet fragrance of her perfume. "You smell so good, Sarah," he whispered, as he pressed closer into her.

Sarah's breath caught as she sensed his slight erection. It wasn't something she wanted to pull away from, and Lance knew it. He looked at her perceptively as their eyes met, and he realized she wanted him now too. Everything after that point would never be the same. There was no more denying it for either of them. They continued to dance through another slow song, even though Mike and Nancy had already sat back down.

"Look at them, Mike," Nancy commented in fascinated confusion, as she watched her daughter and Lance holding each other very close with their eyes shut, lost in the moment as they swayed to the beat of the music.

"Hmm…" Mike simply observed with an upward turn of his one eyebrow, as they continued dancing from one song to the next. He could see that things were finally beginning to change in a good way between Sarah and Lance – and he was very pleased to see that it was happening.

Maybe Sarah is healing - in more ways than one, he thought happily, as Lance spun her around one last time across the dance floor.

CHAPTER 32

Lance lay awake long into the night, after saying goodbye and goodnight to Sarah and her parents. He had undressed her and made love to her several times in his mind, wishing it were really true. Things were at a new crossroads. Lance realized it as they danced and he held Sarah in his arms. He hoped she wouldn't turn on him again, because he didn't know if he could deal with her rejection another time.

Lance looked at his alarm clock and realized it was only 5:30 a.m., and he couldn't sleep any longer. He got up and put on a pair of jogging shorts and a t-shirt, choosing to take a long run on the beach instead of fighting sleep. It has been awhile since he had done so, and even longer since he had gone for a swim. Something had changed in him after Dex's death, and the ocean had lost the magic it once held, being a powerful force that could hold beauty but could turn and kill too. He still was a lifeguard for a few more years after that, but being in the waters came with risks and tragedy that he felt different about the older he became.

The beach was empty, except for a few who had passed out in the sand – probably from drinking too much - and were obviously sleeping it off overnight. He jogged past them, hoping the police didn't stumble upon them before they woke up. The city made its money giving out citations to young beach goers; and he remembered those days clearly, when his dad had to bail him out of jail one night years earlier from drinking and driving. He was fortunate, that he didn't lose his job lifeguarding, but his dad spoke to the police and the situation was "swept under the rug" and kept quiet. That was one of those times, that Lance knew it paid to have John Snyder as his father.

Sarah had a restless night's sleep also, as she thought of Lance and his erection pressed up hard against her as they were dancing. She had not been in a relationship for a while and he turned her on greatly. She imagined him touching her breasts and letting his hand drift between her legs. She shuttered from the thought of it still, as the morning sun peaked through her window.

She opened her bedroom door, finding her parents at the kitchen table having coffee and oatmeal. "Good morning, beautiful," her dad teased playfully, knowing she looked a site in the morning with her ponytail half undone and over to one side.

"Seriously, dad," she chirped as she rolled her eyes, knowing he loved to say that to her every morning.

"How about some oatmeal?" Nancy offered, ready to dish her daughter out a hearty portion.

"Sure, mom. And coffee too?" she replied, waiting for her mother to serve her as she took a seat at the table.

"Sarah, your mother and I were discussing a few things this morning. We were thinking we should go back to Baltimore today."

"Oh?" she answered in surprise, taking a bite of oatmeal and banana. "My cast is still on," she mentioned casually, looking up at her parents, knowing she wanted to stay in Marlin beach until it was removed.

Mike smiled. "Yes, we know that. We plan to go back alone," he explained, getting up to pour some more coffee into his large mug.

"You can handle things here for a while, can't you?" he asked pointedly, while looking at her for the answer.

"Well of course I can handle things, dad, but I thought you were enjoying your time here. Didn't we agree it was our last few weeks together in the beach house before we sell it?"

Mike returned to his seat, thinking out his next words carefully. "I need to go back to Baltimore and check in on the office staff in person. I should see how things are going and gather up a few things to bring back to the beach. I think I will also get by golf clubs."

Nancy stopped eating and looked at her husband in surprise. "You haven't played golf in years."

"I know that Nancy, but maybe I want to start again - after being back around John Snyder."

"Ok...?" She answered in confusion, not following along with the excuses he was making.

"I could join you for awhile, but you would have to bring me back to have my cast removed."

"I think it is best you stay here," Mike insisted. "If you go home, you will start working; and besides, you need to continue to get your rest. Remember in time, we need to put the beach house back up for sale and the place still needs painting."

"That's right! I forgot that I never picked out the paint," Sarah remembered, rising to put her dirty bowl in the sink.

"Don't worry, dear. We will take care of that when we get back," Nancy promised, not wanting to put additional stress on her daughter.

With their bags already packed in the rental car, Mike walked a short distance away from the beach house and contacted Lance.

Lance answered his phone, already in the office on his computer, beginning his day early. "Mike, everything ok?"

"All is fine, but I need to ask you a favor."

"Sure, what can I do for you?" Lance replied, turning off his computer so he could focus.

"Nancy and I are leaving town for awhile. We need to go back to Baltimore and take care of some personal things. Do you think you can check in on Sarah while we are gone?"

"Of course, I will do that. When are you leaving?"

"Actually, within the hour."

"Are you sure it will be ok with her if I stop by?" he asked skeptically, not knowing how Sarah would react.

"Of course she will be fine if you stop by," Mike answered, only telling a half-truth. She knew her parent's were leaving, but she did not know that Lance would be checking in on her.

"It was great seeing you last night, Lance. Hope you enjoyed that seafood as much as we did!"

"Yes, I did, and thank you again for dinner," Lance answered pleasantly, feeling his groin slightly tighten with the memory of Sarah dancing in his arms the night before.

Mike and Nancy had already been gone several hours, as Sarah lay passed out on the couch with a half-drank glass of iced tea sitting on the teak coffee table in front of her. They had left her with plenty of food, and had washed all her dirty clothes before they departed.

Sarah found it strange that there was such an urgent need for them to leave that very day. She understood about the business and the need to check in with the staff, but to go so quickly was puzzling her. *Maybe dad was getting bored*, she considered, as she said her goodbyes and they hurried out the door without hardly a word.

Mike had built quite a successful architectural firm, and staying at the beach house for an extended vacation was no excuse, Sarah rationalized, even if she was recuperating. She was quite capable of taking care of herself, and had learned how to wrap her cast and deal with her bathing and hair, without her mother's help anymore.

She heard a soft tapping at the door and then the doorbell ringing, which made her sit straight up on the sofa. "Who can that be?" she wondered, as she got up and put on her flip-flops. She was dressed in her jeans and a t-shirt - minus a bra, which made her feel more comfortable with her tender ribs that were still healing. She looked in the mirror, and realized her hair could use a re-combing, but the knocking on the door was persistent in its intent.

Sarah made her way to the door, opening it to Lance smiling down at her.

"Hello, gorgeous," he said with a grin, noticing her disheveled ponytail.

Sarah reached for her hair, knowing she looked a site. "Come in, Lance. Have a seat and I will be out in a minute."

He chose the sofa this time as she went into the bathroom, taking the elastic from her hair and bending over to brush it. She gathered it again, but changed her mind, deciding to let it flow down her back.

As she walked from the bathroom, she realized Lance was on the sofa and she didn't know where to sit. "Can I get you an iced tea?" she offered.

"Sure," he smiled. "Do you need some help?"

"I'm fine. Obviously, my parents wouldn't have left if they thought otherwise," she stated matter-of-factly.

She carried the glass of tea over to Lance, looking down at him as he reached upward for the glass - touching her fingertips in the process. She turned to sit on the recliner but Lance stopped her. "Sarah, sit with me," he beckoned softly, with his brown eyes piercing her to her soul.

She turned back and walked around the coffee table, sitting by him as he requested. Her heart was beating frantically as he drank from his tea and gazed affectionately at her. She sat by him quietly, not sure what to do or say.

"I knew your parents were leaving," he mentioned casually, taking another long swig of the sweet drink.

"How so?" Sarah asked Lance with curiosity.

"I just assumed you knew that your dad called me. I told him I would check in on you."

Sarah rose, understanding now the reason for his visit. "I am fine, Lance. You *do not* have to check up on me like I am a child."

Lance placed his iced tea glass down and rose to stand directly in front of her. *"Oh yes I will, and its more than obvious you are not a child!"* he answered firmly, taking her swiftly in his arms and meeting her lips with his own - with a long, over-due, passionate kiss that Sarah couldn't resist and didn't want to.

The drive back to Baltimore was uneventful, except for the early rush hour traffic. "Mike, I just don't understand why we left Sarah in such a hurry," Nancy commented, as she looked at her husband and rested her hand lovingly on the back of his neck as he drove home.

He glanced back at her briefly, knowing he had to keep his eyes on the road. "Do you want your daughter to be happy?"

"Well, of course, Mike. Why would you ask me such a silly thing?"

"Her happiness is right in front of her - in Marlin Beach. And I realize that now."

Nancy was perplexed, still trying to figure out what Mike's motivation was for leaving so quickly. "Your are talking in riddles. What do you mean?"

He glanced at her once more, trying to make things very clear. "It's Lance… Nancy. Lance is the key to Sarah's happiness!"

CHAPTER 33

After a long lingering kiss, Lance broke his hold on her and looked down at Sarah, who was still breathless with what had just happened. Her eyes were still closed, as she stood motionless in a daze, unable to move.

"Why did you just do that?" she asked, reopening her eyes and staring blankly back at him.

"Why not?" he smiled brazenly, realizing she was without a bra and her nipples were hard and poking through her t-shirt, as she was still pressed up against him.

"Lance, we can not do this. What is the point?"

"The point is, we obviously like each other. Do you disagree?" he asked, as he reached out to rub her arm with his thumb, brushing over her t-shirt with its still hardened bud.

"You know my time here is temporary. Why would we start something that will ultimately end?" she asked with confusion in her eyes.

"Sarah, you are over thinking things, just like you *always* do. Let's just enjoy the time we have together."

Sarah broke free, walking over to the granite countertop in the kitchen. "Yes, I find you attractive, Lance. But with all that has happened to us in the past… *it makes this quite impossible.*"

Lance remained in the living room, just staring at her, knowing that she was probably never going to let down on her guard concerning Dex.

"Fine, let's just be friends."

"Seriously?"

"Seriously," he added, keeping his distance as he continued to stand by the couch. "Your parents are away and you are alone. So why not? Let's just be friends. I will help you with whatever needs done."

"And how will you do that?" she demanded, still doubting his sincerity.

"What about your car?" he asked. "You will need a new one before you go back to Baltimore."

Sarah stopped, considering Lance's words. "That is very kind of you, but remember, I still have this cast on," she replied, raising her arm to show him again.

"As you said, it will only be on a few more weeks. We could start looking now - if you would like. And besides, I can help you grocery shop, cook and do your laundry," he offered with a hopeful smile.

Sarah began to laugh. "I don't think my parents will be gone *that* long."

Lance joined her in the kitchen, placing his glass in the sink. "Is there anything I can do now for you before I leave?"

"Not a thing," she said half-heartedly, not wanting to be alone and knowing he was leaving.

Lance walked over and encircled her in his arms, whispering in her ear as he pressed against her breasts. "I'll see you tomorrow, *friend*. Sleep well," he added, as she felt the slight touch of his lips brush the top of her head before he released her.

He walked to the door - opened it - and was gone. She peaked out the window and watched him get in his Jeep and drive off - beeping his horn as a final goodbye.

Sarah sat on edge of the couch, touching her fingers to her lips where Lance had just kissed her with his scorching seductive kiss. She closed her eyes, remembering how it felt as his tongue entered her mouth, stirring a passion deep inside of her again. "This is silliness," she breathed, as she got back off of the couch, trying to shake the memory of it all from her being.

She walked to the refrigerator, pulling out her leftovers from the night before, reheating them in the microwave. As hard as she tried, she looked forward to the next day, even if she didn't need his help – at least that is what she told herself.

The drive along the beach was balmy and pleasant, as Lance watched the sun setting. He parked his Jeep on a side street and made his way down a sandy path, where sea grass and a half-broken fence lined either side of the walkway. No one was on there to intrude on his thoughts. Lance felt the need to sit and watch the waves, as the last lingering moments of sunshine dipped below the horizon.

"God, what am I going to do now?" he said aloud, knowing his growing feelings for Sarah would lead to nowhere and were obviously crazy to even consider. He closed his eyes and breathed in the salty air of Marlin Beach, hearing the noises of sea and surf that he loved so well.

A family passed by, breaking into his thoughts, causing him to get back up, as he wiped his sandy hands off on his shorts. He walked barefoot for some time, with his feet in the water, before replacing his flip-flops and walking back up the path to his Jeep. Lance drove off with the need for food, deciding to stop for a bite at his regular place.

"Hey, brother, haven't seen you awhile," Mark the bartender welcomed warmly, as Lance walked into Old Bay Café for a beer and burger.

"Yeah, I know. Didn't want to run into someone," he confessed sheepishly, as he took a seat at the counter and Mark poured him a cold one.

"If you are talking about Michelle, she always asks about you several times a week," he said with a snicker and a well-intentioned smile on his face.

Lance looked up after a few bits of burger. "That's what I was afraid of."

"She is really harmless, but you obviously have captured her attention," Mark added with a wink as he grabbed the remote, turning the channel on the TV to something more interesting than the news.

The door opened to Old Bay, as if she read his mind, with Michelle standing proudly with her hands on her hips. She smiled at Lance with satisfaction, knowing that she had finally accomplished her goal of finding her prey, as she walked in his direction.

Lance stopped with his beer mug in mid-air, glancing towards her as she beamed happily. "Well hello," he said, not wanting to be rude.

Michelle pulled a barstool close to his side, placing her elbow on the counter as she leaned in close. "I thought you were going to call me?" she purred.

"Sorry, been busy. Lots has been going on," Lance replied blankly, as he continued to sip his beer, acting half interested.

"I can understand that, honey, but I thought we had fun when we were together."

Lance looked at Michelle, with her over-applied face of makeup that was grinning back at him. Her hair was almost white-blonde from being over-dyed, and her scantily clad attire of jean shorts that were up to her ass, and a low-cut orange tank top that showed a little too much cleavage, along with her over-sized, heart-shaped necklace - did nothing for him.

Lance sighed, knowing he had to set things straight with her, as he swiveled sideways on his seat - wanting to make full eye contact with the barfly to gain her undivided attention.

"Michelle, I am very sorry, but this isn't going to work with us. It was a one-night thing. That was all it was."

"Is there someone else?" she asked, with hurt registering on her face.

"You could say that," Lance offered, knowing he was avoiding the truth, but one he would go with just to get her off his back. He turned back to face the counter, taking another swig of beer.

"I just... thought... that maybe we could see where things could go with us. That's all. You seemed like you were into me that night," Michelle added optimistically, while reaching out to touch Lance's arm, not wanting to give up so easily.

"You're great," he lied, pulling away and standing up to release her hold. "There is just someone else - that's all," he replied succinctly, while closing out his tab and looking at Mark with hopes he would not give away his cover.

"Take care," he wished her with a nod, leaving Bay Café as Michelle stared after him with tears in her eyes.

CHAPTER 34

Another busy day was unfolding as Lance pulled into the back parking lot of Beach Dreams. His parents were already there, as he grabbed his briefcase from his Jeep, and made his way into the reception area that was filled with several interested patrons.

"Good morning, Patti," he said cheerfully, as she looked up from her computer, giving him a nod.

"Your parents are with a client," she mentioned distantly, as he walked past her towards his office. He could hear his mother through the wall, talking to a buyer who was agreeing to a price for a highly sought after oceanfront penthouse.

Lance turned on his computer, catching up on his unanswered emails as he drank from his coffee mug.

"Haven't seen you much lately," John remarked, walking into his son's office and glancing around the room.

Lance looked up from his computer with a laugh, taking in his dad who was ready to play golf in a few hours. "I think I can say the same for you, most days," he snickered.

John took a seat, sharing a few moments with him over the coffee they shared. "Anything new?"

Lance sighed, not knowing where to begin. "The Miller's went home."

"Yes, I know. Mike called me, but he said Sarah is still in town."

"She is..." he began, getting up to lean on his windowsill. "I thought I would help her while they are away."

John looked over his reading glasses at his son. "Lance, I must hand it to you... you are persistent," he said with a look of confoundment.

"I guess you could call it that, or maybe dumb as shit - for even trying!"

John got up to join his son, as they looked out of the window together at the few cars passing by. "Is there something more going on here that I need to know about?"

Lance stopped and looked at his father. "Maybe for me, but definitely not for her," he admitted, with a far-off look of frustration.

"Be careful, son. Sooner or later, Sarah will be going back to Baltimore. I know she is very successful and involved in her career," he added with a well-intentioned, squeeze of Lance's shoulder.

"Yeah, I know. She has reminded me of that fact too," he said with a shake of his head. "Mike and Nancy are gone for awhile, and I did promise them I would look out for Sarah. She is recovering, but she doesn't have a car and her arm is still in the cast."

John walked to the door with his coffee cup still in hand. "All good reasons to be there for her... just be careful. That's all I'm saying," he added, closing the door behind him.

Lance returned to his chair and leaned back with his hands woven behind his head - carefully considering his father's words of wisdom. "Be careful...huh? Hope I can," he reasoned, as he returned to his computer and the phone calls he needed to make.

Sarah awoke, having slept in late, with the sounds of the beach repeating the same theme of every morning since she had been there. She could hear the seagulls and the children at play. Someone had a boom box turned up loudly, blaring out a song with a rousing backbeat.

She stretched and yawned and made her way to the kitchen. She opened the refrigerator, choosing some yogurt, granola and fruit for breakfast.

She opened the glass patio doors and walked out on the deck, sitting at the table with her food in hand. She took a few bites of watermelon, feeling the warmth of the sun pouring down on her face as she chewed the sweet luscious fruit. *It feels so good to be here*, she realized. The beach was calling to her, but she hesitated still - not wanting to get past her fears and what could possibly happen if she ventured there.

Sarah heard her phone ringing, as she ran to get it off of her nightstand.

"Hello?"

"Sarah? Good morning!"

"Lance?" she replied anxiously.

"None other," he said with a grin, as he made his way back out to his Jeep. "I am on my way to show a property, but I was wondering if I could take you out to dinner tonight?"

Sarah shifted, sitting on her bed as she considered his invite. "I guess so…" she answered, feeling uncertain if it was the right thing to do.

Lance drove down Beach Highway, ready to pull off into an elite and expensive condo building directly in front of him. "Come on Sarah. You got to eat," he announced - sounding like his dad, trying to lighten her mood. "I will pick you up at six."

"You know, I don't have a lot of clothes with me," she admitted, getting up to look at herself in the mirror and noticing her ponytail that was in need of re-brushing.

"Ok… but I am sure you will look good in anything," he replied, causing her to blush.

"I will be ready, and Lance, *we are just going to dinner as friends.* Please, remember that," Sarah added, as she made her way back out to the deck and her breakfast.

"Thanks for reminding me of that, Sarah," he laughed, as he parked his Jeep, ready to meet a client for another scheduled showing.

Lance had gone back to his place to shower and change after a day of appointments, with two contracts signed - contingent on their financing. He was happy and knew his mother would be also, with the deals that were agreed upon.

He was excited for the evening to take place, and hoped that Sarah would feel the same way. The "friend thing" was not easy to accept, but he would try his best to honor her wishes.

As promised, Lance was at The Dancing Seahorse at 6 sharp. The outside lights on the deck were already turned on, as well as every other light inside of the beach house. He gave himself a quick lookover in his rearview mirror, making sure his hair was in place and his shave was to his liking.

The doorbell rang, as Sarah gave herself two sprays of her favorite perfume to the small of her neck. She had her blonde hair down again and flowing freely, and chose a white sundress and sandals that she had forgotten about, that were purchased on a shopping outing with her mother before Nancy went back to Baltimore.

"Coming!" she yelled, as she made her way quickly to the front door.

Lance stood in the doorway smiling, taking Sarah in from head to toe. "You look absolutely lovely," he complimented, as he made his way into the house.

"Well, thank you. So do you," she replied, realizing how handsome he looked in his sand-colored linen slacks and Hawaiian print shirt that was un-tucked.

Sarah grabbed a teal blue sweater, placing it in Lance's car - just in case she got cold. "So where are we going?" she asked, looking at him as he drove.

"It's a surprise!" he grinned, glancing at her periodically, just to remember how pretty she looked. "I thought I would take you to a marina west of town tonight. So I guess it is good you brought a sweater - just in case there is a breeze."

Sarah smiled back, knowing he was hard to resist with all his charm. "Thank you, Lance."

"For what?"

"For keeping me company while my parents are away."

Lance's gaze drifted towards the soft swell of her breasts that looked amazing in the white dress. "The pleasure is all mine, Sarah," he answered, hoping those words would hold more truth than she bargained for.

CHAPTER 35

The view was superb at the Dockside Marina where the waiter had seated Lance and Sarah. They dined on raw oysters and lemon, and swordfish with asparagus and rice pilaf. Sarah had not felt this happy and carefree in a long time.

"Would you like to see the desert menu?" Lance asked, as he sipped on his chilled Chardonnay.

"I am stuffed," Sarah answered with a shake of her head. "But dinner was delightful."

Lance smiled at her, happy to see that she was finally relaxed and letting her guard down. He was content sitting back and enjoying the scenery in front of him, as he noticed that Sarah appeared to be also.

The boats and yachts were in constant motion at the Marina, as the people on board watched what was going on at the restaurant or decided to steer away and go to another destination.

Sarah shivered from the sudden coolness in the air. "We can leave if you are getting cold," Lance offered, seeing her grab for her sweater.

"Let's stay for awhile. This is so nice and I hate for it to end," she said with a pleasant smile as she threw the wrap over her shoulders.

"Then it doesn't have to end, Sarah," Lance sensuously replied, as he kissed her hand and snuggled closer to her, continuing to watch the boaters and their activities.

Sarah glanced down, watching Lance hold her hand and then back up into his searching brown eyes, not pulling away as he expected. She sighed, realizing he was breaking her will and she was beginning to accept and like it.

They drove back to the beach house, mostly in silence, as they listened to the music playing in the Jeep - feeling the soft breeze that was blowing in from the windows.

Lance pulled into the driveway, coming to a stop, waiting for Sarah to speak.

"Would you like to come in?" Sarah suggested, staring at Lance and hoping he would say yes.

"Sure," he grinned pleasantly, walking over to her car door and opening it for her, assisting her to get down. They walked side by side, as Sarah wrestled to find the house keys deep inside of her purse, fumbling to open the lock.

"Do you need some help with that?" Lance offered.

"I'm fine," Sarah insisted, as she pulled the door open, giving way to the living room in front of them. "I think I have some more wine if you would like another glass?" she mentioned, as she walked towards the kitchen, looking in the refrigerator for the Chardonnay.

Lance had already opened the patio doors, bringing in the gentle breeze. "Let me help," Lance offered, as he opened a cabinet in the kitchen filling two wine glasses, handing one to Sarah and taking the other one for himself. She had replaced her sandals with her flip-flops, and walked towards the deck with Lance following close behind.

"Look at the night sky," Sarah whispered, as they sat in the rattan chairs and looked out over the glistening sea with the bright moon shining in front of them.

"Breathtaking..." Lance answered, with longing in his eyes as he looked at her.

Sarah shivered, as Lance reached out to rub her arm, drawing her close - wanting only to warm her. She rested her head on his shoulder, being lost in the moment. He turned to look at her as she looked up into his searching eyes, not waiting for her response. His lips bent to kiss her passionately, as he took the wine glass from her hand placing it on the patio table beside of them.

"Sarah, let's go inside," he asked brazenly, rising to pull her to her feet.

They walked together, hand in hand, as Lance closed the patio doors and then the blinds afterwards that were never drawn shut. Sarah waited on the couch, looking in his direction, as he turned to see her staring. He met her where she sat, as his lips swooped down to kiss her passionately again.

The kisses became more intense and heated as Lance wrapped his arms around Sarah, lying beside her on the couch as he gazed into her eyes. "You know, I just can't help but be attracted to you. I know you want this to be friendship, Sarah, but I am so turned on by you right now. If you don't feel the same way - now is the time to tell me so."

Sarah paused to look at Lance. "I want you too..." she answered, as she reached out to pull Lance's face closer to her own.

It was his undoing, as he finally heard the words that he longed for her to say. Their legs locked together, as Lance's hand slipped inside her dress, pulling out one of her breasts to his view. He kneaded it until a hardened peak formed, and then lowered his mouth to suckle it, causing Sarah to moan out in delight.

He looked up, wanting to see that she was willing, and then continued to rub not only her breasts but between her legs boldly. He stood and removed his shirt and shorts, looking at her, as she lay hot with passion, waiting for him to return.

He grabbed her hand, challenging her to stand as he removed her dress and panties, standing totally nude in front of him as he looked at her with total lust in his eyes. He removed his briefs last, as Sarah gazed at him – bulging and hard with desire in front of her.

He melted, bending at his knees to the floor while grabbing her around the waist tasting of her wet pleasure. She shuttered as she exploded with an orgasm, bending over repeatedly with deep waves of contractions that were unending. Lance watched in delight, as he rose back up to her level, taking her mouth again, and tasting it with his own.

He carried Sarah to her bedroom, placing her lovingly on the bed. She lay on her side with her hair tumbled in a wild array, breathless from what had just happened. Lance looked at her through the half opened blinds, with the moon slicing through - cascading over her with a flickering sensual glow. He crawled on top of her, turning her over to face him, as he bent to give her another kiss that left her begging for more.

He entered her slowly, not wanting to cause her any additional pain from the accident, as she arched her back and accepted his manhood, wrapping her arms around his neck and pulling him in closer. "Sarah..." he yelled out loudly, as he moved in her quickly, taking her with one final plunge of his own soul-searing, matching climax.

They rested, entwined together - half in and half out of sleep - just content to be together. Lance kissed her hair, wiping it away from Sarah's face. "Sweetie, I hope I didn't hurt you," he said tenderly, as he sat up on one elbow, staring down and realizing how beautiful she really was.

She turned to look back at him, still drowsy from their lovemaking.

"I am fine, Lance. Believe me, if I was in pain, I would have told you otherwise."

Lance grinned lazily, planting a kiss on her forehead. "Well I want you to know that you were amazing," he breathed, as he wrapped his arms lovingly around her, ready to fall asleep.

"And so were you," she sighed, feeling totally secure in his embrace, as she drifted off in total contentment.

A short while later, Sarah awoke from her brief slumber, suddenly aware of her lack of clothes and feeling very shy and vulnerable - even though she had just spent such an intimate encounter with Lance.

She darted from the room as he sat staring at her dumbfounded, hurrying to put her dress back on and throwing Lance's clothes in his face as she returned to her bedroom.

"I need a cup of hot tea. How about you?" she asked timidly, as she smiled contently at the nude, handsome male spread out in front of her - who had just rocked her world.

CHAPTER 35

Sarah handed Lance a cup of mango green tea, as she joined him on the sofa with her own cup. The newness of what had just happened between them was somewhat awkward but welcome for them both.

They sat together sipping from the tasty hot beverage, lost in what just went on a few short minutes earlier. Sarah placed her cup on the coffee table in front of them, turning to look at Lance.

"I need to talk to you about something."

"Ok…"

Lance put his cup down also, looking at Sarah, waiting for her to begin.

"It's about Dex. You see, he was my twin brother and we where very close," she began. "My heart broke in a million pieces the day he got caught up in that riptide. I have never forgiven myself for asking him to come to the beach that week with me. It was our last time together for a few days - before we went off to separate colleges. I just wanted to have some fun before our parents showed up for the weekend, like they normally did," she explained with downcast eyes, looking as if she were going to cry.

Lance grabbed her chin, bringing it back up to meet his own. "I'm sorry, Sarah. I know you blame me for this, but I did try to rescue Dex."

Sarah sighed, knowing that what Lance was saying she felt in her heart to be true, but denying it all the same. "It's just that I was out there also, and I was safely rescued by another lifeguard. I am alive and still here to talk about it - but Dex is dead. How is that fair?" she questioned, with pain-filled eyes.

Lance paused, realizing she deserved an answer. "Sarah, I have a story of my own to share with you. You see this tattoo?" he said, while turning his right arm over and pointing to the tattoo above his wrist.

"Yes," she said, curious as to the mystery behind the tattoo that she remembered from so many years before.

"It is there in memory of my friend. He was a lifeguard too - just like I was. We went to high school together and we were inseparable in sports. After high school, we both decided to become lifeguards here in Marlin Beach. His name was Jeffrey Wells, and he died trying to rescue someone in the ocean. In this case, the guy he rescued survived, but he was the one that died. He got too much water in his lungs and he never pulled through it," Lance said forlornly, looking across the room, remembering and reliving the tormenting memory of his friend's passing. "I wish I would have been close by to help him. But, I wasn't working, and it was my day off."

Sarah reached out to touch Lance's arm, laying her hand on top of the tattoo. "I am so sorry. I didn't know..." she replied sincerely, as he turned back towards her with pain still etched on his face. "What does the tattoo mean?" she asked, trying to figure out the hidden message.

"It is a life preserver – the symbol of a lifeguard - and these are my friend's initials – JW - in the middle," he pointed out. "So, Sarah, I lost someone also that I was very close too. He wasn't my brother, but we were like brothers."

Sarah reached out to hug Lance, wrapping her arms around his waist. "I guess I was wrong, Lance. You understand what I have been through, more than I realized."

Lance held Sarah as she began to cry softly against his shirt, allowing her the release she so badly needed and wanted. He kissed the top of her head, trying to calm and soothe her, as they quietly sat together remembering their own personal loss.

Sarah looked up at him some time later, with her eyes red and swollen, feeling embarrassed by her vulnerability. "Lance, I must look a sight," she said, rising and carrying the teacups to the sink.

"You look beautiful, Sarah," he answered, sincerely meaning it. He kissed her goodbye for the night with another deep kiss of longing, hoping for a repeat of the intimacy that they had just shared some time in the near future.

Lance drove home, feeling well sated from the intimate encounter he had just experienced with Sarah. It was everything he had dreamt of, and then more. He was glad they had spoken about Dex and Jeff. It was a hurdle he hoped they had finally gotten past, and now they could go forward and be happy.

He crawled into bed and lay awake, with his hands woven behind his head, just staring at the paddle fan that was rotating its blades in a continuous circle. He closed his eyes and could see Sarah again at the marina with her white dress and sandals, smiling at him with her pale blue eyes and silky blonde hair that cascaded in soft waves down her back. She was beautiful, and his loins tightened again at the very thought of her. He desired her, but more than that, he knew he was beginning to fall in love with her. This wasn't something he had wanted, but now it was here – unplanned, but so amazing. He was in love with Sarah Miller.

Sarah washed her face and went to her bedroom, pulling up the blind and opening the window so that she could stare at the beach in front of her. It was peaceful, with only the waves rolling in and the glowing moon shining back at her. It had been so long since she had been with a man sexually. Her insides were still warm with desire as she remembered Lance kissing her deeply and holding her intimately. *What if I am falling in love with him and he doesn't love me back?* She pondered, wrestling with her over-worked emotions.

It was some time until she crawled into bed, knowing Lance was in her life now for however long it would last. He had been her enemy, rescuer, friend and now lover. It was quite the amazing transition over time, she knew - and in her heart, he was rescuing her from the past and all the pain it held - whether he realized that or not.

She fell asleep, not with the troubling dreams of Dex that she normally had, but with dreams of Lance who was kissing and holding her again - and never letting her go.

CHAPTER 36

Sarah awoke to the sound of the doorbell ringing. She smiled as she sat up. "It must be Lance," she assumed happily, running to open the front door widely with her skimpy nightclothes still on.

"Hi Sarah," John Snyder greeted, while looking down at her t-shirt, shorts and hair - that all needed adjusting.

"Well hello, Mr. Snyder, I didn't expect you," she replied, crossing her arms in front of her braless chest in embarrassment. "Please come in and make yourself at home. I will be out in a minute," she yelled over her shoulder, disappearing into her bedroom to change her clothes.

It was some time until Sarah reappeared, dressed in blue jeans and a fresh t-shirt and her sneakers. She brushed her hair back into her ponytail and met John in the living room where he was pacing and looking out the patio doors that he had opened.

"Hope you don't mind that I opened them," he smiled.

"Not at all," she replied, making her way to the kitchen to grab a water for both of them.

"What brings you here today?" she asked, taking a seat on the sofa.

John joined her, sitting on one of the recliners, as she handed him the water. "I wanted to check in on you and make sure you are doing okay," he said pleasantly. "But I also wanted to see when you wanted to proceed forward with the beach house listing - since it's been awhile."

Sarah paused, not sure what to say or do after the passionate night she had just shared with Lance. "I guess nothing is stopping us from moving ahead," she reluctantly answered. "But I still need to pick out the paint, which I never got around to because of my car accident."

John shifted in the recliner, leaning forward on one arm. "I am not trying to rush you, Sarah. I just know that was your desire - along with your parents - several weeks ago. I thought I would just check in and see where you are with things, since we are not trying to hold you up on our end. That's all."

She thought for a moment of Lance and what John was saying to her now. *Did he know what had happened between the two of them last night?* She wondered. *Would he be so anxious to have her sell The Dancing Seahorse if it meant Lance was alone again and without her?* And for that matter, *would Lance approve of his father being there, encouraging her to get the ball rolling again with things?* Her mind was working overtime and she couldn't stop it.

"Mr. Snyder....?"

"Please, call me John," he insisted, as she continued.

"John... I will call my parents and see what they would like for me to do, and then I will get back to you in a day or two. Does that work?" she offered, rising to walk him to the door.

"No rush, Sarah. Just get back to me after you talk to your folks. And since we breezed past that first part – how are you doing?" he asked as an afterthought, not being known for being sensitive to such details.

"I am fine," she smiled, growing to accept his rough and callous ways, but realizing he was so different from his son who was thoughtful and kind.

"Good, good," he offered, as he waved and left. "I will wait to hear back from you...you know how to reach me."

Sarah watched as John Snyder pulled out of her driveway, barely missing the curb, as he drove away too fast in his Mercedes - speeding down the road to his next destination.

Mike Miller was busy reviewing numerous blueprints that he had spread out over the entire length of his desk, for a major project that needed to be wrapped up before the day was ended. He stretched his arms high above his head, before rolling his shoulders backwards in several rotations, just to get the kinks out from bending over for so long. His phone rang and he realized it was Sarah calling.

"Well, hello, sweetie. How is my best girl doing today?" he asked her warmly, taking a seat at his desk again.

"I am fine, dad, but I needed to call you about the beach house."

"What is going on?" Mike inquired, waiting for Sarah's response as he focused on one of the blueprints in front of him again.

"John Snyder stopped by today, and he wants to know when we would like to resume things with the listing."

Mike shifted in his chair, turning to look out over the bay of windows in front of him. "Are you up for that yet, Sarah? There is no need to rush things."

Sarah paused, not knowing what to say to her father. "I do not have a car as you know...to go pick out the paint. And of course there is the issue of having my cast still on and needing to get it removed," she added, hoping those several setbacks would buy a little more time before she had to make the decision to leave.

"I think it is too soon. Let's give things another week before deciding. By the way, has Lance been in touch? I did ask him to check in on you," Mike inquired, turning over another blue print.

Sarah's throat caught in her chest. "Aah... yes, he has been by," she stammered, rising to walk to the kitchen for something to eat.

"Well, maybe he can take you to pick out the paint colors?"

Sarah sat silently shaking her head. She wondered what her parents would think if they knew what had happened between her and Lance since they had gone back to Baltimore. "Sure, dad. I will ask him if he can help me with that."

"Well that's good, honey. I'm glad Lance is there to help you. It doesn't hurt to have another friend, you know."

Sarah laughed, knowing her father and mother were always concerned about her social life. "I think I got that area covered, dad, but thanks for the reminder."

"Sorry, for wanting the best for you."

"No worries, dad. And by the way - is everything okay at work?"

"Couldn't be better," Mike lied, not wanting to concern her from the overwhelming amount of work he was now covering in her absence. After it was all said and done - he was counting the days until she was back and ready to take over again.

Sarah called John Snyder, giving him the news that things were on hold for another week with the beach house. He was already busy with his afternoon golf game that she had interrupted, and he did not mind in the least that the listing was being delayed. Snyder's Beach Dreams Real Estate had enough listings and revenue coming in, and one less property made no difference to him in the least. As long as he could play golf and enjoy the lifestyle he was accustomed too, not much else mattered.

Sarah's phone began to ring as soon as she hung up with John.

"Hey there, what are you up to?" Lance asked, as he was already driving towards her place, setting aside any business for the rest of the day just to be with her.

She smiled, happy that he called. "I was just thinking about you," she answered, as she finished up her lunch.

"Hmm... I been thinking about you too," he smiled, remembering again the passionate events of the night before. "Thought I would stop by and take you to go look at some cars. What do you say - can you be ready in 15 minutes?"

Sarah was surprised by his spontaneity, but happily so. "I sure can! Let me grab by purse and I'll be waiting outside for you."

They drove to several car dealerships that Lance had done business with – either through buying a vehicle of his own or through real estate. Sarah walked around a few models that she especially liked, as Lance gave his suggestions and pointed out the nice features.

"All I want is for it to be pretty and get me through the snow," she admitted, looking at him for his feedback.

He laughed and shook his head. "There is more to it than that, Sarah. Engine size, horsepower, front wheel drive, speaker system, leather seats, sunroof – just to name a few," he added, as he walked around several cars also, wiping his hand over the paint finish of the ones he liked.

She giggled, taking in Lance's admiration for the cars he obviously was fond of. "I never thought about those things in the past. To be honest, my dad just helped me pick out what he thought was best for me."

Lance stopped what he was doing and walked back over to Sarah, encircling her in his arms and bending to give her a kiss. It still felt foreign to her, especially out in public. "I am more than happy to help you with this, Sarah. It's been fun picking a car out together."

Sarah looked into Lance's handsome brown eyes as he continued to hold her, wanting to trust and believe him – in all ways, and not just with car shopping.

"A final signature is needed here," the car salesman pointed out, as the three sat together in his office going over everything on the agreement. He handed Sarah the keys to her new sky blue Mazda that matched her eyes. "Your tags should be arriving soon and we already installed the temporary ones."

"Thank you," she beamed happily, taking the package of information that he presented to her that detailed and explained everything about her new vehicle.

As they walked outside, Lance opened the driver's door and offered her the seat. "Your chariot awaits, my dear," he teased with his arms outstretched, as she climbed into her new SUV and he shut the door securely. Lance gazed at her as she looked back at him through her open window, feeling grateful for all he had done.

"Thank you, Lance, for helping me. You made this very easy for me today."

"I'm glad you at least picked out an SUV," he teased, realizing her car choice was not what he would have picked for himself.

Sarah laughed and shook her head. "We like what we like. At least I gave into you, and I'm not driving a sedan any longer."

"You got that right!" Lance laughed, as she started up the car.

Sarah sat for a while in idle - adjusting her seat, mirrors and finally putting her hands on the wheel - looking nervously at Lance as he remained by the car watching her. "I hope I can do this," she said uneasily, having her confidence shaken from the car accident that was still fresh on her mind.

Lance reached in to give her a quick kiss. "Don't worry, I will be right in front of you leading the way. You will be fine," he encouraged.

Sarah took a deep breath and put the car in drive, waiting for Lance to pull out first. He drove slowly, making sure she stayed right behind him, leading her safely back to the beach house.

CHAPTER 37

A week and a half had passed, and Sarah and Lance had seen each other typically everyday, for either lunch or dinner after the end of Lance's workday. True to his word, he did help her with the grocery shopping and laundry, barely allowing her to lift a finger when he was around the beach house.

Sarah had avoided intimacy, and Lance did not press her on the subject, thinking that maybe she was still experiencing pain – even if she didn't want to admit to it. *Maybe thoughts of Dex, or the emotional after affects of the car accident*, he pondered, *could still be crossing her mind*. He was content just to be with her, on whatever level she chose.

What he didn't want to consider, was her pulling away because she was leaving soon. It was inevitable - but for now, he would enjoy whatever time he had remaining with Sarah before she returned to the Baltimore and the beach house was sold.

Sarah drove her new SUV to Logan's Hardware, crossing the very area where her car accident had occurred several weeks earlier. Lance was busy at work and she knew she could pick out the paint without his help. It felt strange to have her cast finally off, and she couldn't stop touching her bare arm that was now free to move. Dr. Owens had said she was fully recovered and able to return to work.

John Snyder had been contacted several days prior, and Sarah had finally agreed to begin the painting of the beach house. She had asked for only a few more days before the painting began and the listing was made live. It was time to get back to her original plan and sell The Dancing Seahorse and get on with her life.

What was difficult, was saying goodbye to Lance. He was a good friend that she dearly cared for, but he had become so much more. Sarah did not want to consider what he was to her – her career took priority, and that was where her direction was to go for now.

She opened the door of Logan's Hardware and walked to the paint counter. "I need to pick out a few paint colors," she greeted with a smile, looking at the older gentleman who was splattered with paint and pounding the lid on a paint can that he had just mixed up.

"Lots to choose from," he waved towards the display stand, showing her the vast selection of paint-sample cards neatly placed in rows of styles and color palettes.

Sarah chose a few, and walked to the front of the store holding them up in a sunny window, trying to get a better feel for what they would actually look like once painted on the walls of the beach house. After selecting a few, she took them back to the paint department and laid them on the counter. "I will take these," she announced. "This one is for the walls and this one is for the trim," she explained, smiling up for his approval.

"Whatever you would like," he answered dryly, as he continued to study her with interest, with his arms crossed.

"Andrew Scott is my painter, and he told me that he already contacted the store with the amount of paint that is needed. Things have been delayed awhile because I was in a car accident," Sarah admitted, as she handed the clerk her credit card, waiting for his response as he rang up the purchase.

"I heard about that. You doin ok?" he asked out of polite courtesy, as he swiped her card and handed it back to her.

"I guess so," she replied, feeling that being *ok* was much more than just the physical that he was implying.

The paint was purchased and Sarah made her way back to Marlin Beach, crossing the bridge that was always picturesque with its many boats and other watercraft that were always nearby – darting to and fro.

"Hello?"

"Sarah? Whatcha doin?" Lance asked, as he was driving to his next property showing.

"I just picked out the paint for the beach house," she answered reluctantly.

"Oh...? Didn't think you were ready to do that quite yet," he replied while looking in his rearview mirror, as he shifted lanes to make a U-turn quickly across to the other busy side of the road, going in the opposite direction.

"I just picked it out, Lance. The work won't start for a few days yet," she added sadly.

Lance just sighed, sensing her mood and sharing in it. "Hey, I have an idea. Why don't we take a walk on the beach today? Your cast is finally off, so the sand shouldn't be a problem now."

Sarah pulled into the driveway, looking towards the ocean in front of her. "You *know* how I feel about that, Lance," she said forlornly.

"Yes, I do, but I will be with you. It is such a beautiful day!"

She sighed, shaking her head and feeling her stomach tense up in a knot. "I guess… when will you be here?"

"One thirty?"

"I will be ready. See you soon," she added hesitantly, as she climbed the steps and closed the door behind her.

The cooler was packed with ice, water bottles, fruit and cheese; the things Sarah typically remembered taking to the beach in the past. She grabbed a beach bag that she found laying on the top shelf of her mother's bedroom closet – placing in it two beach towels, suntan lotion and a large beach blanket - just in case they were needed.

Lance knocked on the door and rang the bell afterwards, which was always the way he greeted her.

"Coming," Sarah yelled, making her way from her bedroom in her green and yellow-stripped bikini that was barely there, with only the ties holding it securely in place on the sides.

"Well, well…" Lance greeted with approving, pleasure-filled eyes, looking her over from head to toe. "Not sure I want other guys on the beach looking at you this way," he teased, gathering her into his arms for a soul-searing kiss.

Sarah giggled as she grabbed his hand and led him into the kitchen. "It's ok, Lance. I'm only yours today," she said, handing him the cooler as she grabbed her beach bag.

"Today and everyday," he answered, wrapping his free arm around her waist and leaning in for another kiss.

They walked to the downstairs shed, and Sarah found a couple of chairs and an umbrella that she wanted to take with her, placing them to the outside of the building before she re-secured the doors with the lock. Lance noticed the boogie boards leaning against the one wall - far to the back, that he guessed were the very ones that Sarah and Dex used to play on in the ocean when they were children. He knew that it was better not to say anything, but found it rather sad that the shed still held those long-forgotten, faded memories of her youth.

The sand was hot as they walked across it, pretty typical for an August day. Lance dug a hole and placed the umbrella pole in the sand, moving it back and forth until it had a tight grip. He opened the multi-colored umbrella, fastening it securely to the pole, as it flapped playfully in the slight breeze of the day.

Sarah watched him, as she lathered herself with suntan lotion, trying to protect her skin from the searing sun. Lance placed all the items that they had brought underneath the shade of the umbrella, plopping down in one of the low-slung sand chairs afterwards, and looking at her as she approached. "Man, that took the wind out of my sails," he said with a handsome smile, as his sunglasses reflected the beautiful vixen that was joining him.

Sarah opened the cooler, extending a water in his direction. "This will help," she grinned, taking a few swigs herself from her own bottle.

They sat together just watching the scene at hand - the couples walking or sitting, and the children at play. Lance grabbed Sarah's hand taking it to his lips. "You know you look so darn pretty today with your little string bikini. I can't take my eyes off of you," he admitted lovingly, as he looked into her beautiful blue eyes and kissed her on the lips."

Sarah smiled contently, not feeling the anxiety that she had anticipated would happen once she was on the beach. "It is good to be here with you, Lance. You were right – it is such a beautiful day!"

He grabbed her hand and kissed it again. "All is well, Sarah. Not only a beautiful day, but a great day!" he smiled reassuredly, as they continued to relax and kick back, trying to ease her worries.

After some time of just doing nothing, Lance rose and took off his t-shirt, exposing his tight, muscular tan chest to Sarah and everyone else on the beach that was staring. "Why don't we take that walk?"

Sarah looked at him with uneasiness etched on her face, shielding her eyes with her hand. "Ummm… sitting here isn't so bad now, is it?"

Lance grabbed her hand and made her stand. He leaned in close, whispering in her ear. "You will be fine. Trust me," he beckoned as he applied some suntan lotion to his arms, before placing some extra on Sarah's back.

They walked along the shoreline, hand in hand, as Lance continued to talk about pleasant happy things to Sarah, trying to keep her distracted from her thoughts. "I think we should go to the boardwalk tonight. What do you say?"

"I haven't done that in years," she answered with excitement in her eyes, looking at him and considering the possibility.

"So tonight is the night," Lance replied, looking very handsome in his sunglasses and royal blue trunks that were reminiscent of what he wore when he was a lifeguard. As they walked, the waves were rushing up around his tight calves, placing a film of sand all around them.

Sarah grabbed Lance's arm tightly and screamed, as a large wave tried to knock her down. He picked her up, steadying her again and holding her tightly as her breathing began to turn rapid. "Shush, Sarah," he whispered calmly, as the waves continued to roll in playfully around their feet.

"I don't like this, Lance," she cried out in fright, clinging to his neck much too tightly.

"Sarah, I am here."

"Lance, please... let's go back to the beach house."

"Sarah, I am here," he said again, brining her chin up to meet his own. "Look out over the water. It is calm today. You played in these waves from the time you were born."

She looked out over the horizon, feeling herself relaxing with Lance's reassuring words. Tears stung her eyes at the thought of Dex once more, but then she remembered Lance's friend too - who was now gone because of the ocean.

"How can you feel this way, after what you shared about losing your friend Jeff?" she asked, turning to look at him again in confusion.

"Jeff loved the ocean," he explained, as they continued to walk. "Death doesn't change that fact."

"And so did Dex..." Sarah admitted, realizing what Lance was saying was true.

"We can still enjoy all this," Lance added with a broad sweep of his hand. "And yet keep their memories alive."

They walked back to their chairs, grabbing the towels and drying off, while they rubbed the sand from their legs. Sarah opened the cooler again, sharing the fruit and cheese with Lance.

"I am glad you suggested this," she confessed, as she popped a grape in her mouth. "And the walk and what you said - did me some good."

Lance looked at Sarah intuitively; glad he could share some of his wisdom. She looked like a tomboy with her ponytail turning off to the one side, with a spray of sand running throughout it. Her skin was now tanned, and a tinge of pink was shining through on the tip of her nose. Her light blue eyes mimicked the color of the sky, and her lashes were still wet from the surf. She was a natural beauty and he couldn't help but desire her again.

He grabbed her hand, as they rested together on the touching arms of the sand chairs, contently looking out to sea and drinking their waters.

"Sarah?"

"Yes?" she said as she turned to look at him.

Lance smiled and removed his sunglasses, placing them on the cooler lid behind him. He hesitated to speak as he studied her beautiful face and trim body as she waited for him to speak.

"I love you," he said plainly and sweetly, waiting for her response.

Sarah sat in silence, not knowing what to say, and could only smile back in return.

CHAPTER 38

One by one, the beachgoers slowly packed up and moved out for the day. As the beach emptied, Lance and Sarah decide it was time to do the same. With the chairs and umbrella placed back in the shed, they rinsed each other's feet and legs off at the outside spigot, making their way back inside the house, just as Sarah had done so many times as a child.

Lance placed the sandy cooler on the floor of the kitchen, wrapping Sarah in his greasy suntanned arms. "Why don't we get a shower?" he suggested playfully, nuzzling her neck.

She grabbed his hand, giving him a mischievous grin, running with him to the bathroom. Sarah turned the shower handle on, making the room fill quickly with steam, as Lance kissed her passionately and fondled her breasts - releasing the back string of her bikini top and flinging it to the awaiting floor. He then too lowered his bathing suit, revealing his throbbing hardness, as the two entered the oversized shower, closing the glass door behind them.

The water slowly washed the sand, salt, and coconut oil from their bodies. Lance lowered his mouth to Sarah's waiting nipples, already firm with desire. She moaned out in pleasure, pulling him closer to her chest, as Lance suckled and teased each bud in his mouth.

It was a time of mutual washing as they kissed and fondled the other, being fully aroused and unable to stop. They stepped from the shower and Lance grabbed a towel, quickly drying the both of them, before dropping it to the floor by the forgotten bathing suits that were already there. He picked Sarah up in his arms, carrying her to the awaiting bed, not bothering to pull the comforter back first.

The last shimmers of daylight poked through the blinds, as Sarah lay on the bed - ready and waiting for Lance. He stood in front of her - fully erect - looking over her beautiful nude body with longing etched all over his face. She rose on her elbows, smiling at him in an alluring way, giving him permission to proceed.

"Oh, Lance, that feels so good," Sarah yelled, as she wrapped her legs around his waist, feeling his manhood deep inside of her - plunging in and retreating back out slowly and deliberately. He grabbed her hips, grinding tightly, crying out with a satisfying release as she mutually did in return.

They lay together wrapped in each other's embrace, as their breathing resumed to a normal pattern. Lance kissed the top of Sarah's hair that was still wet from the shower. "Why don't we crawl under the covers, sweetie?" he suggested as he watched her shiver. Sarah obliged, and they snuggled close beneath the awaiting sheets and comforter.

Sarah's phone began to vibrate as she reached for it on her nightstand, trying to grab it before it stopped. She was still in a daze, allowing her mother's message to go to voicemail.

Lance rolled over, waking with the interruption. "Who was that?" he asked, looking at Sarah whose damp hair was a crazy tumble - falling half over her one eye.

"Just my mom. I will call her later," she smiled contently, reaching down to give Lance another tender kiss.

"Why don't we go to the boardwalk?" he asked, getting up to find his gym bag with his clean clothes that he had brought with him earlier.

Sarah jumped from the bed and headed towards the bathroom, turning to look at Lance. "You wore me out but I think I am up for it," she smiled playfully, running for the shower one more time.

The boardwalk was a flurry of activity. The day's heat was still rising from the splintered boards, creating a heady aroma of wood, salt and tar. Sarah and Lance walked hand in hand, with their flip-flops snapping in unison, mingling with the others in the crowd.

They stopped at a French fry stand that had a long line of patrons off to the one side of it, knowing that the long wait was well worth it for a taste of the salty potato treat. Sarah sprinkled some malt vinegar on top of the large container they shared, with ketchup not being offered - being a Maryland thing.

They sampled fried chicken, pizza and ice cream too, and even stopped for licorice candy along the way.

"Let's sit here," Lance suggested, taking a seat on one of the many benches placed strategically the entire length of the boardwalk, as they finished eating their cones. Sarah noticed the metal plaque that was attached to the back of the bench in memory of a loved one who had passed. It served as a reminder, that her parents had done the same for Dex, but she didn't have a clue where that bench might be or even what was written on his plaque. She wondered if whoever looked at Dex's bench considered the short years of his life, as much as she considered the life of the person where she sat.

Lance looked at her, sensing her change in mood. "Everything ok?"

"Yeah, I'm fine," she answered forlornly. "It's just these benches always make me feel a little weird sitting on them with the plaque and all. My parents had one made for Dex on one of these benches - somewhere along the boards – although, I have no clue where that might be."

Lance reached out to squeeze Sarah's hand. "I think the benches are very special. Your parents did a very special thing to remember your brother like that."

"Yep, they did," she answered, pulling him to his feet and trying to keep the evening upbeat. "You said we are getting on some rides, so now that I'm good and full - let's hope I don't throw up!" she giggled.

Lance began to laugh. "Oh my... I didn't consider *that* while we were eating ice cream. Maybe we should wait awhile."

"I know exactly what we can do until our stomach's settle."

"And what's that?"

"Skee-Ball!" she announced with a big grin, as they made their way towards the Sun and Fun Playhouse. "I usually win, and I am just warning you!" she added, tugging on Lance's arm and leading him past the arcade games and to her favorite bowling game location.

It was quite late until they had made their rounds and did all that they had hoped to do. Sarah won three games of Skee-Ball while Lance won two. They found the crazy mirrors, posing in front of all of them – ones making them look skinny, fat, with long faces and silly grins. They laughed so hard they cried, as their sides hurt from all of the fun. They decided on the antique merry-go-round, with its old hand-painted horses that were each a piece of beautiful artwork, almost too pretty to ride.

"Let's get on the Ferris wheel before we leave," Lance suggested, as they walked towards the ticket both, purchasing two for the ride. They walked together at a fast pace, being the next in line, quickly taking a seat, as the ride rotated and the attendant dropped and locked the bar securely in place over top of them. The ride started to move, making Sarah turn with a slight jump, as she leaned into Lance's arms more securely and he held her close. She looked out over the ocean that was mostly dark, seeing only a few boats with their lights that were burning low.

Lance closed his eyes and just breathed in deeply and relaxed, enjoying the moment immensely with Sarah - not wanting it to end.

"Lance we are up so high," she said with her eyes wide open, almost like a child's trying to regain his attention.

"Yes, Sarah, we are," he answered with an affectionate smile, as he reopened his eyes to look at her beautiful face. *"And that is the point of it all, isn't it?"* he asked, hoping she understood what he was implying. "To be up here - high above everything - seeing Marlin Beach at this angle. Don't you think it is quite spectacular?"

Sarah paused and just gazed at him, trying to understand the meaning behind his words. She looked out over the ocean and the town again, and then back at Lance once more. "Yes, it is really amazing up here," she admitted, snuggling in closer from the slight chill in the night air. "I feel so carefree up here."

"Exactly," he whispered, as he kissed the top of her head, realizing the moments were fleeting and something he would cherish forever once she returned to Baltimore. "It's getting cold. Why don't we get going once the ride is over?"

She stared into his handsome brown eyes, finding it hard to suddenly not please him. "Sure, honey. Whatever you would like," she replied, not wanting to leave his arms or the boardwalk ever.

The blinds were pulled back and the doors were opened again to the sound of the waves and the soft tinkling of the wind chimes. Sarah poured two glasses of chilled Chardonnay, handing one to Lance who was out on the deck waiting for her.

"What a night," he said with a relaxed smile as he drank from his wine glass. "It's going to be another hot day tomorrow. I can already tell from the sky."

"Hasn't rained in awhile," Sarah added, sipping from her wine along with him. "I really have missed the beach, Lance," she said, as she affectionately touched his hand. "If you hadn't encouraged me to go there today, I'm not sure if I would have ever gone back."

Lance set his glass down and looked at Sarah, wanting to make his point. *"I'm glad you did and maybe next time we can get in the water."*

Sarah stopped drinking her wine mid-air. *"I'm not sure if I can ever do that, Lance,"* she said with a tormented look of fear.

"One step at time, and I will be with you then too," he promised.

"Today was big for me in many ways. The beach and then the boardwalk – it brought back lots of memories of Dex, but if felt okay."

"Come here Sarah," Lance beckoned, patting his lap for her to sit.

Sarah crawled onto his lap - wrapping her arms around his neck - sitting sideways and looking out over the waves. They sat quietly together, just holding each other and listening to the sounds of the night.

Lance turned Sarah towards him, finding her lips as he plunged his tongue deep into her mouth. She realized his intentions, knowing the wine was aiding in his aroused interest again. He began to rub between her legs, wishing the jean shorts and her underwear were not in the way.

His breathing became ragged as he reached into her bra, bringing out one of her breasts to see and suckle. The moon shone brightly down on them as Lance continued to caress her. He released his mouth, looking at the saliva encircling her tight bud, and it became his undoing as he watched Sarah arch her head back - lost in ecstasy.

Lance carried her to the sofa and playfully removed her clothes, after which, she reached up and did the same for him too. They lay together, kissing and holding the other, while Sarah became bold in intent, bending down over Lance and taking his shaft into her mouth - molding it perfectly between her tongue and lips.

After some time, Lance rose off the sofa, grabbing Sarah's hand and making her come with him. He sat on one side of the bed and willed her to straddle him, as she slide onto his cock and rode him hard and fast. He grabbed her ass in return - pulling her in closer, sending them both over the edge of no return.

"Oh my God, Lance, this is so good!" she screamed.

"Oh yes, it is, darling!" he echoed loudly, giving way to his own glorious release.

The covers were pulled back once again, and this time they slept soundly, with Sarah on her side and Lance wrapped tightly around her, either barely making a move throughout the night.

The doors to the patio were never closed, as the sounds of the wind chimes still tinkled a melodic song of pleasant harmony.

They rested peacefully, sleeping the night away, with the moon setting and the sun rising – giving way to a new day and a new morning.

CHAPTER 39

Lance woke in the strange but familiar bed, trying to remember where he was. He squinted and sat up, looking to the other side of the bed that was now empty without Sarah. *Where is she?* He thought, as he walked to the bathroom to perform his morning emptying of his bladder. He walked to the living room, where his clothes still laid, grabbing his boxers and shorts, and stepping into them both.

He realized Sarah was on the balcony with the doors pulled shut, which he found strange, as he watched her look out over the ocean from the deck. He left his shirt still on the floor, walking to the heavy patio doors, pushing them back to join her.

Sarah had already showered and dressed, with her hair pulled back into her typical, tight ponytail. She had on white shorts with a black halter-top, and her white flip-flops were back on her feet.

Not a sign of the night remained, with her clothes now gone and the wine glasses washed and back in the cabinet where they originally came from. Even the cooler was missing, that they had left in the kitchen before going to the boardwalk. All was clean, straightened up and neat - except for Lance.

"Hi Sarah," he greeted, with uncertainty written all over his face.

"I made you some coffee," she replied warmly as he joined her by the railing, kissing her on the cheek.

"I woke up and you were gone. Is everything ok?"

Sarah looked at Lance with a false pretense of a smile. *"I think we need to talk."*

"What about?" he asked, feeling confused after the wonderful day previous they had just spent together.

"Why don't we go inside?" she offered, while walking back into the beach house and into the kitchen. She poured two cups of coffee and placed them on the table, remembering to add the French Vanilla creamer to Lance's cup.

He sat at the table, still with his shirt off, just watching her and feeling in a daze - not ready to say goodbye to yesterday quite yet.

Sarah took a sip of her coffee, placing the mug back on the table before she began. "Lance, I want to begin by saying that the beach and boardwalk were so perfect and fun..."

"What is going on here?" he interrupted, reaching out to grab her hand as she pulled away.

"Lance, you must let me finish!" Sarah insisted, rising to walk over to the kitchen counter - resting her backside against it for support. "Everything has been wonderful, but the reality is, I must get back to work - and my life in Baltimore."

Lance sighed, shaking his head silently in frustration as she continued, looking to the floor and then back into her pain-filled eyes that were similar to his own.

She stammered as she continued, feeling a slight mist of tears forming in her eyes. "I spoke with my parents today. There is no sense in delaying things any longer. I am better from my injuries, I have a new car and the paint has been selected for the house. *All is done...*" she resolved, looking now to the floor herself to focus on the task at hand.

Lance got up and joined her by the counter, grabbing her arms and turning her around to face him. "Sarah, you don't have to do this. I love you and we have come so far," he said, with tears beginning to form in his troubled brown eyes.

"Yes, I do, Lance. My dad is counting on me to come back to work. I have a huge overload of work waiting on my desk. *Don't you understand that?*"

Lance lowered his head again and sighed, realizing he had also allowed his work to slide, and his mother was picking up the slack for him. *"Yeah, I guess I do unfortunately understand..."*

Sarah broke from his embrace and walked to the living room, giving them some distance. "I plan to leave tomorrow, Lance. I need to call your father and give him the go ahead to proceed forward with the listing."

Lance joined her in the living room, finding his shirt and slipping it on over his head. "Damnit it, Sarah, why can't we *just try* to keep this thing going? Baltimore isn't that far away. I can drive back and forth to see you, if you are willing to make the effort too."

Sarah began to pace, stopping to consider Lance's words. "What is the point? I need to focus on my job. I don't have the time to devote to a relationship right now," she insisted, crossing her arms in front of her.

Lance encircled her again in his arms, refusing to let her move as he held her close. "Hasn't the last few days changed things for you, and for us? Don't you deserve a life outside of work?" he whispered, as he gazed steadfastly into her sky blue eyes, waiting for the answer he so desperately sought.

"I can't think about my personal life right now," she said quietly, while releasing his arms and breaking free of the hold he had on her. "I owe my parents so much. What would they do without me? I am all they have left..." she said sadly.

Lance angrily grabbed his keys as he walked towards the door. *"What would they do without you?* What about me – what will I do without you? Don't I count in your life - after all we have been through?" he gritted out in frustration.

Sarah began to cry as she tried to hold back the tears. "Unfair, Lance.... You are being unfair. I am sorry it has to be this way," she said determinedly, as she made her way towards the door where he stood.

His hand rested on the knob just waiting for her to speak, as her eyes met his own.

"I will *always* cherish our time we spent together. You have done so much for me - and I will *always* be grateful."

"Don't be grateful to me - for our lovemaking!" he bit out. "At least *for me* it was real!"

Sarah looked at him with hurt registering in her eyes. "It was real for me too, Lance. Don't make this any more difficult than it already is."

Lance turned and grabbed Sarah's arm, bringing her firmly into his embrace, as his lips sought to make her his own one last time. "I will honor your wishes, Sarah, but I know you are making a big mistake!"

He quickly broke their embrace, finding the door and opening it. "Goodbye, Sarah. I will let my dad know you want to speak with him," he added without turning around – before walking out and slamming the door loudly and rattling the walls.

Sarah stood staring in disbelief at the closed door, crying softly to herself. She no longer had to be strong and shield her tears from Lance's view. She was alone and could cry freely with all the pain of regret she was feeling for losing him.

She made her way to the sofa and kicked off her flip-flops, hugging the couch cushion to her face as she continued to cry. Her mind wandered to the night previous, as she thought of Lance touching her sensuously right where she lay and what she did back to him in return. He was so hot for her and she for him. *Why do I have to end this?* She thought in anguish, with no logical reason making any sense to her.

Sleep finally overtook her, since she was exhausted from not having much the night before. Sarah had slipped from her bed early in the morning, as Lance slept peacefully, being unaware of her plans to stop the relationship from going on any further. Now it was done and she was alone again, with only her job and her parents to keep her company.

Dex visited Sarah again in her dreams…. A scrabble game was being played at the beach house kitchen table – just like it had been played many years before. But this time, the game wasn't being played only with Dex. There was a new player at the table – Lance had joined the group - and she knew she was losing at the game.

CHAPTER 40

Sarah awoke to the sound of her cellphone ringing, realizing it was John Snyder trying to call her.

"Hello, John," she greeted, as she got up off the sofa and put her flip-flops back on her feet, after sleeping there all night.

"Lance said you wanted me to call you?" he asked, as he was ready to tee off at the first green.

"Yes, everything is done. I guess it's time to activate the listing."

"That surprises me, Sarah. I thought maybe you had a change of heart," he said with a gruff laugh.

"Why would you say that?" she asked in surprise, as she began to wash up the two coffee mugs that were still left in the sink from the day before.

John straightened, resting on his golf club for support as he spoke to her plainly. "I thought you and Lance were seeing each other."

Sarah placed the mug back in the sink, with the cellphone still pressed between her ear and shoulder. *"Did Lance tell you that?"*

John chuckled, anxious to get back to his game. "No, he didn't *tell me that*, but it wasn't too hard to figure out either. He hasn't been at work as much in the last few weeks, he rarely answers his phone, and he hasn't joined his mother and I for dinner lately. What else is there to know?"

Sarah was taken back by John's straightforwardness. He didn't mince words. She sat on the sofa again, needing it for support. "I think it is best that I do not discuss my personal life."

"Do as you wish. That is totally fine with me, Sarah. But I have a golf game waiting, and if you want to list The Dancing Seahorse then it will be done - as soon as the house is painted. Did you make those arrangements with Andrew Scott?"

"Yes, I did, and I already picked out the paint and paid for it. He said the labor cost you would take care of, and we could finalize what I owe you at settlement.

"That works. Let me know when I can put the lock box on the house and you have finally departed. I will let you know when we have a buyer. I suspect your place will sell quickly, based on the inquiries that we receive daily requesting a nice place like yours."

"I will contact you when I am gone, Mr. Snyder...I mean John. And thank you again for everything you have done."

"No thanks needed. But you may want to thank Lance. I know he has been there for you, Sarah," he said impatiently, as he hung up the phone on her.

Sarah sat on the couch staring at her cellphone, realizing John had cut off the call - once again before saying goodbye - just as he normally did. *"Thank, Lance,"* she said aloud. *"Unfortunately, I think that ship has finally sailed."*

It wasn't hard for Sarah to make her rounds throughout the beach house and gather up all the remaining things that she wanted to take with her back to Baltimore. Her parents had already emptied out their bed and bathroom, so all that was remaining was her bedroom, bath and Dex's room.

She hated to go back into his room and pack up his belongings yet another time. Once was enough, but the car accident had a way of bringing his things right back to where they started. As she folded his clothes on the bed, and emptied the trinkets back again into a box, she noticed the "selfie" picture of her and Dex. She held it close, studying his face, taken back to those last happy moments spent together on the beach right before the riptide hit and changed their lives forever.

She sat on his bed, hugging the picture to her chest, rocking back and forth as she spoke to her departed twin - hoping he could hear her words. *"Oh, Dex, have I made such a mess of things,"* she admitted, with tears stinging her eyes as she looked around the room one last time. *"Someone loves me, but I can't allow myself to love him back. He should have rescued you, just like I was rescued that day. I am here - and you are gone. I can't allow my heart to accept love from a man like this,"* she cried out in misery.

Sarah made two trips back and forth from Dex's room, taking the several boxes that she had packed with her. She took one final glance, looking around the room, before shutting the door tightly – saying goodbye to the room, and all the memories of the house and the beach, that went along with it.

She gathered the remaining things that were left, having to walk up and down the outside steps several times, before loading the boxes and suitcases in the back of her car. She slammed the trunk lid shut and rested on the side of her SUV, just trying to catch her breath from all the work that she had done. All that remained was some food, as she threw a few things into the cooler, leaving the rest for the painter.

Sarah made one last final inspection, checking all the cabinets and closets for any forgotten items, before placing the extra keys under the mat by the upstairs deck. She grabbed her purse, pausing at the front door and looking around one last time before leaving. No detail was forgotten. She knew it was over and wanted things finalized once and for all. It was time to say goodbye to The Dancing Seahorse and Marlin Beach.

Sarah dialed John Snyder's phone as she drove out of town, ready to speak with him again. She got his voicemail instead on the third ring, and was relieved after the way he had just spoken to her.

"Mr. Snyder, this is Sarah Miller calling. I just wanted to let you know that I have left the beach house for the final time, and you are free to begin the listing once the house is painted. The keys are under the upstairs deck mat. If you have any questions or updates, please contact me. Thank you."

The second call was made to her father, but this call was answered right away.

"Dad, everything is done and I am on my way home."

"Great to hear, Sarah! We could meet for dinner tonight - if you are up for it."

"I think I will pass," she answered, as she maneuvered through some heavy beach traffic, heading out of town. Mike filled her in on what were pressing, and the deadlines that they were facing - beginning the next day.

Sarah sighed as she listened intently, as he went on for 15 minutes more without end. She realized she was going back to her busy life, and had said her final goodbyes to Lance and the beach house. As sad as it made her, she knew she had no other choice for either.

"Dad, I gotta run. If you want to see me at work tomorrow - first thing in the morning - I need to get my apartment back in order and buy some groceries yet tonight," she added pragmatically, as she ended her call - driving across the Chesapeake Bay Bridge on her way back to Baltimore and her career at Miller's Architecture.

Chapter 41

Alison Snyder was busy at work trying to keep Beach Dreams functioning while her husband was constantly distracted with golf, and her son was now also letting down on his obligations - much to her dismay. She knew Lance had done his best to help Sarah Miller, but now she was gone and he needed to get back to the business at hand.

John had called his wife, after drinking one too many beers at the clubhouse after his golf game, with the news that The Dancing Seahorse was finally able to be listed. She contacted Andrew Scott and scheduled the painting, delaying the listing for several days yet – with an explanation on the MLS real estate site that painting needed to be done first.

Alison knew that the Miller's beach house would be sold quickly, and then all the distractions and interruptions of the summer could be put to rest, and business could get back to normal for at least Lance and her.

John was another matter. He would never work as hard as he once had in the real estate business. He had heard about one too many of his friends with health problems that had dropped over dead unexpectedly. Since his parent's had both died in their seventies, he decided that he was going to live life to the fullest. Alison couldn't complain - he had given her and Lance both a wonderful life, and she was capable of managing the business exceptionally well without him.

The cardinal rule was as long as they spent dinner together in the evening, she didn't care what John did the rest of the day. Lance had made it habit to join his parents for dinner also - at least several times a week. They always picked up the tab, and it was their time of talking mostly about the business.

The joke was that they had stock in Old Bay Café, since they mainly frequented the place. Not only did it have great food but a fun atmosphere. All of the waiters and bartenders knew the family - calling them by name and giving them free extras – be it a drink or food.

Lance joined his parents after work, as they sat at their normally reserved table, peeling the shells off of the Old Bay seasoned shrimp and drinking a cold draft.

"Hey," Lance greeted, taking a seat opposite them.

John looked up, wiping his sticky fingers on a napkin and taking a swig of beer. "Get my son a Natty Boh and some more of these shrimp," he ordered, pointing towards the bartender who was busy watching an Orioles baseball game on TV.

"Right away, boss," he yelled back at John, grabbing the beer and placing it front of Lance.

"Thanks, Dave. How about a bowl of crab soup and crackers also?"

"You got it, Lance. It will be right out with your shrimp."

John, Alison and Lance relaxed and enjoyed the beautiful evening that they spent together as a family. The garage doors, on the back of the building, had been lifted; while the outside tables with their surrounding fragrant tiki torches that burned brightly, gave way to the majestic bay in front of them. The sun was setting, as a two-man guitar assemble played and entertained the diners.

John sighed, satisfied with his belly full, as he looked out over the lush grasses that blew softly in the breeze. A crane squealed and flew away, splashing a spray of water behind him. "Isn't this the life?" he asked contently, as he looked at Lance and Alison while smoking his cigar.

"Yeah, its pretty special living here in Marlin Beach," Lance replied solemnly, with sadness etched all over his face as he stared out over the glades.

Alison interrupted, looking at Lance with concern. "Speaking about *pretty special*, what happened between you and Sarah Miller? I thought you were seeing her."

Lance looked intently at his mother and then towards his father. "What's up with everyone thinking we were dating? We *obviously* were just friends - and nothing more."

John placed his arms on the table, leaning in towards Lance as the cigar smoke swirled around his head. "It doesn't matter what anyone else thinks. You did right by her and her family, and you helped her in her time of need. If she chose to leave, then that was her decision. Just like we have a family business that needs to be attended to, so do the Miller's. Sarah is a crucial part of their company."

Alison began to laugh and clap, standing up for affect. "Bravo, John! *A family business that needs to be attended to* – oh, how I can relate! And speaking of family businesses, I could use some help with ours - if you catch my drift!" she added with a raised eyebrow while looking at Lance, before slipping off to the ladies' room for a much needed break from her family.

"I guess it is time I get back involved with things, if I want to keep mom happy," Lance said with laugh and a shake of his head, as he looked at his dad and took his last swig of beer. "Give her my love. I'm off to get a good night's rest. Tell her I will see her first thing in the morning."

"Will do, son," John waved, as he signed off on the bill, taking one last puff on his cigar before smashing it out in the ashtray in front of him.

It had seemed like forever since Sarah had been in her apartment. She stopped by the Harris Teeter and picked up the necessities, realizing several trips to the grocery store would be more practical with her arm still healing and feeling somewhat weak. The boxes she took from the beach house would stay in her car overnight. *There was always time to deal with it after work tomorrow*, she had decided.

A good night's sleep was all she desired, after such a long and tiring day of packing and driving. Her father had already emailed her about several pressing projects that required her attention, and a meeting had been schedule for the afternoon. A bid was in the works for a large hotel and resort that Sarah had devoted a lot of time and effort to, before she had gone to Marlin Beach to sell the beach house. Mike had asked for an extension of time, based on Sarah's accident and the crucial part she played in it all. If they could land the job - it would make their year financially.

Sarah planned to set her alarm for an hour earlier than she typically did, so that she could go into the office to prepare and finalize her proposal and presentation. While she was away in Marlin Beach recuperating, Mike had laid the preliminary groundwork with the investors, buying time until Sarah was back at the firm.

They knew of her car accident, and had agreed to delay a final decision until Sarah was working again. After several meetings, they grew impatient and wanted to proceed forward, which Mike knew would open the door to other architectural firms with less attractive proposals being considered.

Now Sarah was back home in Baltimore and making her re-entrance at work - on board, and ready to pick up where she had left off with the project again. If all went as planned, she would win them over and wrap up the deal, leading to a finalized signed agreement. The word would get out and it would become the envy of every other Architectural firm bidding on the same job. Keeping Miller's Architecture at the top in reputation - as one of the best firms - known for their excellence in superior design and quality workmanship.

CHAPTER 42

Andrew Scott picked up the paint from Logan's hardware, along with the other supplies he needed to paint the Miller's beach house. The lockbox was already in place. He opened the front door, after tapping in the combination that Beach Dreams used on all of their properties - which he really didn't consider being safe.

He found Sarah's note and decided to make a sandwich from the loaf of bread, meat and cheese that she left in the refrigerator. Andrew turned on his boom box, blasting out the Top 40 music that kept him motivated, as he painted each room. He stood back with his arms crossed, admiring his handiwork. "A fresh coat of paint is just what this place needed!"

Lance noticed the white work truck with "Andrew Scott Painting" printed on the side, as he pulled into the driveway. *Sarah is no longer here. So what does it matter if I stop in to check on things?* He thought, taking the steps two at a time. He opened the front door as Andrew turned in his direction.

"Hey, Lance, was just finishing up."

"I can see that. It looks great!" he mentioned, walking through the place and checking out each room, while Andrew cleaned up and removed the paint cans and drop cloths.

He paused as he went into Sarah's bedroom, remembering their intimacy that was still fresh on his mind. He missed her. The love that he felt for her was still very real and fresh, much like the paint that was now drying on the walls. *Her comforter was still in place on the bed*, he realized, as he shook his head in disbelief that what just started unfolding between them was already over.

Lance remembered the amazing last day that they spent together on the beach and the boardwalk. He honestly thought they had made a major breakthrough with trust, but obviously with her leaving - he couldn't be more wrong. Then there was the sex. He took it for granted that the attraction was mutual. *Or at least she pretended well*, he concluded bitterly. He remembered holding and sleeping with Sarah throughout the night, and it felt so perfect with her wrapped in his arms. It had only been a few short days, but it already felt like an eternity, and he ached with the memory of it all.

He sighed as he walked from her room, trying to shake it from his being so that he could go on with his day. "My father wants me to pay you," Lance explained, extracting ten – one hundred dollar bills from his wallet - handing it to Andrew.

"Thanks a lot," he nodded, as he balled the money up and shoved it in his painter's pants pocket.

"No problem, and we will have more work for you in a couple days," Lance added, as he made his way back outside to his car.

He looked up at the deck, remembering his last night with Sarah there too - as they drank wine and he fondled her breasts. It was magical as the moon shone bright, illuminating her in a sensual glow. He realized she had wanted him as badly as he had wanted her, whether he doubted himself now or not. There was no denying that it was true for at least that one evening!

For God's sakes, what has made her attitude change so drastically?
He questioned in frustration, as he pulled his Jeep away from The
Dancing Seahorse. Soon the place would be sold, and all would be lost –
with only distant, pleasant memories fleeting through his mind from
time to time, as he would drive by the place.

Sarah Miller was dressed in a tan suit with a white button down
shirt, and tan matching pumps that she slid on over her pantyhose. Her
blonde hair was pulled back in her trademark tight ponytail, and she
wore small diamond stud earrings, and a small dab of lip-gloss. She
gave herself a quick glance in her floor-length mirror, approving of her
look before she walked out of her apartment with her briefcase in hand.

Her father had met with her early, as they mutually prepared the
room for their meeting with ZAMS Hospitality Group International. The
plans were designed for a large 250-room hotel resort - complete with
world class dining, conference rooms, spa and an indoor heated
swimming pool. Outdoors, there would be an additional swimming pool
and tennis courts, with spacious grounds displaying fountains with
statuaries, tropical trees, flowers and walking paths.

Sarah had been working on the project for months, before going to
Marlin Beach to list the beach house, and never did she guess that her
efforts would be put on hold from the unfortunate series of events that
occurred. Her father had even encouraged her to keep her laptop at
home, saying she needed a break from the project and to focus on the
sale of the beach house for a few days. Little did she guess, that her
computer would be smashed in a car accident after insisting to take it
with her.

A few days turned into several weeks, and the broken arm had left
her without the ability to do her work. Mike, and the other associates,
had made a few small changes to the resort layout - based on the
requests of the investors - but Sarah's workmanship was unequivocally

without flaw or error. He was very proud of his daughter and her dedication to the company and her trade.

"Please come in and find a seat," Sarah greeted pleasantly, as the ten-person panel made their way into the conference room. High above the Inner Harbor, the sun attempted to shine brightly through the tinted windows of the 12th floor conference room, as the lights were lowered and the PowerPoint presentation began.

Each picture was set to music as it flowed from screen to screen, showing the depiction of what the new resort would look like completely on the inside as well as the out. Each suite was laid out with an excellent view – many with balconies overlooking the ocean. The kitchenettes were designed with granite countertops and black stainless appliances, along with a dining table and chairs. The sitting area held a sleeper sofa with two accent chairs, a coffee table and a flat screen TV that was to be mounted on the wall. The bed choice was either a king or two queens, depending on what the guests preferred. The presentation depicted beautiful artwork, draperies and comforters on each bed. No detail was missed and the panel seemed to be impressed.

The restaurant was to employ award-winning chefs, and the swimming pools were to be Olympic in size. The spa facility would come equipped with a team of professionals that would provide massages and facials, and there would be a full assortment of exercise equipment, a sauna, steam room and hot tub. The outside grounds and gardens would be designed for parties and weddings - with romance being the central theme with its walking paths, statues, waterfalls and intimate sitting areas.

The response from the visiting executives was well received, as they applauded at the end of the presentation, with several even standing and shaking Sarah and Mike's hand. Lunch was served as the talks continued, with a wrap up and review afterwards conducted by Mike. Sarah concluded the day's events with her final thoughts, as she stood confidently in front of the group of guests.

"I want to thank you for taking the time to join us here today at Miller's Architecture, and for allowing me the opportunity to present to you what we feel is an outstanding resort experience. What we would like for you to take away today, beyond your packages in front of you, is how the presentation made you feel personally as you watched each slide. Did you feel like it was a place you would like to visit on your vacation or even host a business meeting or wedding at?" Sarah asked passionately, as she paced the room in front of the decision making panel, driving home her point with outstretched arms. "If the answer is *"yes"* than I would suggest your review the information - sleep on it - and let us know your decision as soon as possible. The project will take two years to complete - once we begin - so time is of the essence that a decision is reached very soon."

The group rose in unison as the presentation concluded with each panel member filing past Sarah and Mike and shaking their hand goodbye. The receptionist stood at the door, leading from the conference room, and handed each participant a takeaway packet of information before they departed.

Sarah sat with her dad and associates after the visitors had left, trying to regroup after such a stressful day, and asking for their feedback.

"Job well done, Sarah," Mike congratulated, as the co-workers joined in and applauded unanimously in response.

"I couldn't have done it without the help of all of you," she offered humbly, looking at each person present, and knowing they had put forth many extra hours of overtime to help her out while she was away recovering.

The group departed and Sarah was alone with her father sharing a cup of coffee, suddenly feeling worn out and yet relieved that the meeting was finally over. "So now that it is just the two of us, how do you think things *really* went?" she asked of him.

"Honey, you did an amazing job! Daughter or not, I couldn't be any prouder of you today and what you have accomplished. I feel that we will *definitely* win the bid now. They know our pricing is very fair and that our reputation speaks for itself. It is no secret to them, what we stand for and what we will provide."

Sarah looked at her dad with an equal sense of pride, as she placed her coffee cup on the conference room table. I hope you're right dad, or we have some major work ahead of us to pick up the slack from this lost bid. Other big deals will have to happen, that is for sure – if this falls apart."

"It will happen, Sarah. Don't worry your pretty little head about this! You just wait and see," he answered reassuredly, patting her arm. "I got all the confidence in the world with you being back in charge, and that is half of the battle."

"Thank you, dad. That means a lot coming from you."

Mike rose from his seat, walking over to the large expanse of windows that overlooked the cityscape, turning back to look at his daughter once again. "Welcome home, Sarah. We couldn't be any happier that you are finally back - because we *do know* that you make things happen and you do get deals done around here!"

CHAPTER 43

With the painting competed, the listing was finally made active for The Dancing Seahorse. Beach Dreams started to receive calls almost immediately for showings by interested clients, as well as other real estate companies and their agents.

"Lance, there is another call on Line 3 for the Miller place," his mother yelled from her office, knee deep in work from other properties that were up for sale, keeping her overwhelmed and busy.

"Hello, Lance Snyder. How may I help you?" he asked, as he turned his computer back on to the listing in question. "Yes, it does have three bedrooms and two nice size bathrooms. Yes, the deck wraps around a good portion of the house and the view *is amazing* of the ocean," he added, remembering all the vivid details almost too well. "Yes, I would be happy to set up a showing for you tomorrow at 3 p.m. - if that will work?"

Lance tabbed to his scheduling calendar, and typed in the contact information of the couple that was coming from Pennsylvania to see the Miller's Beach house the following day. They did not have an agent, so if they liked the house – Snyder's Beach Dreams Real Estate would receive the full commission on the property. He saved the information and closed his laptop, before saying goodbye to the potential buyers.

"Mother, I am out," he announced, as he leaned halfway into Alison's office.

She cupped her hand over her desk phone receiver, whispering to Lance. "Did you set up an appointment?"

"Yes *mother*, and the Elliott's do not have no agent," he grinned.

"Fantastic!" she answered, waving him a fond goodbye.

It had been awhile since Lance had been on active volunteer duty with his EMT work, since his free time had been devoted to Sarah while she was still in town. But now that she was gone, he decided that he needed to get re-involved again with his other activities. He made the call to Marlin Beach Ambulance, and they immediately asked him to stop by the station to assist with a fundraiser that they were trying to organize.

The group sat casually in the kitchen of the ambulance house, discussing the details over coffee and donuts.

"Well, look what the cat just dragged in," one paramedic said with a sarcastic laugh, as Lance made his way over to the coffee pot and poured himself a cup of the freshly brewed coffee.

"Hasn't been that long," Lance announced with an awkward grin, taking a seat at the long table where the others were already sitting.

"Yes, it has," the group agreed unanimously in one voice, laughing good-naturedly as he joined them.

"What's been going on, Lance?"

"Not much, Ed. Just been busy with some personal stuff," he replied nonchalantly, looking up at the supervisor who was now studying him.

"Ok, I understand. We just know you used to help out one day a week, and then it suddenly stopped – that's all."

Lance felt somewhat uncomfortable with the line of questioning from the supervisor, since Sarah was now gone. *Maybe the time I spent with her wasn't even worth it in the long run,* he concluded.

"Well, I'm here now," he answered, trying to change the subject. "So what is this fundraiser you are trying to put together?"

Ed stood up and addressed the group. "We have decided to work mutually with Marlin Beach Humane Society to do an adoption day. Whatever proceeds we make in donations and adoptions, we will split 50/50 with them."

"So how will the money come in, boss?"

"We are going to make some phone calls to local businesses, and then set up a stand that I need you guys to man on the boardwalk where you will ask for donations there also. We will have pictures of the animals, and hopefully we will get interested applicants to adopt the cats and dogs, after we complete a thorough background check on each one of them." He paced the room trying to make his next point. "Then we will coordinate the final adoption day and actually bring the animals to the boardwalk that will be adopted. By doing so, it will hopefully generate more interest, and other people will go to the shelter in the future and adopt a pet."

"Now that sounds like a great idea! I'll be happy to make some contacts," Lance agreed, signing his name to the list of those wanting to get involved in their own way.

Ed handed Lance a list of 50 patrons from years past that had been loyal and generous in making a sizeable donation to Marlin Ambulance. "Start with these and maybe add some of your own. You may want to ask you dad also, if he knows a few of his golfing buddies that would want to make a donation."

Lance sat at a desk in a private office calling all the names on the list, leaving many voicemails but getting a few excellent responses.

"Hello, Is this Mrs. Martin?"

"Yes, it is."

"Mrs. Martin, this is Lance Snyder calling. I think I went to high school with your daughter Debbie?" he began.

"Lance? Oh, my word, we haven't seen you in years!"

"Well, I am calling on behalf of the Marlin Ambulance Association. We are having a fundraiser that will benefit the ambulance company, but also the animal shelter in town. We are not only asking for a donation of money, but we are trying to find homes for the animals at the shelter too."

"Lance, I just lost my dog last week that I had for 17 years," Mrs. Martin admitted sadly.

"I am so sorry to hear that, Mrs. Martin. It must be tough," he replied sympathetically. "I would suggest you visit the shelter and see if you can find a new dog or cat to adopt. They desperately need homes."

"Maybe I will do that, Lance. And pencil me in for a one hundred dollar donation. I will drop the check off tomorrow."

"Well, thank you, Mrs. Martin. And please say hi to Debbie for me."

The phone calls were all made on the entire list and a few extras besides that Lance had in his contact list on his phone. He even called his mother and she agreed to a five hundred dollar donation from Beach

Dreams, even though he couldn't convince her to adopt a pet because of her hectic work schedule. Lance always wanted a dog while he was growing up, but life was very busy working in real estate, and no amount of coercing was going to make Alison change her mind on the subject – then or now.

"Want me to hang in here for emergency calls?" Lance asked, as he walked from the private office over to Ed's desk.

"We got it covered today, Lance. Thanks for all your hard work, though," he said, glancing up from the list of calls that he had just made also. "I'm sure it will make a difference!"

"Think nothing of it, and I will drop off my mom's donation in the next day or so. And you can bet, I will work on my dad also when he isn't playing golf," he grinned.

"Sounds good. And, oh by the way - I'm glad *your friend* has made a full recovery," the supervisor nodded with an understanding wink, as Lance shook his head and walked out the door.

Sarah was back in the office early for a second day, already considering the next project up for bid - which was a remodel for a restaurant in Fells Point. The owners wanted to open the walls and bring the kitchen with its staff into direct view and operation with the diners. It was a concept widely accepted and used, but it came with its challenges, especially with an older warehouse building that it was situated in.

She had already drafted her initial plans, and had passed them off to her team for additional concept ideas and revisions that they would discuss the next day. Lance crossed her mind, as she walked from her desk and looked out over the city. *Maybe I should call him*, she considered, but dismissed the thought just as quickly with her large overwhelming workload ahead of her.

"Sarah, you have a call on 105," the secretary paged, as she broke into her thoughts, turning to answer the call.

"Sarah Miller, how may I help you?"

"Sarah, this is Mr. Walters from ZAMS Hospitality Group International."

"Mr. Walters, so good to hear from you!" Sarah greeted, taking a seat at her drafting desk again. "Did you get a chance to review the take away materials and consider the proposal?"

"That is why I am calling you. The group has reviewed the materials and *we have* reached a decision."

"Yes?" Sarah asked anxiously, sitting on the edge of her seat, waiting for his reply.

"Based on your amazing and thorough presentation, cost analysis, and additional takeaway materials that you sent with us to review - we have decided to give Miller Architecture the contract for the design and building of our next resort."

Sarah was beaming with joy and happiness at the news. If all went as planned, it would be the biggest year for Miller Architecture in profit. "Thank you, Mr. Walters. I cannot begin to tell you how extremely pleased we are that you would entrust us with your project."

"The choice was quite simple. You are the best at what you do, and your reputation precedes you."

"Well, that means a lot! We will be getting back to you with the contract agreement, and set up another meeting within the next week to finalize things. And, Mr. Walters?"

"Yes?"

"You will not be disappointed!" she added, feeling on top of the world.   The conversation continued, as the two discussed the tentative starting date for the beautiful new resort - that Sarah Miller would be in charge of - in Marlin Beach, Maryland.

CHAPTER 44

Sarah hung up the phone after talking with Mr. Walters for over an hour, and then walked to her father's office to let him know that they landed the deal on the resort. His office was empty, and with the excitement of everything, she had totally forgotten he would be out of the building and away at lunch. She could hardly contain herself, and just wanted to share the good news with him along with the others in the office.

Sarah went back to her office and decided to take her lunch break also, since Mike was gone. She knew that she was too excited to eat anything substantial, so she grabbed a granola bar and banana from her desk drawer instead, and washed it down with some water just to tide her over. Her cellphone was tucked away in the drawer too, and she took it out and began to read some of her old text messages, looking at the exchanges between her and Lance. She smiled fondly at what he wrote, suddenly realizing how much she missed him - wanting to share her good news that she had just received.

"Hello?"

"Lance, it's Sarah."

"Sarah, how are you doing?" he asked in pleasant surprise that she reached out, as he drove back to his office from the fundraiser duties.

"I am fine. Back to work and very busy, but fine."

"Well that is good to hear that you are doing ok."

"How are things in Marlin Beach?" she asked with curiosity.

"Not much going on here. I am involved with a fundraiser for Marlin Beach Ambulance. We are trying to raise money for the Ambulance Company, but also the local animal shelter."

"Well that is a worthy cause," Sarah replied, never ceasing to be amazed by Lance's caring nature and selfless ways. "I would like to make a donation if that is possible?"

"Well... sure, Sarah. Not necessary, but if you would like to do so, you can call Marlin Ambulance and they can take your donation over the phone."

Lance continued to drive, passing The Dancing Seahorse on his way back to Beach Dreams. "Your place is up for sale now and we are getting a lot of calls for showings."

"Already?" Sarah asked in surprise, having to face the reality of his words. "I didn't expect this so soon."

Lance was dumbfounded. *What did she think would happen after abruptly packing up and leaving, and giving the go ahead to list the house?* "Sarah, you wanted this..." he said quietly, shaking his head in utter frustration that she was actually gone.

She bent her head at her desk, feeling her resolve breaking. "I am sorry, Lance. I didn't mean to upset you. I just wanted to talk and catch up – that's all."

Lance sighed, knowing he couldn't change what was happening.

"It's fine, Sarah. Well, I gotta go. I am back at the shop and I'm sure my mother has a few showings that she has arranged for me. But, the good news is - your place should sell soon and Marlin Beach will soon be a distant memory, and one less thing you have to worry about.

Sarah grabbed her forehead, feeling the tears welling up in her eyes. "Take care, Lance. It was good talking to you."

"Yeah, you too Sarah. Take care of yourself," Lance replied distantly, as he hung up his phone, much like his father – not waiting for her response.

Mike Miller was back from lunch and walked into his daughter's office, taking note of her busily looking down over her phone with a troubling look. "Everything ok?" he asked, as he took the seat opposite her desk overflowing with papers.

Sarah wiped her eyes, trying to toss the thoughts of Lance from her mind. "I am more than fine, dad," she announced, as she rose from her seat and held onto her desk and leaned forward for affect. "I heard from ZAMS Hospitality Group International while you were at lunch…. Dad, we got the contract!"

"No way!" Mike replied in utter delight, raising from his seat and *high-fiving* his daughter in the air. "Now the fun begins. What did they say?"

"They were impressed with everything – the presentation, financials, overall design, and what we are offering! I told Mr. Walters that we would meet again in a week to have the contract signed and to discuss all the other details."

"Sarah, I am so proud of you!"

"Thank you, dad," she genuinely answered, while taking a seat again. "But you know, that after the accident - you, as well as the rest of the team – jumped in to help with my work load."

"Not another word, Sarah. You had the majority of work done before you left for Marlin Beach. We need to announce this to the others," Mike commented, as he made his way to the door to leave. "They will be very pleased. If all goes as planned, we will be giving out big bonuses at the end of the year, and more when the project is completed."

Sarah smiled happily, glad that her dad was pleased with her performance. "How about a meeting at three and we will give the team the good news?"

"I will send out an email," Mike answered. "And Sarah, let's celebrate tonight over dinner with your mother. She will be thrilled!"

"Sounds good. See you in the conference room at three."

At three o'clock, Sarah entered the conference room to a standing ovation from her co-workers and father. Her mouth dropped open in surprise from their applause, as she was taken back in gratitude that they cared and were honoring her.

"The thanks goes to all of you, too," she offered, taking a seat at the one end of the large conference table opposite her father. "I know this project is going to be a major undertaking once it begins, but what we have already done is a major accomplishment already. It is no secret to you, that I was in a car accident, and needed your help for a while on this project while I was away recovering. I thank every one of you for that. Your kind words, cards and flowers kept me motivated during that difficult time," she said sincerely, looking around the room to each one present.

So now we go into the next phase. ZAMS Hospitality Group International will return next week to sign the necessary paperwork and contract, and we will have a tentative date as to when the project will officially begin. In the meantime, we need to start getting the necessary permits with the city of Marlin Beach approved so that the excavation can begin. We need to keep the lines of communication open, and I will need all updates sent to my email or by text as soon as they are forthcoming." Sarah rose, standing at the head of the table, pausing to smile at the group. "Congratulations, team. Job well done! Now, let's dig in and make this the best darn resort that Marlin Beach has ever seen!"

Sarah left the room and made the call to her mother, as per her father's request. "Mom, it's me. Dad wanted me to call you and set up plans for dinner."

"Wonderful, Sarah. Where would you like to meet?"

"How about the Boat House at 7?"

" I assume I will meet you and your father there?"

Sarah smiled, taking a seat behind her drafting table again. *"Yes, mom.* You know dad and I are always here putting in long days and hours."

Nancy nodded her head silently in agreement. *"Yes, I do dear, and I can't be any prouder of you and your father's efforts."*

Sarah and Mike walked into the Boathouse and joined Nancy who was already sitting in a booth overlooking the harbor. The many lights of the boats and yachts, were casting a warm glow that could be seen from the windows in front of them.

They dined on prime rib and bay scallops, au gratin potatoes and Caesar salad; with lump crab served first as an appetizer to everyone at the table. The waiter brought champagne to Nancy's surprise, as she looked towards Mike for an explanation.

"What are we celebrating?" she asked in curiosity, while the server popped the cork and poured a generous libation into each glass.

"I think you should ask your daughter that question," Mike responded with a coy grin, lifting his glass - ready to announce the toast.

Nancy raised her eyes, uncertain as to what was happening, as she looked to Sarah for guidance and the answer.

Sarah smiled, as she unraveled the mystery. "Mom, we got the contract today for the project we have been working on for close to 6 months. The one for the resort that is being built in Marlin Beach."

"Oh my word!" Nancy exclaimed with excitement, placing her hand over her mouth, hardly able to contain herself. "I know how hard you have both worked on this," she said with admiration in her eyes, as she looked at her daughter and then to her husband in pride.

Mike raised his glass - as did the other two – as he gave the toast, and they clinked their glasses together in unison. "To Sarah – for all you have done to make this dream become a reality for Miller Architecture - we salute you!"

The merry trio talked and dined and finished their wonderful celebration dinner, ending with a desert of chocolate mousse cheesecake and small cups of espresso, before hugging and saying their goodbyes and going home.

Mike and Nancy left the Boat House happy and content from a great dinner and a time of celebration with their daughter. But Sarah went back to her apartment alone, sadly missing Lance. She thought of her great day and how it felt to finally be at the top of her industry, landing the deal with ZAMS Hospitality. With all the praise and accolades that she had received that day, she questioned why she still felt unfulfilled, as she wrestled with sleep. Only Lance could fill up the void that she was running away from, and as much as she tried to forget him and deny it - she knew it was true.

CHAPTER 45

Lance unlocked the combination on The Dancing Seahorse, extracting the key and opening the front door. The beach house still reeked from the smell of fresh paint, and the blinds were shut tightly as he fumbled with the light switch.

"Watch your step," Lance announced, as he turned on the lights to Harry and Leigh Elliott, who had traveled from Allentown, Pennsylvania to see the place.

Lance walked over to the blinds, pulling them back for the Elliott's, allowing them to admire the vast expanse of the ocean that was spread out in front of them.

"Oh my…" Leigh gasped in delight, as she and her husband walked towards the patio doors that were now pulled open wide, allowing the ocean breeze to blow in gently and rustle the vertical blinds. "We really would have an amazing view of the beach," she mentioned, as Harry nodded back in agreement.

The three continued to the deck as they looked out over the railing, bringing back memories again of Sarah to Lance's mind. The patio table and chairs were now neatly tucked together, but the citronella candle remained where it was left, even if the flame was now extinguished.

"I think I want it!"

"Now Leigh, let's not get ahead of ourselves, dear," Harry said pragmatically, with a pat to his wife's hand. "Let's at least see the rest of the place," he laughed, "before we decide."

Lance escorted the pair from room to room, each one gaining the approval of the Elliott's. Closets were opened in the bedrooms, and the blinds were raised for another glimpse of the ocean outstretched in front of them. The bathroom toilets were flushed, and the sinks and showers were turned on. Each drawer and linen closet was opened, as the potential buyers considered if the property was workable for their own wants and needs.

"Why don't we proceed to the kitchen?" Lance suggested, as he gave them a more thorough tour of that area of the beach house. He showed them the custom-made cabinets and tested each appliance – gaining the Elliott's approval.

"Harry, I love the place!" Leigh exclaimed, already having her mind made up and not needing to see anymore inside or out.

Harry looked at his wife and then at Lance with a concerned smile. "She knew she wanted the place when she saw the pictures online. Can we at least see the outside before we make an offer?" he suggested with a frustrated grin, knowing his wife was getting ahead of herself - at least in his mind.

Lance had to chuckle at the merry pair, knowing the buying signals were all there. "Let's go outside through the patio doors and I will show you how the deck wraps around a good portion of the house facing the beach, and then we will walk down the outside steps to the ground level."

They followed Lance around the deck and down the steps towards the shed and outside shower, as he gave a detailed tour. He did not miss any of the features, since he knew them all by heart. He opened the lock on the outside shed, pulling open the doors to a mast array of chairs, umbrellas, boogie boards, bicycles and even a forgotten cooler. The inside was dark and smelled musty, as they peaked their heads inside for a look.

"The owners don't want these items?" Harry asked, as he curiously looked around at all that was contained in the shed.

"They are part of the deal - along with the inside furnishings and outside patio furniture. All of it, will be on the contract and convey with the property," Lance announced methodically.

After walking around the entire outside of the beach house and down to the beach, the Elliott's were both smitten as they looked back up at The Dancing Seahorse from the view of the beach itself.

Harry grabbed Leigh's hand, bringing it to his lips for a kiss. "Is this what you really want, dear?" he asked tenderly, as he looked into her eyes for her approval.

"Yes, I do, honey! It will be so perfect for us and the children; and I know our relatives will love it too!"

Lance looked at them as they lovingly related to each other, feeling disillusioned that his dream had died for him and Sarah. "Would you like to go back inside and write up a contract?"

"Yes!" they both replied in agreement, walking hand and hand back towards The Dancing Seahorse, ready to make the Miller's an offer.

The conference room at Miller's Architecture was a flurry of activity. Mike, Sarah, their lawyers, and Mr. Walters from ZAMS Hospitality Group International, reviewed and revised several items on the documentation and contract; but finally a binding agreement was reached and was signed off on by all parties concerned, for the new resort in Marlin Beach, Maryland.

"Thank you," Mike said sincerely, as he reached out to shake Mr. Walter's hand one last time, as he escorted the entire group from the room. "The start of the project will begin within a few weeks, once we get the final go ahead from the city. The engineers feel the structures and surrounding property should be within code, so there will be no unforeseeable issues or concerns for the city's approval."

"I will constantly be on the premises overseeing things. So don't worry - I will make sure you receive daily updates, Mr. Walters," Sarah promised, as they walked together towards the elevator.

"A daily update will not suffice. I will be expecting updates throughout the day, Sarah!" Mr. Walters advised, with a firm, but resolute look on his face.

"Of course, Mr. Walters, whatever you need," Sarah answered, feeling somewhat apprehensive by his demands.

Mr. Walters proceeded into the elevator looking one last time towards Sarah. "We have entrusted you with a very big undertaking. Success on this venture is our only option. I expect no less."

"I live by that creed of excellence. You will not be disappointed," she vowed, as the elevator doors closed, leaving Sarah alone to think of the major responsibility and undertaking she was now facing. She was thrilled for the opportunity and up for the challenge, but uncertain as to what the next two years would hold.

As she made her way back to the conference room to speak with Mike about Mr. Walter's demands, her phone began to ring. "Hello, Lance," she said with a smile, disappearing into her office with a wave to her father.

"We have an offer on the beach house," he said matter-of-factly, forcing Sarah to sit down at her desk with the news.

"We do? What kind of offer?" she asked in surprise, still not considering that the sale would happen so quickly after being caught up in her own issues at work.

"A decent one. It would be a cash sale," Lance added, as he drove towards Beach Dreams. Their names are Harry and Leigh Elliott and they are from Allentown, Pennsylvania. He owns a textile mill and money is no issue for them. They are set on buying the beach house and they do not want anyone else to offer you more for it. So they are willing to give you $50,000 beyond the asking price - which makes their total offer one million dollars – if you agree exclusively to their offer."

Sarah stared out her office windows, feeling suddenly nauseous. "I will to speak with my parents about this, Lance. This is their decision too, you know," she said quietly, not wanting to deal with it so soon.

"I realize that, Sarah," Lance replied impatiently, since conversations with her anymore were never easy. "The Elliott's are having lunch right now. I'm not sure if you can contact your parents about this, since they were hoping we could have a signed and agreed upon contract before they left town."

"Sure, Lance. I will get back to you within the hour," she resigned sadly, knowing this contract was not one she wanted to agree upon like the one with ZAMS.

Sarah walked from her office, finding her father in his own. Mike was busy reviewing some blueprints with another worker - deep in thought. "Try to get this to the contractor as soon as possible," he advised, handing a stack of rolled-up papers to the other architect in the room. "He needs this for the extended area of the restaurant that was never considered until the owner changed his mind."

She walked over to glance at what was in the works, as they were finishing up. "Tell him the exposed beams with barn wood would look great in that room," she suggested, as her co-worker walked from the room with a confirming nod.

Mike smiled at Sarah as she took a seat. "Dad, Lance called, and we have an offer on the beach house. He wants to have an answer in an hour if we agree to the price."

"So soon?" Mike asked, as he also took a seat and joined her.

"The potential buyers are in Marlin Beach now, and they want a ratified, signed contract before they leave town."

"How much are they offering?"

"More than we listed it for. One million dollars."

Mike shifted in his chair, not anticipating an offer that high. *"Well, that is an unexpected surprise."*

Sarah rose from her seat and paced the floor. "Yes, to say the least. They own a textile mill in Allentown, Pennsylvania, and it would be a cash sale. I guess you need to contact mom and ask her what she thinks," Sarah suggested, turning back around to face her father.

"It's hard to say no to this, Sarah," Mike admitted, taken back by the offer.

"I agree," she said with some reluctance, knowing it was a smart business decision being part owner of the beach house.

Nancy was contacted, and after some discussion, the three decided that they would consent to the offer - allowing the Elliott's to purchase The Dancing Seahorse for one million dollars.

"Lance?"

He picked up the phone as he closed his laptop, waiting for her call. "Yes, Sarah?"

"We have decided to accept the Elliott's offer of one million dollars for the beach house."

"Are you sure?" Lance asked.

"Yes... we are sure."

"Fax us the papers and we will sign off on them today."

"The Elliott's are hoping for a quick settlement."

"Whatever they need," Sarah added sadly, feeling like she was losing a very big part of herself.

CHAPTER 46

Several weeks had passed and the settlement was fast approaching for The Dancing Seahorse. A deposit of one hundred thousand had been place in an escrow account, and the Elliott's had agreed to no additional changes needing to be done on the beach house.

Sarah prided herself in her decision that the current furniture would not affect the sale of the house. Her instincts, as well as her architectural background, had proven again that she had a good eye for design and what worked.

She did not have it in her to contact Lance and let him know of her plans to return to Marlin Beach for the overseeing of the construction of the resort. Sooner or later, he would find out - since everyone in the town knew what was going on. But for now, she would focus on work and getting things organized for her soon departure from Baltimore once again.

What Mike and Nancy hadn't considered was where Sarah would stay now that the beach house was being sold. Mike found it strange having to contact a beach rental agency, after owning an oceanfront beach house for so many years. To keep Sarah comfortable though, was the main objective and well worth any cost to Miller Architecture. She would take up residence in another beach house that would need to be rented for two years until the resort was completed. Then she would return back to Baltimore and her apartment. The rental was fully furnished and only a short distance away from The Dancing Seahorse, which Sarah had mixed feelings about - being only walking distance away from her childhood beach home.

As she packed up her many bags and numerous totes, she took a seat on her bed, just to look around at the slightly empty room. It felt strange to be leaving again so soon.

Don't do it…. she swore she heard a voice whisper, as she turned around to see if someone was present. Sarah shook her head, finding the words troubling but very real.

"Don't do what?" she said aloud, as she rose back up off the bed.

She walked from her bedroom, shaken by the message that would not leave her. She went to the refrigerator and threw out the remaining food, emptying it in the trashcan.

Her subconscious called to her again… *don't do it!*

Sarah sat on her couch, lowering her head as she began to cry. "If this is you Dex - trying to tell me something - I need to know what you are trying to say to me?" she pleaded, breathing deeply with her heart racing, trying to regain her composure.

She grabbed the last remaining empty tote, and walked towards her end table beside of the sofa, dumping the contents into it. *There it is…again!* She realized. *That last selfie picture of Dex and I. On that life-changing day on the beach, right before the accident!"*

"You *are* talking to me, Dex!" she blurted out, as she stared down at their picture, with uncontrolled tears streaming down her face.

Sarah went to the kitchen again and found her cell phone and immediately called her father.

"Dad, I need to talk to you. I will be in the office within the hour!"

Alison Snyder spent the morning organizing the final papers for the settlement that would be occurring on The Dancing Seahorse in only two days. The Miller's would not be present, and their lawyers had reviewed and signed off on the contract, giving Snyder's Beach Dreams Real Estate the right to represent them at closing. The Elliott's had already planned on an open house welcoming party with their extended family, and the ownership would be transferred in only 48 hours.

Lance walked around his mother's desk, realizing what she was finalizing. "The Miller place?" he asked curiously.

"Yes, Lance, it is," she answered, looking up at her son who seemed distracted. "Is everything ok?" she questioned.

Lance sighed, not knowing how to answer her. "I guess I just never thought the Miller's would have went through with selling the place... That's all," he added, as he sighed in frustration.

Alison leaned forward, studying her son. "You haven't stopped caring for her, have you?"

"Unfortunately... I do still care," he admitted, feeling very torn with his words. "I haven't been able to forget her, mom. But I can't change what is happening, and she left here and returned to her life in Baltimore."

"Lance, you never did anything to stop her!" Alison said adamantly. She rose from her desk chair, coming around to look down at him. "Every woman wants a man to fight for her! Did you even try?"

Lance stood up again, joining his mother as the two stood eye to eye. *"She has never gotten over the past with her brother Dex! I could only fight his ghost so long... even if I do care deeply about her."*

"*Care deeply about her?* Lance, for heavens sakes, you are in love with Sarah Miller! And for the life of me, her brother Dex would want her to be happy too - if he was still alive. Enough of this foolishness!" she yelled over her head with her hands in the air, as she left the room, leaving Lance alone with his thoughts.

Sarah joined her father in his office, as he was finishing up his lunch. "Hi honey. What is so pressing?" he asked, as he looked up at her with concern, noticing her tear-streaked face.

"I think Dex reached out to me today in the apartment."

Mike studied his daughter, thinking maybe she was overworked and hearing things. "Why do you feel this way, Sarah?"

"I was packing up my final items and taking them out of the apartment, when I *plainly* heard these words – *don't do it* – not once, but twice, as I was packing. I know you must *think* I am losing my mind," she explained, "but I asked Dex to let me know for certain if it was him trying to communicate with me. I emptied the last remaining drawer from my end table in the living room, and there it was – the selfie of Dex and I before the riptide accident!"

Mike sighed as he looked at his daughter, lacing his fingers together under his chin while resting his elbows on the desk, considering what she was saying. "Sarah, I know the last few weeks have been very demanding – between projects, your accident and the beach house listing. Do you think your imagination is just slightly overworked?"

Sarah looked at her father with hurt registering on her face. "*Seriously, dad?* You know I am not given to that sort of thing! But I am telling you, I felt Dex's presence, and I think he is giving me a definite message."

"So if that be the case - what is the message?"

She choked back the tears. "I feel it is about The Dancing Seahorse. I think Dex was telling me that we shouldn't sell it."

Mike rose from his seat, coming around to reach out his hand to her, requesting for Sarah to stand as he wrapped her lovingly in his arms. "It's ok, Sarah," he whispered. "Let's call your mother and ask her to come here, and we will talk."

"Thank you, daddy," she whispered back, finally feeling a wave of peace and release cascading over her.

Nancy Miller joined her husband and Sarah, as the three sat in his office contemplating what to do next. "I have felt all along it was wrong to sell the beach house," she admitted sheepishly, looking at her family.

"Seriously, Nancy, why didn't you tell me this sooner?" Mike replied with a shake of head, knowing that he felt the same way.

"We worried about you, dad. Your heart and all... We thought it was for the best," Sarah admitted, looking to her mother for support.

"How can we change things now with the settlement being in less than two days?"

"I will take care of things," Mike answered firmly, knowing it was time to call his old friend, John Snyder.

John Snyder was just finishing up a round of golf when his phone began to ring in his pocket.

"Mike? Hey, bud, settlement is almost here, and you can take that lovely wife of yours on a cruise or something to celebrate once you get the check," he said with a boisterous laugh, as he unlaced his golf shoes, throwing them in the back seat of his Mercedes and putting his duck shoes on in their place. "So what can I do for you?"

"John... you will need to cancel the settlement in two days. We have just changed our minds - we no longer want to sell The Dancing Seahorse."

CHAPTER 47

John Snyder sat in his car, looking over his beloved golf course, as he listened to Mike Miller giving him the surprising news.

"We have just had a change of heart. Not sure why we wanted to sell it in the first place," he sighed. "Is it too late to get out of the contract on the beach house without any issues?"

John adjusted his ball cap, considering the dilemma. "This won't be easy, my friend. The Elliott's really like your place and they could actually sue you at this point."

Mike paced around the room, hearing the impact of John's words, while glancing at his wife and daughter who anxiously looked on. "Is it worth the risk?" he asked.

"Before I answer that, the bigger question is - why the change of heart? Although, I must say we didn't want to see you go," he added with a gruff chuckle, as he pulled away from the clubhouse.

"Maybe just a reality check that we were making a big mistake – that's all," he replied, not wanting to peg it all on Sarah.

"I am heading back to Beach Dreams now, and I will talk to Alison about this and see what we can do. Let's hope the lawyers don't have to get involved," he added as he hung up - which seemed to be John Snyder's way with everyone.

"Alison, where are you?" John spoke in frustration, as he looked around the office unable to find his wife and son, before picking up his cell and calling her.

"Hi John. Lance and I are across the street at Old Bay. Care to join us?" she greeted happily.

"I'll be there in a minute. We need to talk," he stated, grabbing his brief case and the papers off of Alison's desk.

Old Bay Café was busy with the happy hour crowd gathering for drinks and appetizers. A singer was standing at a mike and crooning a happy beach tune to the attentive listeners. The garage doors were up, and the view of the bay was stunning, as the sun was sinking low on the horizon, and the birds of flight were mingling and playing amongst the reeds.

Lance and Alison were dining on their usual fare of crab cakes with Old Bay seasoning, peanut oil fries and cole slaw. They had already ordered the same meal for John, along with a cold beer that was waiting for him on the table.

As he sat down and took a long swig, he looked at both of them with a solemn face. "Well, you won't believe this... but the Miller's have changed their minds. They don't want to sell The Dancing Seahorse after all."

Lance stopped mid-air, with his fork halfway to his mouth and a bite of succulent crab cake just hanging from it. "Whaat?" he yelled out in disbelief over the fray of the noise-filled room, thinking he wasn't hearing his dad correctly.

"Yep. Got a call from Mike Miller just a short while ago and the family have changed their minds. They want to hold on to their place," he stated matter-of-factly, taking another long swig of beer.

Lance shook his head and looked at his mother. *"What are we going to do now?"*

Alison rose immediately, pushing back her chair. "I guess we need to go back to the office and contact the Elliott's. Hopefully, we can resolve this peacefully without a fight," she said sternly, as she looked towards John, directing him to pay the tab.

"And Lance, it looks like Sarah Miller *still wants the beach house*. Will wonders ever cease!" she added with a wink, as she walked away.

John and Lance joined Alison in her office, as she made the call to the Elliott's over her office phone - turning on the speaker for all to hear and to take part in the conversation, if need be.

"Hello? Harry Elliott."

"Mr. Elliott, this is Alison Snyder with Snyder's Beach Dreams Real Estate. How are you doing this evening?"

"I am fine, Mrs. Snyder. We plan to be in Marlin Beach tomorrow. Leigh wants to get there a day early before settlement - just to enjoy the beach."

Alison sighed, looking at John and Lance, not sure what to say next.

"Well about that..." she began, hesitating to break the news. "The Miller's have changed their minds about selling their place."

There was dead silence on the other end of the phone.

"Hello? Mr. Elliott are you still there?"

"Oh yes, I am here, but I am *not sure* I heard you correctly. *Did you say that the Miller's have changed their minds about selling?*"

Alison shifted in her chair, knowing she needed to stay the course. "Yes, you heard me correctly. It has been a very difficult time for the Miller family. You see… they lost their son while he vacationed with his sister at the beach house so many years ago, and it hasn't been easy for them to say goodbye to the place after all."

Harry looked at Leigh who was questioning his solemn look. "I need to talk to my wife about all of this. Can I get back to you within the hour?"

"Absolutely, I will be waiting on your call."

Alison hung up the phone, looking at John and Lance both in frustration. "We may want to say our prayers - about now - that this doesn't blow up in our faces. The last thing we need is *bad* publicity for Beach Dreams."

"It will be ok," John reassured. "We have always gotten through tough times, Alison," he added with a confident nod, as they waited together for the call.

Lance excused himself and went outside to clear his head, not understanding what was going on but feeling certain that Sarah had something to do with it. He paced outside and took his phone out of his jean's pocket, finding Sarah's number.

"Sarah?"

"Lance. Hi," she answered in surprise, as she heard the voice that she missed and longed for.

"I just heard the news that you changed your mind about selling?"

Sarah walked over to her office windows, looking out over the Inner Harbor with its many shining lights, as she continued. *"Yes... we all did,"* she replied quietly, waiting for his response.

Lance reached up nervously and ran his hand through his wind-blown tousled hair. "My folks are waiting on the call back from the Elliott's. They know about your change of heart, and we are just waiting on an answer."

"I am sorry, Lance... for all of this," she answered despondently, knowing she had told him that so many times before - and for so many other reasons.

He sighed, realizing the same thing too. "Sarah, I still miss you and I'm glad you changed your mind. If it matters."

She felt herself breaking with his words, wanting to tell him of her upcoming plans, but still hesitating to do so. "Lance, I miss you too," she confessed. "Maybe it doesn't mean anything, but I want you to know that there has been no one other than you since I left Marlin Beach. My life has been consumed with only work and projects, since I have been back in Baltimore."

Lance felt a sense of relief, knowing the same was true for him. "Sarah, I will be in touch as soon as we hear something."

"Thank you, Lance."

Lance returned to his mother's office, overhearing her deep in conversation again with the Elliott's, as his father looked on.

"Of course we will refund the $100,000.00 as soon as possible...Yes, I am sure the Miller's will agree to pay the closing cost fees that were incurred, along with the other expenses that you made."

Lance leaned against the wall, anxiously listening to what he thought was good news, watching his father drink a cup of coffee - shaking his head *"yes"* at his wife as she spoke.

"Goodbye, Mr. Elliott. And again, I am so sorry for the inconvenience of all of this. Thank you so much for your understanding in this matter, and I will be sure to let the Miller's know what you shared with me."

Alison hung up her office phone and looked at John and Lance, who were waiting for her response, as she breathed a sigh of relief. "We are damn lucky that the Elliott's are kind and understanding people. They too lost a son. In their case, it was from a drug overdose a few years ago, and they can relate to this difficult situation of letting go. They are only asking for a few concessions, which I am sure you heard me discussing with them. We are *very lucky* that the situation didn't get sticky. And by the way, Lance, they do like the other place you showed them on 20th street. So maybe we can come up with another contract, once the dust settles with The Dancing Seahorse."

Lance looked at his parents and knew he needed to focus at the task at hand. "I'm going to call Sarah and give her the news. I am sure these terms will be more than agreeable with her and her family," he said with a cheerful smile, looking very relieved.

"Great, son. We know you can handle it," John said with a nod of encouragement, turning to wrap his free arm around Alison who had already gathered her things, as they walked from the room.

"You know, my dear, our son is in love - if you haven't already figured that out."

Alison laughed, looking at John and shaking her head, finding him utterly amusing. "I'm glad you are *finally* up to speed on that. Now lets hope Lance does something about it!"

Sarah finished packing up the last remaining items from her office, before closing her briefcase and walking back into her father's office. Mike and Nancy sat together on a leather sofa on one side of the room, just talking softly to the other as they waited for the call.

"I'm all packed and ready to go tomorrow," she announced with a pleasant smile, as they glanced up at her."

Nancy looked up her daughter, with the sad reality settling in of her soon departure. "We will miss you, Sarah."

Sarah pulled over a chair, joining her parents. "You can always come and visit me, mother. I am sure the place that I will be staying at will be nice enough," she added, patting her mother's arm.

"Of course we will visit. I will have to be there from time to time anyway to check up on things with the resort. The company's profits are riding on this for the next two years, and a lot of people are depending on us," Mike added on a serious note as he looked at Sarah.

"Yes, dad. I haven't forgotten."

Sarah's phone rang again, as she realized it was Lance calling. "Hello, Lance?" she answered anxiously.

"Sarah, I have some very good news! The Elliott's have agreed to cancel the contact, with the understanding that your family pays for all expenses they incurred with the upcoming settlement, along with some other miscellaneous things. Is that agreeable?"

Sarah looked at her mother and father, before responding. "Lance, I feel that is *very* agreeable! I am with my family now and I will let them know what you just shared. Thank you so much for working this all out for us!"

"You are welcome, Sarah. The Dancing Seahorse is still yours. I hope you are happy," he sincerely wished her, before hanging up the phone.

Sarah looked at her parents with jubilant tears flooding her eyes, finding it hard to tell them the news. "We still own the beach house," she said happily, grabbing both of their hands in joy. "The Elliott's have agreed to release us from the contract, and we just have to pay the closing cost fees that were already processed, along with a few other extras that the Snyder's will figure out for us."

"Well that is wonderful news and a small price to pay to still own our place!" Mike agreed, as the three stood together hugging each other in relief and happiness, from the profound change of events that fate seemed to have a positive hand in.

CHAPTER 48

Sarah packed the last remaining plastic tote in her trunk before slamming the lid shut on her Mazda. *Thank god I listened to Lance and got a SUV*, she breathed in relief, knowing it held a lot more items than with her last vehicle.

She had said her goodbyes to her mom and dad the night before, and then spent the night in her apartment for one final time for a while. All was packed and she could barely sleep, knowing she was on her way back to Marlin Beach.

The rental agent had been contacted and was notified already the night previous, about the place she had intended to stay at for the next two years. A one-month security deposit would not be refunded, which Sarah felt was fair. She was free to break from this agreement also, without any repercussions. For all intensive purposes, things appeared to be going very right. At least that seemed to be the case – except for she and Lance.

Sarah drove out of Baltimore, passing Annapolis on the way, heading for the Bay Bridge. She thought of her motivations and if she only wanted to be with Lance again because she would be in Marlin Beach for an extended period of time. *Would she have come to that same conclusion if she had stayed in Baltimore?* That was the question that plagued her as she continued to drive, stopping at Mom and Pops for produce before driving on.

She loaded her car with the bags of corn, tomatoes, watermelon and cantaloupe as she got back on the road, knowing her destination was only an hour further. Sarah passed by the place of her car accident, shivering slightly from the memory. The bridge was soon to follow, as she passed over it with the floating caravan of boats and other watercraft lazily drifting by.

She felt free and truly back home, returning to the place she loved and adored. Within a short distance, she pulled into the driveway of The Dancing Seahorse, just idling with her car in park, not turning off the ignition as she sat staring at it. She could not believe the house was still theirs. Never did she think she would enter it again – but this time, she promised, never to be sold - if she could help it!

She climbed the steps, opening the beach house door, finding the key first that was placed under the upstairs mat again. The house smelled of fresh paint, and she yearned to open the blinds and patio doors, bringing in the familiar smells of salt and sea.

After some effort, she unloaded her car and sat on the patio deck with her feet propped up against the railing, drinking a water from the cooler that she had brought. Nothing had changed really. The beachgoers were still there and the children were at play amongst the waves, having a magical time. She reflected on what she saw, not fearing the scene any longer – being at peace with the ocean in front of her.

She went to her bedroom and looked at herself in the mirror. She needed a shower and a change of clothes from her morning of travel. Sarah chose a strappy sunflower blue sundress and slid on her white sandals. She pulled her hair tightly back into a ponytail and applied some pink lip-gloss. She felt refreshed and pretty, as she climbed back into her SUV and made her way down Beach Road.

Sarah drove to Beach Dreams and pulled into the front of the building, nervously anticipating her reunion with Lance. As she left her car, she checked her appearance one last time, making sure it met with her approval. She opened the door of the real estate office, giving way to the familiar surroundings. "Is Lance here?" she inquired, as Patti looked up from her magazine that she seemed to be fascinated with.

"No, he's not," she replied curtly, realizing the pretty woman had been there before and was a past bother. "Do you want me to leave him a message or something?" she added rudely, only wanting to pry in Lance's personal life that she knew she could never be a part of.

Sarah looked disappointed. "No, that's ok," she replied defeated. "But thanks anyways for your help," she said with a kind smile, as she turned to leave and return to her vehicle.

"But thanks anyways," Patti mimicked, squinching up her nose in jealousy - glad she was gone.

Alison made her way to the front reception area and looked at Patti. "Who was that?" she asked with interest, finding the voice very familiar that she had heard from a distance.

"She asked for Lance, and I told her he wasn't here. She didn't say who she was, but I don't think it had anything to do with real estate," Patti added, directing her vision back to the article she was engrossed in.

Alison returned to her office and peaked out the window, immediately recognizing who it was. She smiled to herself. *"I see you are back. Let's hope this all works out,"* she added with a nod, placing the blind back in its place.

Lance was on the boardwalk, packing up the last remaining items from the long anticipated fundraiser of Marlin Beach Ambulance in cooperation with the Marlin Beach Animal Shelter. It was a large success, with 20 dogs and 15 cats being adopted out into well-deserving homes - that they previously background checked and approved.

"Thank you, Lance," Isabelle squealed, as she held securely to her new kitten that her mother was ready to place in the awaiting cat carrier.

"Take good care of her, Isabelle. She will be your best friend as long as you feed her and change her liter," he winked knowingly, as mother and daughter walked from the boardwalk together with their new pet.

Lance could not believe that he stumbled upon Dex's bench that he and Sarah had talked about only several weeks prior. With the help of the other volunteers, he had set up all the animal cages - placing them under a tent - along with an information table with the necessary adoption paperwork, an assortment of animal carriers, and take home care packages that included a few toys and food.

What was the likelihood of that? He considered, as he looked at the bench again that was right beside of the fundraiser area, before folding up the table and tent, transporting them back to his jeep.

His phone rang as he placed the last things in his trunk, realizing it was Sarah Miller who was calling. "Sarah, how are you?" he asked, pleasantly surprised by her call.

"I am great, Lance. If you have the time, I need to talk to you about something though."

"Ok...what's up?" he asked, walking back up to the boardwalk and taking a seat on Dex's bench, as he looked out over the ocean.

"I'm back in town and I wanted to talk with you in person, if that is possible?"

Lance was glad he was sitting, as Sarah gave him the unexpected news. "Where are you?"

"I just left Beach Dreams. I went there to find you."

Lance got up and started pacing the boards, mingling in with the many walkers who were passing by. "Meet me on 5th street - on the boardwalk."

"Sure, Lance," she answered, feeling somewhat confused, as she hung up and drove to where he was located.

She parked her car beside of Lance's jeep, nervously checking her face one last time in her rearview mirror, before walking to where Lance stood waiting on her.

She noticed his appearance. He looked somewhat weary but tanned, rugged and handsome – and more so, than she had remembered. He had on khaki shorts and a white t-shirt, with his flip-flops on his feet. His hands were placed defensively on his hips, as she approached him. "Why are you here, Sarah?" he inquired apprehensively.

"I have some good news," she smiled happily, as she tried to lighten the mood. But he only stared back with unbending resolve. *"Can we just talk about this?"* she pleaded.

"What is this about?" he questioned sternly, as they began to walk together on the boardwalk.

"I'm back, Lance, and I'm overseeing a large project," she beamed. "I have designed a large resort that is being built right here in Marlin Beach!"

Lance stopped to stare at her – suddenly remembering how pretty she really was. He had heard about a group coming in with a new hotel. "You got that contract, huh?"

"Yes, I did, and I will be here for two years!" she added with a bright smile, hoping he would lighten up and share in her joy.

Lance looked away, feeling torn by her words. "Sarah, I must ask you something. Would you have sought me out if you hadn't gotten this contract?"

Sarah stopped, and met his eyes with her own. "Yes, Lance - I would have. I know now that I have been foolish… and my time back in Baltimore has made me realize… how alone I truly was - without you. Lance, I have missed you so much, and I know I am in love with you!"

Lance looked away and sighed, finding it hard to accept the sudden change of heart that she was now showing. "Come here," he beckoned, while grabbing her hand and leading her across the boardwalk. "I found Dex's bench," he said softly, as she looked at the bench in shocked disbelief - reading the plaque that was in front of her.

Dexter William Miller – Beloved son and brother.

"Keep dancing upon each wave – until we meet again."

Love, Mom, Dad and Sarah

Sarah looked again at Lance, and began to cry. *"How did you ever find this?"* she asked, as she took a seat on the bench and touched the plaque.

"The fundraiser today for Marlin Beach Ambulance and the animal shelter, led me to it. The animals were in their cages right beside of it."

Lance took a seat beside of Sarah, looking at her with concern in his eyes. "How can I be sure you won't change your mind again, Sarah? I do care for you, but after the resort project is done, you will probably go back to Baltimore and your life there. You walked away once and gave up on us. What is to stop you from doing that again in the future?"

Sarah searched his attractive questioning face, not knowing what to say. He got up from the bench and glared down at her - ready to leave. "I can't take you walking away again. It just killed me when you left the last time! *Do you know that?*" he asked her passionately, as he turned to walk towards the sea wall alone.

"Lance, I couldn't sell the beach house because of you!" she yelled in his direction, as she got up and joined him by the cement barrier that overlooked the ocean. "I came alive again, after we were together. I found happiness with you, as much as I tried to deny it - after you took care of me and showed me how to love again," she pleaded with tears in her eyes.

Lance turned to stare at her, wanting to believe what she was saying was true. "Do you really mean that, Sarah?"

"With all my heart," she answered tenderly, placing her hand lightly on his arm. "When I am done with this project, I promise - we will work things out... As someone wise once told me before, Baltimore is not really that far away," she said with a brand-new resolve and loving smile.

Lance looked at his arm that she was touching and back into her searching, beautiful light blue eyes, melting with her words. "I love you too, Sarah, and I have never stopped," he answered, as his will was broken, and he encircled her in his arms, for a long overdue kiss.

They walked from the boardwalk, hand in hand, as Lance nuzzled against Sarah's neck, whispering to her playfully.

"I know a fine place with a deck that has a magnificent view of the dunes and ocean, where the moon shines crystal clear and the wind chimes tinkle out a sweet melody for all to hear. The wine there is sweet and the citronella candles burn brightly. Romance and passion

constantly fill the air. Any interest in going to a spectacular beach house like that with me?"

Sarah looked lovingly at her man, realizing her world was suddenly perfect and everything she wanted it to be. "Everyday and forever, my love," Sarah whispered back in return, as they kissed and walked away. Ready to start again – overlooking a balcony at The Dancing Seahorse.

EPILOGUE

2 years later…..

"Sarah, wake up," Lance beckoned, as he pressed his *hard-on* against the inside of her legs. "We got an important day ahead of us, love," he reminded, as he straddled over her, placing his mouth over one breast.

Sometime later after their lovemaking was completed, they showered and dressed, eating bites of toast and making two coffees to go. Sarah hurried to Lance's Jeep, knowing their lingering moments in bed would make them late if he didn't drive quickly.

She looked at Lance, nervously anticipating the day ahead. "Do I look alright?" she asked, as she re-applied her lip-gloss to her lips that were still swollen from being over-kissed earlier.

He smiled, looking at the woman he adored more than anything in the world. "You look amazing, sweetie. I am so proud of you and all you have accomplished. This day wouldn't be happening - if not for you," he praised, as he parked his Jeep in a reserved spot marked only for them.

The executives of ZAMS Hospitality Group International, the city officials of Marlin Beach, the Miller's and the Snyder's, along with a host of many other citizens and friends of the town and beyond, were there for the ribbon cutting ceremony of *The Dexter Hotel – Resort and Spa.*

Sarah walked up to the podium as the mayor of Marlin Beach introduced her, expressing his gratitude for all that she had done to provide additional jobs and revenue for the city.

The 250-room resort was completed, along with a convention center and restaurant featuring a world-renown chef. The grounds were amazing, with palm trees and gas lite torches that lined the walking paths, mingled amongst the beautiful flowers, waterfalls, statues and benches.

The health spa and aquatic center, with indoor and outside pools, along with several tennis courts, was dedicated to Lance's friend - Jeffery Wells – that had died in the ocean trying to rescue someone while he was a lifeguard. It was a surprise that Sarah had kept secret up until that point, as she and Lance made their way towards the indoor pool. The plaque hung on the wall right beside of the double doors leading into the swimming pool for all to see.

THE JEFFREY WELLS AQUATIC CENTER

GREATER LOVE HAS NO ONE THAN THIS - THAT SOMEONE LAY DOWN

HIS LIFE FOR HIS FRIENDS. JOHN 15:13

Lance stared at the plaque, reading each word as tears moistened his eyes. "Sarah, you are amazing! Thank you for remembering my friend, just as you did your brother, Dex," he said softly as he kissed her, truly touched by the sentiment.

She smiled back tenderly, looking into the kind brown eyes of the man she loved. "They will always be a part of this place now and the beach that they loved so much," she added with another kiss, as they walked back to the front entrance lobby, hand in hand, to find the others that were waiting in the lobby with its huge crystal chandelier.

"How about a celebration back at Old Bay Cafe?" John asked cordially of the group, as he looked at Sarah, Lance, Alison, Mike and Nancy.

"Of course! That is the perfect choice!" Sarah agreed merrily, as they drove away and met at their favorite hangout for an early dinner.

They sat together at a large table with citronella candles burning that overlooked the bay with its picturesque view. The music played softly, as the crab cakes were served, with all reminiscing over the day's festivities.

Lance stood, taking his knife and tapping it lightly on the side of his champagne glass, raising it in a toast, while looking lovingly down at Sarah. "To my wonderful, beautiful lady, who I am so proud of! *The Dexter* - with all its grandeur, is here now - because of you!" he exclaimed, as the table mutually took a drink and agreed.

He bent to one knee, grabbing Sarah's hand, before withdrawing the velvet box he had concealed in his light blue, linen sport's jacket. He opened it, revealing a beautiful two-carat diamond that shone brightly before her. "Will you marry me, Sarah?" Lance asked, with tears of happiness glistening in his eyes.

Sarah rose to stand with him, as she agreed and he placed the ring lovingly on her finger. "Yes, my love. I most definitely will marry you," she answered sincerely, as Lance kissed her and the room applauded - joining in their happiness.

THE END

ABOUT THE AUTHOR

Roberta lives in Western Maryland surrounded by her family, friends and cats. She loves to read and write romance novels. She is also a decorator, and loves to cook and garden.

With the writing of The Cutting Tide, Roberta has tried to share with her readers her love of the beach and the Eastern Shore of Maryland. Ocean City, Maryland which was her inspiration for the story, has a very unique boardwalk and beach culture that she invites you to visit and enjoy!

Made in the USA
Middletown, DE
03 August 2020

14262334R10184